OPERATION ROYAL BLOOD

BARRY DAVIES

OPERATION ROYAL BLOOD

JB

JOHN BLAKE

Published by John Blake Publishing Ltd,
3 Bramber Court, 2 Bramber Road,
London W14 9PB, England

First published in paperback 2001

ISBN 1903402 16 6

British Library Cataloguing-in-Publication Data:

A catalogue record for this book is
available from the British Library.

Typeset by t2

Printed in Great Britain by
Creative Print and Design (Wales),
Ebbw Vale, Gwent.

1 3 5 7 9 10 8 6 4 2

Papers used by John Blake Publishing Limited are natural,
recyclable products made from wood grown in sustainable forests.
The manufacturing processes conform to the environmental
regulations of the country of origin.

CONTENTS

For Mary

AUTHOR'S NOTE

So many people ask the question, why did Diana die? Was it an accident . . . or an assassination? One thing is certain; had Diana not married Prince Charles, she would still be alive today.

Furthermore, without having married into the House of Windsor, would she have become the icon of beauty the world's media perceived? I think not. You would have passed her in the street without giving her a second glance. The media created a legend in Diana. She was hounded by the press from the moment that rumours started to circulate about her romance with Prince Charles. From being a complete unknown, she was elevated to the status of a major Hollywood star with all of the glamour, and sex appeal, that entails. Diana, although shy at first, soon co-operated and was ultimately able to use the press attention, even encouraging it and manipulating the media to suit her own purposes. The media have been accused of being partly responsible for Diana's death, and if you accept that as being true you must also accept that Diana shared that responsibility. Having worked so hard to create the legend, of course, the media would never have wanted to bring about Diana's death. Others, however, might well have.

This book was started in November 1996 and was due for publication on September 18, 1997. The original manuscript presented to the original publisher caused some debate. They did not like the idea of Diana being shot with a high-tech crossbow and infected with a deadly virus, although this was integral to the plot and clearly stated in the original synopsis. On July 1, 1997 the book was postponed and I was asked to come up with a better ending. The final version entailed the princess's car being forced off the road and over a bridge. Divers lurking in the water below would make sure all the occupants died of natural causes, i.e. drowning. On August 30, 1997 the princess died and the publisher cancelled the book. I then set the project aside and it was three years before I decided to resurrect the book and change the ending yet again, this time to mirror the actual events surrounding Diana's death in Paris. I am grateful that the publisher, John Blake, saw merit in Royal Blood and that the story has at last made it into print.

The book was designed to be, and still is, a work of fiction. The original synopsis outlined an ongoing struggle between an American and renegade members of the British SAS. Their conflict leads to the discovery of the Sovereign Committee, a covert organisation tasked with solving the embarrassing problem of an errant princess. When the prospect of marriage to a Muslim comes to light, Diana, Princess of Wales is targeted for assassination. That was the fictional part.

The fact is that from the July 14, 1997, when Dodi Al Fayed arrived to join the family holiday in the Mediterranean, he and the Princess of Wales were almost constantly together. Whether through loneliness, manipulation, or true love, in Dodi Al Fayed Diana appeared to have found her Prince Charming – a man whom, had they both lived, I have no doubt she fully intended to marry. Although most of us, I am sure, would have hoped that she had finally found happiness and wished her well, to some among the British 'establishment', the marriage would have been unthinkable. In order to marry a Muslim, she would have to embrace the Muslim faith. The mother of the future King of England (head of the Church of England and Defender of the Faith) a Muslim? Intolerable! To avoid such a situation there could be only one solution – assassination. 'Never happen,' I hear you say. Well, take a look at your history books.

Covert operations are carried out by the security services every day, but you never see them and they rarely make mistakes. There was, however, the time when a foreign diplomat was found bound and drugged in a packing crate at Heathrow airport; or when the French Secret Service was caught blowing up a Greenpeace boat; or when Mossad assassins shot and murdered an innocent man in Norway mistaking him for a Palestinian; or when that spy had a poison pellet shot into his leg while walking over a bridge in London. Added to which, you should see what the security services get up to in Northern Ireland.

Be honest, when Diana died, how many of you thought something was amiss? Still not convinced? The day after Diana's death I went with a friend to a military exhibition in London. Word had leaked out about the nature of Royal Blood, and the fact that it had been put on ice, and I was being bombarded with phone calls from journalists looking for support for assassination theories. The exhibition visit was to help me dodge the press for a while. I was walking with my friend through the exhibition halls when a man cut across my path, bumping my shoulder. I looked at him, my face clearly showing my displeasure – he stared right through me. Two paces later and I collapsed. I vomited with such force that my breakfast landed two metres away. The room began to swim. Every time I tried to sit up I would vomit. I found it impossible to control my balance. As a result, I finished up in Cardiff Hospital where I was told I had a viral infection under my brain. It took me two weeks before I could get out of bed and it was a month before I could drive or even walk in a straight line.

I normally enjoy robust good health and the mystery illness struck with suspiciously convenient timing to keep me out of the way for a while – or had I just been given a warning?

PROLOGUE

'Target turning off the M4 at junction 16, speed 70-75. Who's backing?'

'Tango-three is backing.'

'Roger, Tango-three. Target has taken the B4042 as expected, speed now 45-50. It looks like Control was right, he's going to Highgrove. Tango-five, what's your location? Over.'

'Tango-five, sitting in a lay-by, watching the 4042 as it enters Malmesbury. If he's heading for Highgrove, we'll get in front.'

'Roger that. As soon as he gets close to the house, pull off. I'll inform the static team to expect him shortly. In the meantime, let's not get sloppy – keep it coming.'

The conversation continued for another thirty-five minutes, keeping the car under observation right up to the point it entered the walled grounds of Highgrove.

'All stations, this is Zero – target housed. All cars pull off, repeat pull off. Sierra-three the target has arrived.'

'Zero, this is Sierra-three – that's a Roger.'

She felt excited; he would be here soon. In anticipation her mind drifted back in time to when they had first met. It had all been so innocent – or had it? He was a dashing cavalry officer, an expert with horses, and the offer of private riding lessons meant time away from palace life, moments of freedom. Not that any event in her world could be classed as totally free. There was always her lady-in-waiting and the police escort tagging along. The 'Royal Watchers' shadowed them even during their intimate cup of coffee in the Officers Mess; they were everywhere, always reporting back. Despite this close scrutiny, her friendship with him had blossomed, bringing with it strange new desires. Each time she saw him, the warmth of his presence filled her soul, it made her feel whole, and so excited. From the very start they had shared this mutual feeling and when, after several months, their hands had finally touched, she knew in her heart the barrier had been breached – and that they would now become lovers. Yet the rules determined that he could not approach her. She made the first move. With bold decision she invited him to Kensington Palace for dinner; an invitation she planned and prepared in detail. He had accepted eagerly, and with that acceptance came the clear signal that there would be no turning back. That evening they had made love, and she had been happy.

Happiness, however, commands a high price, and theirs was separation; the army posted him to Germany. His leaving ensured she would fall back into the entanglement of Palace life, and without his love for support her situation became unbearable. Then, just before Christmas, she had discovered that he was home on leave. She called, inviting him to Highgrove, and he accepted – she had missed him so much.

In what seemed like an endless day, she waited for him to arrive, deliberately busying herself, fussing over the smallest of details, her mind full of intimate fantasy and anticipation. It was a wonderful day marred only by the presence of several workmen who turned up at Highgrove to work on the electrical wiring. Her first reaction was to dismiss the men, a decision she reversed when it was pointed out that there was a major fault with the wiring, something dangerous, something that might easily cause a fire. Eventually the workmen left and everything returned to normal.

Later, she dressed with care, in a style that made her feel confident, a style she knew he found provocative. Before leaving her bedroom, she spotted fragments of fallen plaster on the bedside dresser. For a moment her anger flared. She cursed the workmen's sloppiness before fetching a tissue from the bathroom to dust the blemish away. Relaxed again, she walked downstairs, content at last that everything would be perfect. She dismissed the staff and sat waiting for him, feeling like a schoolgirl on her first date. He arrived and they talked, then they dined, and soon afterward they made love.

The air was thick with dust, and the space was confined, yet despite their discomfort, the two men lay perfectly still. Luckily for them the attic floor at Highgrove had been sheeted with chipboard, and the soft foam sleep mats they had brought with them cushioned their bodies against the hard surface. Side-by-side, they lay partially hidden by several large storage boxes. On top of one was balanced a small television monitor, several black leads snaking from its rear. These fed in the signals from hidden cameras. A separate cable was linked directly to a video recorder, while yet another was connected to a small, hand-held device that the camera technician was holding. The second man was wearing headphones, and busily adjusting the knobs of a tape recorder that lay in front of him.

'What's he saying?' asked the cameraman.

'He's giving her some shit about fighting with his unit in the Gulf War. If you ask me, he's playing the hero bit, trying to get her legs open – you got any sandwiches left? I'm starving.'

'Help yourself.' Without moving his eyes from the screen, the cameraman pushed the Tupperware box in front of his companion.

'Thanks,' said the soundman, lifting the corner of a sandwich and peeking inside. 'Is this all you have? You know egg makes me fart.' He paused suddenly, raising his hand to press the headset closer to his ear. 'Stand by, sounds like they're about to come upstairs,' he whispered to the cameraman, who had temporarily lost interest in the sandwich and was now busy watching the monitor. The couple on the settee had disentangled themselves from their passionate embrace, and walked out of view.

'I hope this isn't going to be a long session. I could do with getting some sleep,' complained the camera operator, flicking the switch on the box he was holding. Immediately the screen image changed, displaying a wide-angle shot of the bedroom.

'That camera is well positioned, you can see right under the canopy – Trescott should be pleased with the results.' The sound technician's words where muffled by a mouthful of sandwich. 'Can you zoom in on the bed?'

'No problem. Ask me nicely and I can get in close enough to show you the spots on his arse – here they come.' The camera gave a bird's-eye view of the couple entering the bedroom. 'He seems in a hurry.'

'With a body like she's got, so would I be, mate.'

For almost two hours the men lay watching the screen. During this time they witnessed the couple's passionate love for each other, yet throughout the erotic display both lay emotionless, as if devoid of any feeling. Their only action had been to faithfully record the couple's wantonness – E4 had trained them well. When at last the man had risen from the bed and dressed himself, they powered down the equipment.

'Hello, Zero, this is Sierra-three. Target on the move. Over.'

'Roger that, Sierra-three. Maintain your position. I will arrange for you to exit Highgrove early tomorrow morning. Out to you. All mobiles stand by.'

'Well, that's our bit done,' said the soundman, 'I don't suppose there's any chance of getting a copy of that film.'

'Don't even think about it.' The cameraman crawled into his sleeping bag and rolled over on the soft mat. A dull burping noise ripped from his companion's lower torso, and rank fumes filled the dusty air.

'You dirty bastard.'

'Sorry, mate, it's those bloody eggs.'

They both fell asleep.

'An interesting night, Collins?' Trescott asked mildly, sipping his morning coffee and indicating that the man should take a seat.

'Yes, sir, very. It's all in the report, but in brief outline; the target arrived at Highgrove early and was met by the princess at the door. They had drinks in the sitting room before moving into the dining room for dinner. It's all recorded, but no physical activity out of the ordinary at this point in time. They returned to the sitting room approximately one hour later. They sat talking for a short time – flirting would be a better word – then they both went to the princess's bedroom where they had sex. There is a full transcript of the conversation, plus a video tape from both the sitting room and bedroom. As yet, we have been unable to secrete a camera in the dining room but we are working on it. Likewise, due to the rush, the technicians have not had time to synchronise the sound.' Collins finished his report with a yawn. 'Sorry about that, sir, but it's been a long night.'

Trescott smiled sympathetically. He had chosen his man well. Collins could be relied upon. 'Are these the original and only copies?'

'Yes, sir. We made a hard copy of the dialogue but, as per your instructions, I personally purged the computer files immediately after printing.'

'Excellent work,' said Trescott. 'Not a pleasant task for any of us, but you appreciate the need for the strictest security.'

'Yes, sir.' Collins stood, noting the unspoken dismissal, and left the office.

With Collins gone, Trescott moved over to where the television and video recorder sat in the corner of his functional office. Having fed the first tape into the machine, he picked up the remote control and returned to his desk. After a few minutes and several playbacks he managed to loosely synchronise the picture with the printed text. His head bobbed up and down as he swiftly read through the 23 pages of text, trying hard to watch the video at the same time. There was little to read as the couple on the bed reached the height of their passion, and Trescott sat emotionless watching the screen. He had been correct. 'This little madam is getting out of control,' he thought, and sighed. 'Now we must move to permanent surveillance.' He would recommend such action at the next meeting.

CHAPTER

1

Gulf War, February 9, 1991

In the Gulf, Iraq was suffering violent retribution for its invasion of Kuwait. The Gulf war raged, albeit principally an air war. When the air force failed to stop Iraqi Scud missiles falling on Israel, General Wayne Downing, commander of Special Operations Forces in Iraq, deployed his troops. To avoid accidental conflict the Americans operated mostly in the north, an area they Christened 'Scud Boulevard', while the British were sent to roam the southern 'Scud Box'. For safety, liaison officers were exchanged, and the special forces embarked on their patrols deep behind enemy lines. It is in the nature of war that casualties will be sustained. Some of the men on these covert patrols become separated from their units, and were forced to run for their lives, evading the enemy at every turn, striving against hypothermia in the worst weather the region had experienced in living memory. Some reached the safety of a friendly border, while others died of their injuries. Some were captured and, in the worst of nightmares, these men were tortured to the point of insanity.

The cold continued to grow out of the ground, slowly consuming his whole body. It fused with his brain and told him to sleep, yet he knew he must remain conscious. He wanted to move, yet self preservation instincts still controlled his movements: stay still they warned, and you may yet live. He realised with some dismay that his breathing was ragged, and again the inner voices warned: breathe consistently. He fought to control the rhythm. Slowly, raising his face from the icy ground, he opened his eyes, focusing on where his head had lain in the snow. A strange sculptured impression remained, as if the petrified likeness were his death mask. But he was not dead. His body shivered of its own accord, steeling itself against the icy wind which cut straight through his frozen garments.

His left hand moved, reaching out numbly to touch the snow.

Another bout of shivering took him.

His world was surreal, everything was so white and silent.

His mind was drifting.

At last he became aware that he was moving, dragging his stiff body over the white surface. There was pain but he was so cold that he felt detached from it, surrounded instead by a frosty haze that sealed off the hurt. His memory returned in flashes but comfort battled constantly with reason over whether to lie down and sleep or force his body to go on. The freezing wind cut into him afresh, and his resolve crystallised. He had gone no more than a few metres, crawling out of the small depression in which he had lain. He rested for a moment, confused, half hoping this was only a dream. The moonless heaven shed little light on the falling snow, instead it cast a dull glow that distorted the landscape. In his mind he thought he heard distant thunder, and he concentrated on the sound. He crawled a few more metres until his path was blocked by a small mound. Lacking the strength to climb over the two-foot high obstacle, he moved to his right. Inadvertently, his hand brushed against the snow-covered mound and the snow fell away.

He stopped. Startled.

The frozen face of a young soldier stared blindly at him. Then, like a flood breaching a dam, his memory returned and full recollection washed over him.

This was the Gulf War and he was deep behind the Iraqi lines.

He had been shot.

A British soldier, named Bulloch, had shot him in the head.

His brain felt like a giant football, and there was a strange indefinable singing noise, yet he felt no pain. The absence of pain worried him. How was he supposed to measure the damage? Gently raising his left hand, he touched his forehead searching for the wound. His fingers found the mass of frozen blood two centimetres below the hairline and directly above his right eye. Searching further, he tenderly brushed his open palm over the rear of his skull, searching for an exit wound. It would be massive, and he was prepared for the worst. He felt more frozen blood yet, oddly, his skull was still intact. So great was the relief, that he felt physically sick and wanted to vomit. At the same time, the realisation of his present plight revived him, making him aware, filling him with a strange new alertness.

He must think.

The distant thunder grew louder for a moment, and small lights danced on the surface of the snow. He watched the lights grow in size and strength, fluctuating until they became solid beams. His fuzzy brain told him that the column had returned – they had come back for him. Dropping his head to the cold snow once more, he rested. Help was at hand.

After what seemed like an eternity he lifted his head once more. The snowy surface around him glittered brightly, transformed by the lights of the vehicles. Yet he heard no sound. As if by some sixth sense, he knew and felt the estrangement of sudden danger. They could not see him in the snow. He crawled forward, lifting his arm as he did so, his voice dry against his throat. His eyes focused on the form of a man walking towards him, his silhouette black against the light. The man stopped directly in front of him, no more than three metres away. He spoke once, the voice hard and bitter – an Iraqi voice.

He could see the shadowy figures moving around searching the area; why didn't they help? When at last one of the figures slowly walked towards him, he felt afraid. He could see the man's legs, and focused his eyes on the boots that trod softly on the desert's carpet of snow. He stared, unable to move. Without warning, the leg swung up at his face, and the toe of the boot struck him on the left temple. The lights burst in his head and he tried to cry out, but the sound would not come. Once more his mind went plummeting into the red darkness.

The Iraqi soldier continued to kick, lashing out at the unconscious body, stopping the savage attack only when he saw an officer approaching. 'He is still alive, Major, but not for long,' The soldier reported in short breaths, his voice flushed by the exertions.

The officer looked annoyed. 'Fool. We need him alive. Some of our men have been brutally tortured. Baghdad will want to question this American. Get the others loaded, then take him to the truck – see that no further harm comes to him. We will return to Al Sya immediately.'

Aware that he was moving, he very gradually opened his eyes. A picture began to form, it was foggy and not at all clear, but he felt as if someone was beating his head, slapping his face in an effort to rouse him.

'Get up, get up,' the voice ordered.

He grunted an answer without hearing the words himself – they just seemed to form in his throat and spill out. His mouth was dry, burning, he needed water.

'No water, no water,' hissed the voice.

He struggled desperately to recollect what was happening. Again it came back to him, he had been wounded. With his eyes now fully opened he slowly focused on the bizarre surroundings, remembering the snowy night, with its bitter wind. Then he saw the tracks made by his own legs, as two Iraqi soldiers, holding him by the arms dragged him backward across the ground. They stopped before half lifting, half throwing him into the rear of a truck. Luckily for him, his head hit the metal floor; unconscious once more, the pain stopped.

He had no recollection of how he had been transported from the freezing desert to the room in which he now lay. Entombed in the underground structure at Al Sya, neither had he been aware of the carnage the Apache helicopters had wreaked on the surface installation. Falling in and out of consciousness, he had lingered on day after day, unwilling to give in. He knew he was close to death, but the longer he hung on, the better his chances. The pain in his head had receded a fraction, to the point where it was almost bearable. He could recall several times when they had lifted him, dragging his limp body, to the filthy toilet, even so he had fouled himself several times. The stench reached his nose as, for the first time, he became fully awake.

He recognised that he was lying on his back looking up at a single light bulb hanging from the ceiling. The room was constructed of unpainted concrete with a rough, uneven concrete floor. It appeared windowless. Except for his trousers, they had removed all of his clothing, including his boots and socks. He lay on the cold floor, yet he felt numb rather than cold. He moved slightly, only to discover that his hands were bound behind his back and that his feet were lashed to the leg of a metal-framed bed. He must have lain in the same position for some time. With consciousness returning, his muscles screamed for relief. In an effort to roll over he rested on his left side . . . only to observe that he was not alone.

The guard sat on the edge of the bed, his bright young eyes staring down at the prisoner. On seeing the American move, he jumped up and ran to the door, shouting excitedly until several others entered the room. They all stared at the man lying on the floor as if he was some wild beast. Then, while the others shouted encouragement, one rushed forward placing a well aimed kick at the wounded man.

In trying to defend himself, the prisoner tried rolling under the bed, letting his back take the punishment. As the others joined in, a coarse voice rang out above the clamour and suddenly the soldiers were still. The voice spoke again and all but two of the soldiers left the room.

'Good morning, Captain Wesley. You must forgive my soldiers, but the men you tortured and killed at the outpost were their friends, and the raid last night killed 37 more – you understand.' The man came forward and stood looking down at him.

It seemed strange for Caleb Wesley to hear his name spoken. Confusion filled his mind, he needed time to think. 'I am wounded – some water, please.' Cal kept his voice even, and made his request simple.

'You shall have water and a doctor, a very fine doctor, one trained in your own country. It is Baghdad's dearest wish that you remain alive, so that you may answer for your war crimes. But first you will tell me who you are, and what you were doing in my country.'

Cal observed the man. He was obviously an officer, his uniform smart and clean, displaying a shoulder rank he could not, as yet identify. A major or maybe a colonel, he thought – show a little respect, Cal.

'You will forgive me, sir, but you can see that I am wounded and I find it difficult to speak.'

The Iraqi Officer looked down at his quarry with dark, smouldering eyes, his thick blue-red lips curled in a lazy smile. It was a look that some might call cruel, but Cal recognised it for what it really was: savagery. 'Oh, I will make you speak, American, with or with out water. Guards!'

He recognised that they had placed him back in solitary confinement and while he was alone in his cell, a strange inner peace calmed his life. It was only when he heard the footsteps that he became scared. Their presence signalled more interrogations: beatings and torture, administered by those with dark looks of hate. At times he would drift through the rhythm of day and night, his world a mixture of dreams and fantasies. Some were good dreams, where he was happy, and he found himself playing as a child again. He had visions of his father returning home on leave, a tall imposing figure, smartly dressed in military uniform. Other memories were sad. The tears he had cried, sharing his mother's grief, when his father went missing in Vietnam. Cal held on to his thoughts, clinging to them as if they were the thread of life. Throughout his dreams they came for him; sharp footsteps in the corridor – evil men framed in the cell doorway. The sight of them brought a sickness in his stomach, even before the torture had begun. But the thread held and in his moments of reason, he knew that he was still alive.

Caleb Wesley's interrogation continued for four days. At times he was unsure to whom he was talking, or even if he was talking at all. It was all so dream-like. He would answer his interrogator with a blank name, rank and number – that much he knew. The rest of his story he had secretly whispered to his father. Through his dreams he knew his father would understand for, like Cal, he had been a prisoner of war.

'When did you cross the border and enter Iraq?'

'Wesley, Captain, 238794, born 11th November 1966.'

They assigned me as liaison officer to the British SAS, Dad. My own unit was to operate to the north of Baghdad, while the British were tasked to hunt south of the Euphrates. The liaison exchange was to avoid any accidental conflict with friendly forces. They were looking for volunteers and . . . aahhhh!

Words would not come, either in reality or in Cal's mind. The suffering lacerated his body demanding only involuntary screams.

'When did you cross the border and enter Iraq?'

'Wesley, Captain, 238794, born 11th November 1966.'

'When did you cross the border and enter Iraq?'

The voice echoed off the walls of his brain.

I volunteered to be with the British, Dad, just like you had done. They flew me and two others directly to the SAS base. When I got there, I reported to the British commander. He had welcomed me more as a son than an allied army officer. He talked non-stop about you, Dad, telling me about the fun you had when you were seconded to the SAS back in the '60s. I remembered what you told me about the SAS, but I was sure surprised at the British ingenuity. They had formed themselves into strong fighting columns. Their sole task was to operate deep behind the enemy lines and create havoc. The men looked cool and professional, 'hot-to-trot' as you would say. They quickly assigned me to Major Robin Carney's column, callsign Delta two.

'When did they enter Iraqi soil? How strong is their force? How many others are there?' The voice demanded in a distant dream. Seconds later, the pain burnt Cal's back and the stars exploded within his brain.

'Wesley, Captain, 238794, born 11th November 1966.'

When I found Delta Two, they were almost ready to move out. The column consisted of eight Land Rovers, which the British referred to as pinkies or wagons. They were heavily armed with a variety of weapons, including automatic grenade launchers and Milan anti-tank missiles. A Mercedes Unimog served as the mother vehicle and two motorbikes were used as outriders. It all looked very professional but I wasn't happy for long. Major Carney placed me with two men named Bulloch and Norris. He'd done this for no other reason than theirs was the only wagon with a spare seat. I was warned that both men could be a little obnoxious but I was not prepared for the open hostility they showed me. As I came closer, I could see the two guys busy loading supplies onto their wagon; they stopped working as the major and I approached. Major Carney explained that I would be travelling with them as their rear gunner; they weren't pleased. Both Bulloch and Norris acted as if I were invisible, concentrating instead on confronting the major. Eventually Bulloch appeared to capitulate and shrugged his shoulders.

'Load your kit on the wagon,' he said, acknowledging me for the first time.

For the first few days they hardly spoke to me. Not that it mattered, everyone was far too busy concentrating on their work. We crossed the Saudi border into Iraq on Sunday, January the 9th.

'You will talk, American – you will talk! What was your objective? What were your orders?'

'Wesley, Captain, 238794, born 11th November 1966.'

By day the column would hide, selecting some deep ravine, before camouflaging the vehicles to blend in with the desert, although this wasn't like any desert that I had ever seen before. It was a desolate, barren landscape, suffering the worst winter in thirty years. It was cold; so bitterly cold. But if any of the SAS soldiers felt it, they never complained. Sentries were posted, messages sent back to base, weapons cleaned and made ready. I was impressed with their professionalism. As Bulloch and Norris were not talking to me, I spent most of the time with the commander. He briefed me on his intentions for attacking the Iraqi installations.

'Did you say installations? What installations? Where?'

Somehow Cal knew that pain would follow the questioning voice. He arched his back trying to delay the inescapable, even for a second – then it came.

He screamed and he heard his voice speak.

'Wesley, Captain, 238794, born 11th November 1966.'

On day five, at about 3 o'clock in the morning, we had our first encounter with the Iraqis. The column had sat in ambush watching a motorway when a small Iraqi patrol came along. It was escorting two mobile Scud launchers. We attacked.

You should have seen it, Dad! It was like something out of an old cowboy movie – you know, when the Indians chase the train. Two of our wagons gave chase, trying to get in front of the Iraqis and force them to stop, while the rest of the column rained down death and destruction from their heavy weapons. In less than ten minutes, the Iraqis were all dead. The SAS column moved back into the darkness, leaving nothing but a pile of blazing vehicles sitting on the motorway. I was stunned by the ferocity of the fire-fight and, in spite of their hostile attitude towards me, I couldn't help commend Bulloch and Norris for their daring. They took our wagon directly alongside one of the Iraqi rocket transports and blew the hell out of it.

'You are going to die, American! Talk to me.' The fuzzy voice was angry. The open palm of a hand slapped at Cal's face. 'What was your mission? Why did you murder Iraqi prisoners?'

'Wesley, Captain, 238794, born 11th November 1966.'

A few days later, while the column waited for a re-supply in order to repair two of the vehicles that had been damaged during the fight, they received new orders. Special Forces Command in Saudi had radioed instructions for a planned attack on an Iraqi communications installation at Al Sya. This task required a close target reconnaissance, a job that was allocated to Bulloch and Norris, which obviously included me. I tell you, Dad, I really didn't relish being alone with those two thugs but there was a job to be done. The tension between us had not improved over the past days, and I felt the pair were playing a game of cat and mouse with me. It was Bulloch, for some reason, who really hated me. I found out later, he hated all Americans.

That evening, just as it was getting dark, we drove off heading north. The night was bitterly cold but it was exceptionally clear, giving good visibility and allowing us to make good progress. The target area lay some 30 kilometres away, and for almost an hour we drove in silence. Bulloch, who occupied the passenger seat, continued to observe into the darkness using the night vision scope. Every few seconds he would indicate with his hand for Norris to turn left or right, this helped guide the wagon over the rocky terrain. Suddenly, Bulloch indicated that the vehicle should stop. I strained my eyes to see what he had detected through the night scope, but all I could make out was a small ridge silhouetted against the dark sky. Bulloch and Norris were now in deep conversation, whispering to each other. I asked what he'd seen. It turned out that there were several buildings positioned on the small ridge immediately to our front. Bulloch thought it could be an early warning post and wanted to take a look. With that, we grabbed our weapons and set off quietly up the slope. By this time the night sky had become overcast and small snowflakes started to fall. It all seemed so bizarre. I remember pulling my collar around my ears to protect them from the cold. Snow in the desert; you would not believe it, Dad. Hunched awkwardly against the wind, I stepped over the jagged rocks, doing my best to steel myself against the weather. As I peered up the ridge there seemed no sign of danger and we continued. When Bulloch and Norris, who were ahead of me, stopped and lay down in a small area of broken rock. I dropped down behind them and looked out over the desolate horizon. It gave me a strange feeling. Although we three were alone, somewhere out there, beyond the Saudi border, was the largest military force in recent history.

We climbed again. The terrain grew steeper until some eighty metres from the huts we were forced to crawl. Norris was directly in front of me. He moved like a snake, his body slithering over the broken, sharp rocks without a sound. By the time we reached the final cover of a large boulder, the huts were in full view. From what little I could make out, they looked like typical prefabricated Portakabins; the Iraqis used them everywhere. We rested a moment. I was grateful for the break. Both my knees and elbows had been rubbed raw and the cracks in my fingers, caused by the cold, were bleeding again. I wriggled forward to where Bulloch and Norris were peering over a lip of their rocky concealment. In front of them stood the Portakabins, not ten metres away. Using the night scope, Bulloch swept the area for movement. From his vantage point he looked out over the desert below, checking for signs of enemy patrols and to see if he could locate the main Iraqi installation. He found nothing and turned to concentrate on the buildings immediately to our front. There was dull light coming from the one but Bulloch could see no vehicle and thought it was most probably nothing more than an observation post. At best there would be no more than ten Iraqi soldiers inside.

Bulloch told me to stay where I was and cover them while he and Norris used the dead ground to move forward. When they reached the door, they could hear soldiers talking inside. Bulloch put his finger to his lips and indicated that they should check out the other cabin. The second unit was locked and appeared to be empty. Both men returned to where I lay covering them. Bulloch quickly outlined the simple plan. I was to cover them, while they took on the soldiers in the occupied cabin. Bulloch stressed the point to Norris that he wanted prisoners.

'You spoil all my fun,' whispered Norris, taking two grenades from his belt. I watched them approach the occupied hut for the second time. Once they were in position Norris silently nodded, Bulloch moved quietly to the door and slowly turned the door handle.

Despite the noise of the wind, I heard the soft click as the door opened.

Norris tossed in the grenades. Immediately, both men threw themselves flat on the ground. Several cries erupted from the cabin. Suddenly, one man was framed in the doorway. At that precise moment, the night sky lit up as both grenades went off. The cabin disintegrated, disappearing in a blast of flame.

The explosive force catapulted the Iraqi soldier towards me, as if he had been fired from a cannon. He hit the rocky outcrop with a dull thud, and his shattered body fell limply to the ground. In a flash, Bulloch and Norris were on their feet, their weapons trained on the burning hut. Bulloch shouted something, before both men raked the blazing hut with gunfire. Their Minimi machine guns were on full automatic and most of the enemy were killed instantly.

Then, unexpectedly, four soldiers burst from the flames. One was nothing more than a ball of fire. Steve Norris, twisting at the hip, discharged a single burst into the fiery mass. It fell in a heap.

I heard Bulloch cry out for prisoners and the remaining three soldiers fell to their knees. They looked frantic, waving their hands in the air and crying out with hysteria. They looked so young – nothing more than boys. I ran forward to cover them. Bulloch told me to take them prisoner, indicating that I should start driving them down the ridge in the direction of our wagon, while they *checked out the other Portakabin.*

'Ahhhh!' Without warning, the burning pain returned. It came before the question was asked. Unthinking, Cal responded.

'Wesley, Captain, 238794, born 11th November 1966.'

It was almost midnight when we got back to the wagon. I tied the prisoners' hands behind their backs and made them kneel. By this time the others had caught up with me. Norris was busy looking for something in the wagon, while Bulloch just stood there watching the prisoners. I asked if we were taking the prisoners back to the column. Bulloch just smiled.

'Steve is an Arabist. He can do the business here.'

At first I didn't understand. Then Bulloch instructed me to go back to the wagon and keep an eye open for any Iraqis, pointing out that fire could be seen for miles around. I didn't like Bulloch giving me orders, but what he said made sense. I walked the 20 or so metres to the wagon, making a mental note to report Bulloch's behaviour. I remember thinking then that both Bulloch and Norris were acting a little crazy, but put it down to the adrenaline rush from the fire-fight. I had to admit they made quick work of the Iraqi position.

A few minutes passed, I was busy making room in the wagon for the prisoners when, without warning, I heard a barbaric scream. I quickly ran back to where Bulloch and Norris stood in front of the kneeling prisoners. Norris had something in his hand He waved it tauntingly in front of the young Iraqi soldier. Then, whatever it was, he tried forcing it into the soldier's mouth. At first I thought it was a finger, then I realised it was the soldier's penis. The young Iraqi swayed, about to fall unconscious – a dark pool of blood began to spread out from between his knees.

'What the fuck do you think you're doing?' I yelled out. I

couldn't believe such savagery from British soldiers – I had to intervene. As I rushed forward to grab Norris, Bulloch, who was holding a Welrod silenced pistol with which had been covering the prisoners, pointed the gun at me.

'Fuck off, Yank,' he said, his voice razor-edged. 'You don't have the bottle for this, so go back to the wagon.'

A low, long moan swelled from the mouth of the injured soldier. Another, seeing the pain of his comrade, also began to wail, his face upturned and ashen, the eyes rolling irrational in their sockets. They were begging for the right to live, Dad. Norris simply smirked at their pleadings until Bulloch stepped forward. The Welrod made a 'phut' sound as he put a bullet into the tortured man's forehead. The force knocked the prisoner backward, dark blood spurting from his head, staining the freshly fallen snow.

I watched in horror as Norris turned his attention to the second prisoner. At that stage I realised what Norris was holding – a large pair of garden clips, the type used for pruning roses. Pushing past Bulloch, I rushed forward and drove my fist into Norris's face, knocking him to the ground. I fell on top of him, screaming.

'You sick bastards!'

Then I felt a hammer blow to the back of my head; Bulloch had smashed the heavy pistol barrel against my skull Stunned by the blow, I staggered to my feet, trying to confront him, but I was too dazed. The last thing I remembered was rushing to the wagon – I had to make contact with the column and report this illegal killing. I almost made it, when Bulloch fired several shots into my back. The force threw me against the side of the wagon. With my mind numbed and hazy, I collapsed to the ground, falling into a sitting position by the rear wheel. Bulloch calmly walked towards me – lifting the pistol as he did so.

'Twat,' he said, pointing the Welrod directly at me. 'You're

dead meat, Yank.'

Phut. Phut. I heard the bullets hit me and felt my body jump, yet there was no real pain. Norris had followed, shouting encouragement to Bulloch – he seemed to be enjoying this. There was a puzzled look on his face. He came closer, his head bent forward.

'He's wearing a fucking flak vest, John. Shoot him in the head.' Norris advised Bulloch.

I felt weak, unable to move, all I could do was look up at the two grinning faces. Bulloch pointed the pistol just inches from my head. In total disbelief, I asked him, 'Why?' In God's name, surely this man wasn't actually going to kill me?

'Why? Because I fucking hate Yanks!' snarled Bulloch. 'A few years back we had one of you arseholes in Hereford on an exchange programme. I came home from a job overseas to find that my slag wife had moved in with him – took my little boy as well. They nearly kicked me out of the SAS for what I did to both of them, but that wouldn't have looked too good. So they bust me down to corporal, and let me stay. Consider this pay-back time!'

'We'll tell them you were a hero – gave your life to save ours,' said Norris.

Phut. Bulloch fired.

Everything went black. Next thing I remember was the cold and everything covered in snow.

'How many men were in your unit? Where are they now?' The Iraqi colonel gripped the American's chin, raising his head, and looked down at the blooded face. He tried to measure the strength in his obstinate prisoner. Baghdad had insisted he be kept alive. He was a much-needed propaganda item, illustrating to the Arab world the cruelty of the Americans. The colonel noted the man's high, wide cheekbones and the strong features so typical of his breed. He had been told the Americans were weak, but this one was going to be a problem.

'Wesley, Captain, 238794, born 11th November 1966.'

'Idiot.'

The colonel bent down, thrusting his face within inches of the kneeling prisoner. He would make him talk.

'One way or the other, you will talk. Again!' This time the colonel's voice was directed at the soldier standing behind the prisoner.

There was a hissing sound as an electrical device kicked into action. For a second the prisoner steeled himself. Then he felt the pain. It burnt the skin off his back, flayed him until the blood trickled in rivulets to his waistline. Even when the hissing stopped the burning sensation remained and the man continued to scream. He was weaker now; he would not last much longer.

'How many were in your unit, and what was your target?'

'Wesley, Captain, 238794, born 11th . . . Ahhhhh!'

The pain became unbearable. He would talk, talking would stop the pain. Just one more attempt.

'Wesley, Captain, 238794, born 11th November 1966.' The words came out in a single gasp. Then the blessed darkness quelled him once more into silence.

'Take him back to his cell, let the doctor revive him. We have done all we can here. Prepare him for the transport to Baghdad.' The colonel watched as the unconscious prisoner was dragged away, before turning his wrath on the soldier holding what looked like an old electric steam iron. Its flat, perforated surface, designed for removing wallpaper, now glistened bright with blood and small ribbons of human flesh clung to it. Disgusted at his own failure, the colonel slapped the soldier across the face before strutting from the room.

CHAPTER 2

Gulf War,
February 14, 1991

Five days earlier, leaving the American for dead, Bulloch and Norris had dispatched the remaining Iraqis with a single shot to the back of the head before driving off to rendezvous with the rest of the SAS column, whereupon they made their report.

'So we got bumped by a group of ragheads. Outnumbered, we decided to bug-out – that's when Captain Wesley got hit. We made an attempt to get him back but the crossfire was horrendous. Then I saw him go down for keeps – took it in the head.' Bulloch looked at the column commander, his face blank and emotionless.

'You are sure he was dead?' Major Robin Carney asked coldly. He had never trusted these two.

'Yes, boss,' said Norris, backing up Bulloch's story. 'I know we were not too keen on the Yank, but he saved our lives.'

Carney looked at both men. He was silent for a long time,

as if he was about to go over their story in more detail. Suddenly, Carney changed the subject and questioned them about the Iraqi position at Al Sya.

'What is your assessment of the situation? Is it possible that the base at Al Sya could have heard the gunfire? What was the strength of the outpost? Could we be ambushed if I take the column in?'

Bulloch had no intention of going anywhere near the outpost and run the risk of letting Major Carney discover their handiwork. 'We saw vehicle lights heading towards us from the direction of Al Sya. I would suspect that they got a message through. They know we are here; my bet is they will be waiting.'

Again, Carney was silent, inwardly deliberating over Bulloch's words. 'Okay, get your wagon camouflaged up. It will be light soon; then get some sleep.'

They watched Major Carney walk away. When he was out of earshot, Norris asked, 'You think he suspects anything, John?'

'No. He was pretty friendly with the Wesley, but what the hell? Carney's not going to risk taking the whole column into an ambush, so we can relax.' Bulloch had been correct on both counts. Robin Carney was indeed sad about the loss of the American captain; in the short time he had known him, they had got on rather well. As for the column, he had no reason to disbelieve Bulloch and Norris. It was easy to see that they had been in a fire-fight. He would recommend that their mission to raid Al Sya be called off.

When Carney's message was received at the Special Forces Command in Saudi Arabia, it was immediately passed to Coalition Headquarters. The compromise of the SAS column at the Iraqi outpost was untimely. Although the Coalition airforce could take care of Al Sya, the loss of an American life caused more concern, especially as it was Daniel Wesley's son.

Few men in the American army had not heard of Colonel Dan Wesley, his name synonymous with special forces raids in Vietnam. He had led several raids into the North in an effort to release captured American prisoners, for which he had been awarded the Congressional Medal of Honour. At Norman Schwarzkopf's insistence, the message that Cal was missing, believed killed in action, was immediately passed to Colonel Wesley, who was also serving in the Gulf.

While this was done, the task of attacking the Iraqi communication installation was re-assigned to a flight of Apache attack helicopters. At midnight, less than 24 hours after Bulloch and Norris had returned to the column, eight Apache helicopters, laden with Hellfire missiles and multiple chain guns, streaked over the Saudi Arabian border. Their mission, to destroy the Iraqi military facilities at Al Sya. Flying in total darkness, this potent force skimmed the surface of the desert, passing unseen over the Iraqi ground defences. Fifty minutes later, they reached their destination, and the commander gave his orders.

'This looks like a good spot,' he said, checking his navigational instruments. 'I estimate we are some five kilometres from the target. Assume formation.'

Defying the darkness and relying on their passive night goggles, the pilots manoeuvred their helicopters smoothly into their well-rehearsed attack formation. All eight Apaches reduced their speed to a hover, facing north. Using the vast array of onboard night vision aids, including laser tracking and magnified infra-red television, individual targets were selected.

'Select your missile,' ordered the leader. The gunner sitting in the elevated rear seat flicked the switch to the missile position on the fire control panel.

'Missile selected,' came the reply.

'Auto-hover engaged. All aircraft, paint your targets.'

'Lazing now,' confirmed the gunner. He looked through his sight and observed the laser reflection as it beaded brightly around the radar dish on the horizon. He smiled and spoke to the commander. 'Call the ball.'

'All aircraft, standby . . . Fire!'

There was a flash as the first rush of Hellfire missiles was launched. Like a battery of cameras going off, the flash was repeated over and over again. The line of Apaches suddenly became enveloped in a cloud of smoke and dust. Gripping the stick, the lead pilot eased his Apache forwards and cleared the cloud, so giving him a clear view of the target.

'The lock looks good – impact in five seconds,' confirmed the gunner.

At the radar station, the Iraqi soldiers went about their business, totally oblivious to the incoming carnage. The first Hellfire ripped through the installation like a tornado. Seconds later several more arrived. In less than two minutes the whole place was one great fireball. Those men not killed ran in terror, desperately seeking shelter. They had not seen the Apaches, nor even known of their existence. There was simply an abrupt 'whoosh' and those soldiers exposed on the surface died. Out in the desert, the Apaches reformed and headed back to Saudi Arabia. They would be back in time to catch a little shut-eye before breakfast.

Doctor Aziz had spent most of his life in America. His family had put him through medical school there. Although a devout Muslim, America had been his home for many years. For him it was a land filed with joyful memories. He had returned to Iraq seven years ago and, for a short time, he had practised in a Baghdad hospital. Then, as war became inevitable, he had been drafted into the army, with the rank of major.

He did not look like a typical Iraqi. His skin was infinitely darker and his head was topped by curly black hair. His face gave forth a trustworthy smile, providing the warmth that enhanced his bedside manner. Four days ago, the Coalition forces had attacked the communications installation Al Sya, at which time he and his mobile medical team had been rushed to aid the many wounded. He had never before visited Al Sya, although he knew the complex was fairly modern, with most of its construction hidden below the surface. Even so, the American attack had wreaked total havoc on the installation, completely destroying the early warning facility, leaving the surface buildings and huge antennas nothing more than a mesh of broken concrete and twisted metal. Upon arrival, Doctor Aziz had quickly organised the wounded in order of priority; his medical team treated those that were not too serious, while the rest were made ready for transportation back to Baghdad. He was somewhat perplexed when he discovered an American prisoner being interrogated at the base. It was explained to him that the man had been found unconscious near the bodies of three dead soldiers, one of whom had been brutally tortured. From time to time the interrogating Colonel had interrupted his work, asking for the doctor's assistance in reviving the prisoner. Despite the charges laid against the man, Doctor Aziz could not help feeling some compassion for the prisoner.

The American had received several large bruises to his body, most probably where bullets had hit him, a presumption confirmed when he learned that the man had been wearing a protective vest. Then there was the head wound. This puzzled him. The doctor had seen a lot of gunshot wounds since the return to his native land. This was not a casual shot; this had been done deliberately. But by some quirk of fate, the bullet had not penetrated the skull. Instead it had ridden on the cranial bone, cutting through the flesh and exiting behind the ear. He had heard of such a thing, but this was the first time he had seen it. The impact had caused some internal swelling to the dura mater, but with time this would subside. The continual kicking the prisoner had taken to his head had not helped his condition. 'Then,' thought Doctor Aziz to himself, 'how does one prevent common soldiers from seeking revenge?' Having examined the prisoner several times during the interrogation, he had recommended to the colonel that if he wished the prisoner to live, he must stop beating him around the head. The colonel's answer was to try a more sophisticated form of torture – they had used an electric steam iron on the American's back. He had seen similar methods of torture before. Modern power tools such as drills and grinders had become favourite methods of inflicting pain. In moderation it left little physical damage and, if used only on the back or lower abdomen, the prisoner always looked perfectly normal when confessing his sins on live television.

Now that the colonel had given up, it was up to him to make the prisoner fit enough to be transported to Baghdad. As he tended the prisoner, the man's ramblings confused him. The American was not coherent, the only definable words spoken, were his number, rank and name.

'You have resisted well,' said Doctor Aziz. 'Rest is what you need now. This should help.' Slowly the doctor emptied the syringe into Cal's vein.

It was some eight hours before the doctor re-entered the American's cell, and he was surprised to find his patient awake. 'You are so lucky, Captain Wesley, so very lucky.' Doctor Aziz ran his hands lightly over the dark bruises that blotched Cal's body, tutting as he did so. Although the wounds were painful, they were also superficial. It was the head wound that worried him. 'One millimetre more to the left and the bullet would have gone through your skull and not around it. Oh, yes, very lucky indeed.' The doctor repeated himself. He finished wrapping a fresh dressing around Cal's head. 'Now lie down and let me see what damage they have done to your back.'

Cal obeyed, but the pain as he rolled over became so severe that the doctor had to assist him. At last he was lying face down on the bare mattress. 'Allah be praised.' The doctor offered up a small prayer as he saw the torn flesh that was unrecognisable as a human back. The skin had blistered and burst, exposing flesh from the shoulders to the waistline. With a sigh the doctor set to work.

Although in pain, Cal was now fully conscious. He remained silent, unsure if the interrogation had finished or not. Warning voices told him to be close-lipped. Yet the doctor seemed genuinely concerned, and there was no mistaking the treatment he was getting. Cal listened to the doctor's soothing voice, quickly recognising the American accent as well as the sympathy.

'You speak good English, Doctor,' Cal muttered, the words sticky in his mouth.

'My family still lives in America, and I went to medical school there.'

'Why did you come back?'

'For all its faults, this is my country and my people need me – now, more so than ever. While you have been unconscious this camp was attacked, many men died and many more are wounded. You are not a popular man here, Captain Wesley.'

Cal changed the subject. 'How bad is the damage to my back, Doctor?'

'They have burned your back with steam. It is a particularly painful treatment, but the damage looks worse than it really is. You will heal quickly. Then, in a few days time, you will be paraded in front of the television cameras, denounced for your war crimes, but no one will see what they have done to your back.' A strange antiseptic smell filled the air. 'Now lie still. I am going to put some liquid over your back, it will feel cool to start with, then it will hurt like hell.' Cal suffered the liquid as it burnt into every fibre of his body. With a supreme effort, he willed his mind elsewhere. If they put him on television, then at least the world would know he was alive. Somehow he knew they would get him back. A feeling of hope lifted his soul for the first time. Slowly the pain in his back began to subside to a point where it became bearable.

As if he had read his mind, Doctor Aziz bent over his patient and whispered in Cal's ear. 'Stay as you are, do not try to roll over. They are sending you to Baghdad where you are to stand trial for torture and for the murder of three soldiers.'

'I killed no one!' roared Cal, confused, trying desperately to think what he had said during his interrogation. 'Did I confess to this crime?'

'You did not confess. You said nothing more than is required to the colonel. Even I could make no sense of your mute ramblings. Have no fear,' the doctor's voice was kindly.

'But I didn't do it. I mean, I didn't kill the prisoners – it was the others. I tried to stop them. Surely they must believe me.' Cal's voice was loaded with anger and desperation.

'It makes no difference. If it helps, I believe you, though it would do me no good to say so. I spent too long in America – they would only say that I was sympathetic. Besides, they have the bodies as evidence, and these have already been displayed on state television. More importantly, they have you. What do they care if you are guilty or innocent? You are the enemy, you are already condemned.'

He was right, thought Cal, they would use him to prove to the world that the Americans were evil. With a strong enough case, even his own people would desert him. It would not be difficult for Bulloch and Norris to fabricate a story that fitted in with the media. 'Thank you, Doctor. I appreciate your care, without your kindness I would not be alive today. I will not forget it.'

'I do what I can,' said the doctor, humbly, 'but I fear that your medical treatment will come to an abrupt end once you have reached Baghdad.'

'When am I to leave, Doctor?'

'They are preparing the convoy now. It is quite a large one, we have many wounded soldiers, and the journey will be slow. For your own safety, I am placing you alone in one of the small trucks. Due to your injuries, only your hands will be tied, but there will be an armed guard. I am to accompany the convoy. This will allow me to check on you from time to time.

Now get some rest.' The doctor turned and left the room.

Several hours passed before they came for him. He rested, but sleep would not come. When at last two guards entered his cell, he saw that one held a black plastic sack. Dumping it at Cal's feet, the guard withdrew some of Cal's clothing, including his boots. Thrusting them at Cal, he indicated that he should dress himself. The task was difficult, each movement was slow and painful, yet the soldiers offered no assistance. Before pulling on his boots, Cal grunted the word 'socks', pointing at the sack, indicating that he wanted to search. The Iraqi soldier did not understand, but when Cal repeated the single word, the guard nodded. Bending forward, Cal opened the bag, searching for his socks. He was surprised to find that the sack held most of the equipment he had with him when he was captured, including his belt kit. Locating his socks, he finished dressing. When he was ready, the guards lifted him roughly from the bed. With one either side, they dragged Cal to his feet, and staggered from the room. They passed through several corridors, until they came to a series of metal and concrete steps which led upwards. The stairs were particularly difficult for Cal, and several times he was forced to stop. Each time the guards would prod or drag him on. When at last they pushed him through an open doorway out into the cold night air, he felt a sense of unease. He had no idea how long he had been interrogated; it seemed as if he had been down in that cell forever. There had always been light. Now, by comparison, the scene before him seemed unreal. The camp lay in darkness, the only light coming from a few soldiers holding torches. Cal looked up, above him the night sky was jet black, the air cold and clear. As his eyes slowly adjusted, his sense of unease turned to panic.

All Cal could make out was a sea of faces.

They stood in silence, waiting. Some leaned against the vehicles while others sat, or lay on the ground.

They were waiting for him.

The hostility was a real thing, almost tangible. Fear entered his mind and threatened to crush him. In this place he was the enemy, the hated intruder who had tortured their friends. An American, whose aircraft had bombed their camp, causing more to perish. With a jolt, the guards pushed him forward. The action triggered a strange sound, a hate orchestrated from unseen mouths. The soldiers spat at him, while some lashed out. A kick made contact with his thigh and almost sent him to the ground. The guards rushed forwards and with the aid of an officer they forced the soldiers back. Cal staggered on down the line. Through the gloom he noticed a line of Iraqi wounded sitting by a medical truck into which several bodies were being loaded. He staggered on, following the line of vehicles. The damage caused by the Coalition air raid was everywhere what else could he expect, other than to reap the enemy's vengeance? As he passed down the line, he could see that each vehicle was packed with Iraqi wounded. Many were covered with blood-stained dressings. One man, who had been standing in a small group, hobbled forward to block Cal's path. With his head bowed, Cal could see that the soldier's left boot was full of blood. With each dragging movement, the man's foot oozed gooey liquid from between the lace holes. Unable to avoid the confrontation, Cal raised his head and looked the man squarely in the face. Despite the grey guise of death that washed his face, the soldier was defiant. His lips stretched tight over clenched teeth, forcing his words to hiss out at Cal, 'You, American devil. *Devil.*'

For a moment both men stared at each other. To Cal the pigeon English sounded bizarrely theatrical, yet he realised that the words were sincere. Unexpectedly, he felt ashamed. This man was close to death. What answer could he possibly give? The answer to war was always death. Stepping to one side, he moved on. At last they came to a small jeep and Cal allowed himself to be manhandled into the back. He crawled into a sitting position, facing the rear, and one of the guards threw in the sack containing Cal's equipment. Finally, the soldier climbed in as well, closing the canvas flap behind him.

Ten minutes later the convoy started its slow journey to Baghdad. Cal recognised the vehicle he was sitting in as a Russian-built Gaz 69 and, although the rear covering was made of canvas, the vehicle had a good heater. He sat with his back against the metal bulkhead that completely separated him from the driver's cab. Like Cal, the guard sat on the metal floor. He squatted near the tailgate, nursing an AK 47. The ride was not unbearably uncomfortable. The convoy was travelling along a well-surfaced road. Cal leaned forward, resting his head on his knees, thus preventing his back from coming in contact with the metal partition. Although it was dark, Cal's eyes had adjusted enough for him to make out the silhouette of the guard. From time to time the man's head would nod, as if he was asleep. Very slowly, Cal shifted his position, trying to lift his left boot and place it on top of the sack that lay between him and the guard. Silently, he continued to paw at the sack, using his heel in an effort to tear through the plastic. A rough stretch of road caused the vehicle to bounce, reanimating the guard, putting him back on alert. Cal ceased his actions, dropped his head and pretended to be asleep. It was not a good move. Whether it was the warmth from the heater or the pain killer the doctor had given him, he became more and more drowsy and eventually drifted into sleep.

Cal's head snapped up abruptly.

Several massive explosions detonated close by, and the vehicle in which he was travelling started to swerve erratically. Something was very wrong. He could hear the two Iraqis in the front shouting, screaming to each other.

Several more explosions ripped through the air – closer this time.

Panic electrified Cal's body. The Iraqi convoy was being attacked by Coalition aircraft. After all he had been through, it was inconceivable that he should be killed by his own side. Outside, the mayhem continued. Then, without warning, the jeep swerved sharply to the left, throwing him sideways against the guard. The young soldier pushed Cal away, his face full of fear. The vehicle was now bouncing wildly, a sure sign that they had left the road and were travelling across open country. Cal rolled towards rear of the truck, while the soldier screamed, and tried desperately to unclip the canvas flap.

Cal took no notice. Through the mayhem a single thought had entered his head – *escape.*

It was now or never, the Iraqi guard was half bent, leaning out over the tailgate, trying to assess the danger. Mustering all his strength, Cal rolled on his back, drew back his knees, and with a mighty kick, struck out at the soldier. Unbalanced by the force, the Iraqi was instantly propelled from the vehicle, disappearing into the darkness. Almost surprised by his luck, Cal struggled to grip the sack and work his way to the rear of the truck. Despite his injuries, his blood surged with adrenaline, driving him on. A new lease of life shocked through his body. Standing, he pushed his head through the open canvas, steadying himself to jump. At that precise moment the truck lurched sideways and, like a demented puppet, Cal toppled over the tailgate and out of the jeep.

He hit hard, landing on his right shoulder, but the momentum of his rolling body continued carrying him half to his feet. For a moment he staggered and half fell, tripping over the sack, then he was up and running. Unable to check his direction, he let the noise and bright flashes guide his way. Keeping them behind him, Cal ran until his lungs felt they would burst. Despite his hands being tied, he clung desperately to the sack. Finally he stopped and dropped to his knees. He fell forwards landing in a shallow dip in the ground. He fought hard to control his breathing, wishing desperately for a mouthful of water that would ease his burning throat. Out in the darkness he could hear the sound of voices intermingled with the bright flashes of automatic gunfire. Then another sound, distant but distinctive, caught his attention. It was the chopping sound of helicopter rotor blades. They were Americans, he just knew it. 'Oh, God, so close,' he said to himself, yet knowing they might as well be a thousand miles away.

Grabbing the sack, Cal started forward once more. He could no longer run. His body ached with a myriad of pains; his back burnt; his head throbbed and his throat felt as if he had swallowed hot sand. Still, his survival training dictated that he must get away; he must put as much distance as he could between himself and the enemy. He walked on at a brisk pace. When he had been moving for about an hour, the excitement in his body lessened and he suddenly became aware of the cold wind eating at him. A few paces more and he stopped again. Feeling safe for the moment, he pulled the sack towards him, hoping to find an extra piece of clothing. The sack had been sealed with a simple knot, which he quickly opened. Feeling inside, his hand touched the webbing of his belt kit, and he hauled it out. On first inspection, he was surprised to find that only the M16 magazines had been removed, everything else seemed intact. With simple optimism, he checked both the water bottles. Finding one half full, he took a long drink from the plastic canteen. The cool water washed the back of this throat before descending, ice-like, down into his stomach. Fumbling in the darkness, his hands searched through the other equipment pouches still attached to the belt. Cal fingered several familiar objects, and located the small pocket knife attached to the belt. He removed it, pulled the blade open with his teeth and clumsily manipulated the knife in order to sever his bonds. As his hands came free, he picked up the belt and fastened it around his waist. This simple act gave Cal hope, the belt clipping into place like a long-lost friend. He had no doubt that the Iraqis had searched his equipment, for as he rummaged in the left hand pouch, he discovered both his handheld GPS and compass were missing. It was then that his hand gripped a small flexible wire. In that single moment of disbelief, Cal knew he was destined to be free.

What he had felt was the aerial of his PRC-112, survival radio. About the size of a Walkman, it could transmit a locating beep, and allow him to call friendly aircraft. Used carefully, the battery would allow him to operate for several hours. For some inexplicable reason, the Iraqis had left the emergency radio attached to his belt kit. With shaking hands he felt the pouch-clip slip open, allowing him to pull the device free. He held the small radio up close to his face and removed the pin. Instantly the emergency signal started to transmit a low, steady sound. Still clutching the radio, Cal pressed the voice button.

'Coalition forces. Coalition forces. This is callsign Delta two-seven, repeat callsign Delta two-seven. I am an escaped prisoner. Over.' Cal whispered, repeating the British callsign his unit had been assigned. He looked around the empty night, fearful that someone would hear him, but there was nothing. The Iraqi desert was like no other he had seen, no real sand or flies, no burning sun during the day. Just a hostile, freezing landscape, its surface littered with small dips and ravines that gashed the ground now all now eerily illuminated by frost-misted moonlight. He was not equipped for such weather, and the bitter cold had already started to crack his fingers, causing small breaks in the skin which invariably became infected, leaving them pus filled and raw. Cal tightened and relaxed his finger muscles several times around the radio, in an effort to increase the blood circulation. Numbly he tried again.

'Coalition forces, this is callsign Delta two-seven, repeat callsign Delta two-seven. I am an American escaped prisoner. Request assistance. Repeat, I request assistance. Over.' Cal waited, but there was no response. Disappointed, he switched off the radio to conserve the batteries, before slipping it into his trouser hip pocket where he could easily grab it should the need arise. Returning his attention to the sack once more, he found it empty. Using his knife, Cal cut a slit in the sealed end, and two more part-way down either side. Then, slipping the plastic bag over his head, he pulled it over him like a sleeveless jacket. With both his GPS and compass missing,

Cal had to rely on his survival training in order to navigate. Despite the cold wind, the night sky was clear. He easily recognised the lazy 'W' cluster of stars that formed Cassiopeia. Next he pin-pointed the four stars that made up the pan shape of the The Plough, allowing him to locate the north star. By always keeping the north star behind him, he knew he would be heading south. Finding the emergency radio had given Cal a new lease of life. Now, stumbling along in the fierce cold, Cal battled to make his brain think clearly. If he could only make contact, they would know that he was alive – and they would come for him.

After an hour, Cal reached a large, rocky mound. Exhaustion was taking its toll and the pain screamed at him to stop and rest. His lungs burned and his body ached. In the back of his tired mind came the overwhelming anguish that the Iraqis would catch up with him. Slumping to the ground, he looked back in the direction he had travelled. For a moment he saw nothing, his vision impaired by sweat-clouded eyes. Without warning the distant sky lit up in a bright but silent flash. Some seconds later he heard the rolling echo of thunderous explosions. Although some way off, and oblique to the direction in which he had been travelling, his first thoughts were that the enemy was still with him. His stomach contracted with panic, forcing back the anxiety of recapture. Instantly he was on his feet, pain and tiredness dispelled by fear – Cal was running for his life. At that moment, the ground beneath him trembled and the mighty roar of jet engines screamed over his head. For a brief second Cal caught sight of twin jet flames. Like him, they were heading south. He grabbed fanatically for the emergency radio and switched on the beacon.

High above the Saudi Arabian border, the AWACS aircraft intercepted the message from the returning F-16.

'Eagle, I'm picking up a strong SAR signal on Alpha.'

'Roger,' confirmed the AWACS operator. 'What's your fuel situation?'

'2000 pounds above cut-off. You want we should make another pass?'

'Roger that, see if you can establish voice contact.'

'You getting that, Tom?' the F-16 pilot asked his wingman. 'We're going around for another look.' Both jets climbed slightly, circling to the west before altering course to cap the area where they had picked up the signal. The pilot was about to summon the AWACS operator, telling him of a negative response when he clearly heard Cal's voice break through his headset.

'Hello, jet. Hello, jet. This is Delta two-seven. Do you read me? Over.'

'Roger, Delta two-seven. I have you loud and clear on the SAR alpha. Identify yourself.'

'Captain Caleb Wesley, American Special Forces. I am an escaped prisoner. I am wounded and need help. Over.'

'Roger, Delta two-seven. We have your position pinged. Wait. Out.' The pilot flicked over the frequency allowing him to talk to the AWACS operator; he relayed Cal's name and position, before adding. 'He sure sounds like an American.'

The operator was already running his finger down the list of missing personnel. His finger stopped on Wesley's name. 'We have him down as missing, killed in action. We need to authenticate. Have you enough fuel for one more pass?'

The pilot had anticipated the request and was halfway through a tight turn when he answered. 'Roger that, Eagle. We have enough fuel for one more pass. Wait. Out.'

'Hello, callsign Delta two-seven, this is Bandit six-one. Authenticate your mother's name. Over.'

Cal clung desperately to the small radio as the pilot's voice came back to him. Holding it close to his mouth, as if he were kissing a bible, he quickly keyed the speech button. 'My mother died in 1982. Her maiden name was Duffy – Sharon Duffy.' For a brief moment, Cal became angry, wanting to shout at the pilot; forget this shit, just get me the hell out of here! He took a deep breath, allowing time for discipline and reason to regain control of his mind. Then, without thinking, he told the pilot his situation.

'Bandit six-one. I was a prisoner in Al Sya, and was being taken to Baghdad when choppers beat up the convoy about five hours ago. Do you copy?'

'Roger, Delta two-seven. We have you down as killed in action.'

'Negative. Negative,' Cal cut in, desperate to convince the F16 pilot of his authenticity. 'I was left for dead but I was found by the Iraqis. Over.'

'Roger that, Delta two-seven. Stay loose, help will be on the way. Bandit six-one out.'

The radio went silent. He listened, his senses searching for the sound of their jet engines. There was only the wind. He was alone once more. 'Well,' he said to himself, 'at least they know I'm alive.' Cal looked around. Although it was still dark, the first grey strands of dawn were already touching the sky, warning him that he should find a place to hide. He had not noticed the change in the terrain. Here the flat open crust of the desert floor had been rippled into a series of low, jagged ledges. He moved to his left, realising that he had started to climb. Somewhat breathless and utterly exhausted, Cal finally collapsed. He had fallen into a small breach that had been formed by two large rocks on the side of the ridge. He slept. He awoke around mid-morning to find that the weather had changed. It was still bitterly cold but the sun was shining and what little warmth it provided felt good. Albeit it by accident, had chosen well, he thought, checking out his new hide. He lay in a small depression on the forward slope of a ten metre ridge. From this position he could watch the enemy approach from any direction. Looking across the terrain over which he had passed the previous night, he could see no sign of anyone following him. Although there was no sign of the enemy, he knew that the Iraqis would continue to search for him. Resting once more, Cal unclipped his belt kit and carefully checked its contents. He estimated that one canteen was at least quarter full. Raising it to his lips he swallowed several mouthfuls, slowly savouring the wetness. Searching further, he found the packet MRE, a ready-to-eat ration of chilli con carne, which he had stuffed in his belt kit almost two years earlier. He started to consume it cold, but after several mouthfuls, he found he was unable to digest any more. He resealed the bag and stored the remains safely away in the bottom of his pouch. His search also revealed a bar of chocolate, but Cal decided against eating this, reserving it for later. It would help ward off the cold if he was forced to spend another night out.

Settling back, he tried to estimate the distance he had put between himself and the convoy. He was still pondering his position when he heard a noise. Cal's body went rigid, straining to detect the noise. At first he could not distinguish it – a truck, or maybe a car. Then he saw it; a jeep moving forward roughly in his direction. For a while it disappeared hidden by a small ridge. It was much closer when it re-emerged, and Cal recognised it as a civilian vehicle. With some relief, he relaxed, burrowing deeper into the crack like some frightened rabbit. He was well hidden between the two large rocks, so he settled down to wait for rescue. The longer the day progressed, the safer Cal felt. By mid-afternoon, with the sun still warm on his face, and using his belt kit as a pillow, Cal slept once more.

It was almost dark when he finally awoke. With infinite caution, he raised his head and looked out over the desert. All was quiet. Picking up the small emergency radio, he switched on the beacon. Next he clipped on his belt. The plastic sack that had protected him against the cold was now badly torn and lay in tatters around his upper body. He tried to repair the worst holes by tucking the ends into his belt. Without warning, the silence that surrounded him was broken.

'Delta two-seven, this is Bandit six-one. Do you copy?'

Cal grabbed for the radio as the mighty engines roared above him. 'Bandit six-one. Bandit six-one. This is Delta two-seven. I hear you loud and clear.' Cal shouted into the small radio, looking up at the heavens searching for his saviour. There was a slight delay before he received an answer.

'Delta two-seven, this is Bandit six-one. Glad to see you're still with us. How you doing down there?'

'Fine, Bandit six-one. Just get me the hell out of here.'

'Choppers are already on the way. Request that you leave your beacon switched on. ETA your location, one hour. They will call you when they get close. Stay calm, Delta two-seven and don't worry. There's going to be a lot of air activity around you for the next hour.'

The rescue team consisted of two enormous CH-53E Super

Stallion helicopters. In each of these 16-ton, seven-blade monsters sat twenty Marines, their faces covered with camouflage paint. As they crossed the Saudi border two Marine AH-1W Super Cobra helicopter gunships, hostile with missiles and chain guns, tagged onto the Stallions as escort. Above this six British Harrier jump jets hovered like angry hornets, ready to punch a fire lane for the rescue mission should the enemy intervene. The AWACS operator looked down at his screen, plotting the progress, orchestrating the movement of some 12 aircraft towards where Captain Caleb Wesley sat.

Around 45 minutes after they had entered Iraqi airspace, the lead Stallion locked on to Cal's signal beacon. The pilot spoke to the Marines' commander, 'Stand by. Five minutes.' The commander turned to the Marines and raised his thumb, indicating five minutes with the fingers of his other hand, anticipating the 'Go' which would send his men scrambling out to secure the landing perimeter.

Cal waited, the time seemingly endless. Momentarily, he though he heard a sound in the distance, but it was just the wind playing tricks. He flopped down, curling into a ball, desperately trying to keep warm. With a start, his head came up. Listening hard, he heard the unmistakable chopping sound made by a helicopter's rotor blades cutting through air. Instantly he was on his feet, searching the night sky – nothing. Yet the noise grew louder.

'Hello, chopper. Hello, chopper. I hear you. You are to the west of my location. Over.' Cal yelled into the radio.

'Roger, Delta two-seven. Can you confirm that the area is clean?'

'Not a raghead in sight,' shouted Cal, feeling totally elated.

He was going to make it. With a roar, two jets flashed overhead, the noise making him look up. Then he saw the huge machine floating towards him. No more than 80 metres away, it was slipping sideways, looking for a place to land. For what seemed like an age, the helicopter maintained its hover, the fine sand particles smashing up into the blades, lighting the whole chopper with an eerie static glow.

'I see you, I see you!' Whooped Cal excitedly, deciding it was time to move. 'I'm breaking cover.' With that, he jumped up and began to run. His legs almost gave out as he stumbled down the rocky slope; twice he slipped and fell. Angry with himself, half afraid that the helicopter might leave without him, he staggered on. There was a sudden shift in the volume, as the whirring noise changed to a steady thump and the helicopter settled on the desert floor.

As the marines deployed, the pilot sat and watched from his elevated position in the cockpit. Then he saw movement, out of the gloom a lone figure was running toward him. The man was 50 metres away, racing over the rocky ground as if pursued by the devil.

Somewhere in Cal's mind it registered that a second helicopter had landed. He could hear the sound of men shouting, while what sounded like several aircraft flew above him. A figure stood in the helicopter doorway flashing a small torch. With 20 metres to go, and Cal made a single dash. One last, mighty lunge and he collapsed on the floor of the helicopter. Scrambling to his feet, he floundered unsteadily. Someone grabbed his arm and dropped him into a canvas seat. Quickly, the Marines climbed back into the helicopter and took their seats. One man was standing, doing a quick head count, then the Super Stallion took off. As the helicopter gained height, sweeping its way back towards the Saudi Arabian border, someone came forward and wrapped a thick blanket around Cal's shoulders. The man, a 40-year-old Marine sergeant major offered him a canteen of water, and between bouts of uncontrollable shivering, Cal consumed the whole bottle. The big Marine, who had remained kneeling in front of Cal, noticed the cold-split fingers, now pus-infected and caked with dirt. Gently, extending his hand, he reached up to touch the tangle of soiled bandage that still crowned Cal's head. He watched Cal's body suddenly retch, his eyes bringing forth swollen tears that spilled down his cheeks washing clean in the dirty mask of stubble on his face.

'What the hell have they done to you?' asked the Marine. 'What the hell have they done?'

CHAPTER

3

Gulf War,
February 15, 1991

The Coalition war room, two floors below ground in Riyadh, operated in air-conditioned comfort, despite the fact that everyone was wearing protective clothing for potential nuclear and biological attack. The scene was subdued enough to resemble nothing more than a large NATO exercise, yet this was a very real war. At the centre of a long table sat Norman Schwarzkopf, flanked by his deputies of the Coalition partnership. Little moved within the room, only the faint hum of communications and the odd whispered voice broke the silence. The main focus of everyone's attention was the large bank of television sets directly in front of the generals. These screens displayed continual updates, as the huge military plan was played like some giant chess game. This was a night war, and by breakfast time the pilots who had flown countless sorties in total darkness reported their targets. Each successful strike was flashed up on the screens, with Scud sites capable of attacking Israel holding top priority. Amid all this calm activity, for ten minutes each day, information co-ordinators would also update the commanders on additional raids carried out by special forces. Almost a week ago to the day, they had reported the circumstance and probable death of Delta Force officer Captain Caleb Wesley, who had been attached for liaison purposes to the British SAS. Suddenly the AWACS were confirming the message that he had escaped and was still alive. This information had immediately been passed to the Coalition commanders.

'May I suggest we tell the boy's father, sir? You will recall Colonel Wesley is a Coalition co-ordinator on board the *USS Bunker Hill*, out in the Gulf.'

'You do that, Chuck, and while you're about it, I want you to personally organise the rescue mission. America owes Colonel Wesley a great deal. Make sure we get to his boy before the Iraqis do,' replied Schwarzkopf. Turning, he addressed the rest of the assembly. 'What we have here gentlemen, is a young American running for his life. He has set us a challenge we have to meet. Get that boy home.'

Standing by the outer door to the bridge, Colonel Dan Wesley heard the weapons officer's voice over the speaker. 'Freeway 121 loose!' He watched yet another cruise missile perform its dog-leg manoeuvre as it climbed away from the decks of *USS Bunker Hill*. It shot skywards, leaving behind it a trail of billowing smoke as it found its way towards a distant target in the heart of Iraq. The million-dollar missiles were new technology to him. He had been schooled in the art of special forces raids, fighting in the jungles of Vietnam. Now, aged 48, he was too old for ground combat, and they had made him target co-ordinator for the Coalition. The US Navy had not taken kindly to the air force hogging all the action in this war. As an army man, Dan Wesley was the Coalition's best choice. Since learning about Caleb's death, he had lost count of the missiles and air sorties launched by the US Navy. He had not slept properly since the news arrived. Despite trying hard to concentrate, the loss of his son was an inward battle which threatened to rip him apart. No matter how many Iraqis the missiles killed, it was never going to be enough.

The sound of a man shouting stirred him back to the present. He must pay attention. There were a lot of men on this ship and they were all someone's son.

'Sir! Sir! He's alive – your son, Caleb, is alive!' In defiance of ship's etiquette, the young officer grabbed the colonel's sleeve, waving a slip of white paper in front of him. 'Message from Coalition Headquarters, sir. He was captive, now he's free and running. There's a rescue mission planned for tonight.' The young signals lieutenant was out of breath, his flushed face grinning as he repeated himself. 'He's alive, sir!'

Dan Wesley took a pace forward, he felt unsteady. Gripping the handrail with some force, he held it until his knuckles turned white. 'Run that by me again,' he said, looking directly at the signals officer.

'Your son, sir, he's alive.'

Next moment, the Captain of USS *Bunker Hill*, who had been within earshot walked over, placing his hand on the colonel's shoulder. 'That's got to be the best news we've had since this war started, Dan. Praise be to God.' The captain was fully aware of the sorrow this man had suffered since the reported death of his son.

Dan Wesley steadied himself, bringing up his left hand in

an effort to conceal the approaching tears. 'Caleb is alive.' As he absorbed this single fact, the empty feeling that had invaded his chest slowly started to retreat.

Only 24 hours earlier, the SAS fighting column to which Cal had been attached lay hidden in a small, dry ravine. They were still some 200 miles beyond the Iraqi border. The first rays of sunlight had already penetrated the huge camouflage nets, throwing a mottled pattern of light over the vehicles and men. Major Carney, having checked his men while it was still dark, was now busy making a brew of tea. Despite the weight of command and the constant patrolling, Carney never seemed to tire. He was always there for his men.

'Tea's ready, Mal.' he said to the man sitting nearby. Mal, the signaller, was busy transmitting the results of their latest nocturnal raid against the Iraqis.

'You'd better take a look at this, boss,' Mal replied, handing Carney the sheet of paper he had just ripped from his pad. 'It looks as if Captain Wesley's still alive!'

Exchanging the mug of tea for the slip of paper, grabbing at it eagerly, Carney read the three lines.

FOR OC B2. WESLEY ALIVE. ESCAPED PRIONER. RUNNING. REQUEST YOU VECTOR NORTH-WEST 40K TO ASSIST SHOULD SKYHOOK FAIL.

Carney jumped to his feet, overjoyed by the news that Caleb had somehow made it. In the short time that he had known the American he had come to admire the man's intellect and laid-back temperament. When Bulloch and Norris had returned without him, he had cursed himself for putting the American in their wagon. The loss of Caleb Wesley had left him feeling somehow responsible, and although there was no evidence to the contrary, he had never quite trusted Bulloch's story. Clipping his belt kit around his waist and grabbing his weapon, Carney ducked from under the camouflage net and made his way to where Bulloch's wagon lay hidden. As always, theirs was the last vehicle in the column. It stood concealed, covering the mouth of the ravine in which the column was hidden. Most of the men were already getting their heads down, or picketing the high ground, acting as early-warning sentries. Carney, well aware that since crossing the border into Iraq, none of his men had had much sleep, took pride in the way they operated. Patrolling at night and sleeping by day put a lot of strain on the men. The loss of the American had only served to put everyone on edge – everyone except Bulloch and Norris that was.

They appeared to be sleeping soundly as he approached but the noise of his boots, crunching on the coarse ground, disturbed them. He raised the camouflage net that covered the vehicle and crawled inside. Squatting down, Carney studied the two men as they awakened. For some inexplicable reason, he enjoyed a feeling of intense gratification at telling them the good news – as if to say, 'I knew you were lying.'

'It would seem you two were mistaken. Captain Wesley is alive. I have just received a signal from Special Forces Command. He was captured by the Iraqis, but somehow managed to escape. They are going in to pick him up tonight. There are no further details as to what exactly happened, but we should get a better idea of his condition later this evening.' Carney watched as both struggled in their sleeping bags to sit up. Although both full of sleep, their expressions changed completely as his words registered. Carney noted with some distaste that they looked worried, not relieved. He had never told them that he wasn't happy with their story – maybe Caleb would enlighten him at a later date. 'Be ready to move at last light. They want us to assist if they can't get him out by chopper.' Turning, he stepped from under the camouflage net and walked away.

Bulloch and Norris sat in dumbfounded silence; not until Carney was out of earshot, did Norris speak, his voice full of alarm. 'Holy fuck! What we going to do? If they get the Yank back, we are really in the shit.'

'Shut the fuck up. Let me think,' Bulloch said, half standing and gripping the camouflage net for support as he wriggled out of his sleeping bag. 'Obviously the Yank hasn't had time to tell anyone the truth yet,' Bulloch reasoned, trying to remain calm, 'but all that will change when they pick him up. What time is it?'

'Just gone nine. Why, what's on your mind?'

'It's time to disappear. What's our fuel and water situation?'

'Plenty of food and water and if I top up our long-range tanks I reckon we could go some 500 miles. What direction are we going?'

'West, across the Syrian border, then we keep going until we reach the Lebanon. Better we take our chances out there. We know what we can expect if we stay here. If we travel at night and hide by day, a lone vehicle well camouflaged will be hard to spot. Three, four days should see us in Beirut.'

'What if we get caught?' Norris was still not convinced.

'No reason we should. This column has nine vehicles and we've been here for three weeks undetected. But if we get caught by the ragheads, we take our chances. We can always try and make a deal, or fight our way out. If we cut due west, clear the Syrian border, keep north of Damascus, we'll make it into Beirut. We have a 110 Land Rover, with a Mark 19 grenade launcher and two heavy machine guns – any of the outfits there will be glad to see us. They're not stupid, they need men like us. We should do well in the Lebanon. Where there's a war, you and I can always find work. Now get your arse over to the Unimog, grab anything you think we'll need. Plenty grenades for the Mark 19 will do for starters. I'll plan us a route.'

Eight hours later, Carney considered it dark enough to move. Earlier that day, Special Forces Command had passed the column the rescue co-ordinates in order that they could rendezvous with Wesley. In turn Carney had briefed his men, stating that if for any reason the helicopter rescue were to fail, the column was to act accordingly. Moving off into the night, their course took them north-west. The two motorbikes, acting as outriders, went speeding across the desert, searching for any sign of the enemy. Every so often, Carney signalled a stop. This gave him time to observe through the night scope, and double check that the way ahead was clear. He was pushing the column hard, eager and excited to help rescue Caleb. They had been travelling for some two hours when one of the bikes reported their path blocked by Iraqi troops. Once again, Carney checked with the thermal imager, observing the bourne that had been constructed by the Iraqi engineers. It was about five metres high, and six metres thick – a major obstacle for the vehicles. Throughout their time in Iraq, he had seen many such earthworks and each one had indicated a sizeable enemy force. Cutting the engine, he radioed for the rest to be silent while he studied the problem. Out there was the Iraqi army. He could see the antennas, armoured vehicles, soldiers in trenches, and all of this no more than 400 metres away. Through the spyglass, he could identify the hot images of the Iraqi vehicles moving around. Quickly flicking the switch from wide angle to zoom, he re-focused. 'Shit, there are fucking thousands of them out there. We'll have to go round.'

Carney was still contemplating the obstacle when someone tapped him lightly on the shoulder. Reluctant to be distracted from his observations, he turned to see one of the bike riders facing him. 'What is it?'

'Bulloch's wagon is missing.'

'What do you mean missing? Have they broken down?'

'No – they're missing. I rode back to our last stop. They were with us then. Now there's no sign of them.'

'Okay. Now listen. There's a large concentration of enemy directly in front. We'll withdraw back to our last checkpoint. You and the other bike sweep out to the flanks, find me a way past this lot,' Carney whispered, 'and do it quick.'

'No problems, boss. What about Bulloch and Norris?'

'Fuck Bulloch and Norris, they can take care of themselves. Now move.'

CHAPTER
4

June 6, 1997

Sitting at a time-scarred wooden table behind the polished glass window of a Parisian café, Bulloch glanced across at his old mate, Norris. It had been six years since they had detached themselves from the SAS column and disappeared into the darkness. Hiding their wagon by day beneath the huge camouflage net, they travelled only by night, heading east. Only once were they spotted, when a youth out minding his goats stumbled across them. Norris cut his throat. Using their training and experience, they vanished into the wastelands, reappearing eight days later as Bulloch guided them safely into the Lebanon. Seeking refuge in the predominantly Christian East Beirut, Bulloch and Norris quickly sold their talents. In such a place, where religious factions tore at each other like wild beasts, with sanity and reasoning long forgotten, there was always work to be found for professional killers. They lived their lives amid the continuous thunder of exploding bombs and shells. Debris filled the streets and burning ruins cremated the dead. Here, where peace was destroyed by suspicion and hatred, Bulloch and Norris prospered.

Less than a year after the Gulf War had ended, intelligence agencies around the world started receiving the first reports of a new team of contract killers operating in the Middle East. For the most part, while Arab killed Arab, the western agencies were content to sit and watch. Mossad, the Israeli intelligence service, reported that one of its Arab agents had been assassinated in Lebanon. Through this action the killers' nationality become known.

The Israeli agent had worked at the French embassy in Beirut, and had been present when General Michael Aoun was granted asylum. The General, a bitter foe of the Arab League's peace plan, had until recently commanded the fanatically loyal Christian forces in East Beirut. He remained holed up in the embassy for more than a week, despite the Lebanese President insisting that he remain in the country to face trial for, among other things, pilfering 75 million dollars from the government treasury. It transpired that the Israeli agent, while at the embassy, somehow convinced General Aoun to part with the location of the hidden loot. Not long after, news of the agent's departure, together with a large sum of money, spread swiftly through the Beirut underworld. The two British gunmen, their reputation for stealth and expertise in the art of murder well established, were hired.

Since their arrival in the Lebanon, several Middle Eastern governments had already acquired their services, creating a mysterious trail of shootings and bombings throughout the region. For Bulloch and Norris, it was all in a day's work. If they accepted a job, it was payment first, then the hit. Twice they had been set up, and twice they had spotted the trap. In each case they had terminated the opposition, before paying a visit to terminate the original contractor – they could never be seen to allow a double-cross to go unpunished. That would have been very bad for business, so such activities were to be discouraged.

They had eventually caught up with the Israeli agent just as he was about to make good his escape. Dragging him to a deserted, bombed-out building, they discovered that he was only carrying a fraction of the stolen money. While Bulloch kept watch, Norris skilfully used his garden pruning shears, trying to coax from the man's lips the location of the remaining fortune. He had already removed two of the man's fingers when several other Mossad agents arrived on the scene. Unbeknown to the British assassins, the Israelis had been sent to assist their colleague safely over the border, and to make sure his affiliation to Israeli security was not tarnished by the temptation of carrying so much money. In the short fire-fight that ensued, the agent was shot dead and Bulloch and Norris simply disappeared.

Their brush with Israeli intelligence had been brief, yet it made both men realise that they had long outstayed their welcome in Beirut. Moreover, they had wearied of their monastic, Middle Eastern lifestyle. Living conditions in the besieged city were growing worse. It was time to move on, taking with them, of course, the substantial accumulation of cash they had earned over the past six years.

Travelling on forged British passports, they had moved without hindrance into Europe. Here they spent much of their time drinking or whoring in the red light districts of Paris or Amsterdam. Their past was almost forgotten until Bulloch received an approach from a contact in the Middle East offering them work. The job, on the surface, looked pretty simple, a straightforward execution. Through drink and laziness Bulloch decided minimum planning was required. In the event, this was to prove a terrible mistake.

They had arrived in Paris at the end of February, when frost capped the great lawns of Versailles, each tiny blade of grass covered in white, while beneath bare trees that showed no sign of life, frosted leaves littered the ground. Transformed by the morning sunlight, the ice crystals shimmered like jewels, sending shades of amber to warm the stone-cold statues. At first the pair had enjoyed the icy scene that was Paris, but after four months and regardless of the gathering summer warmth, they had grown weary of the French capital. Satan had led them a dance through the Parisian nightlife making them bachelors of the dark. Rigid with excessive alcohol they fed on young girls, girls without virtue, whose only interest was money. Having sated themselves of drinking and debauchery, they discussed their next move. Predictably, their conversation would turn to work in progress or pending, or to the vast amount of money they had made. Discussion on how they should spend their wealth was always a popular topic of conversation. When their operation in Paris was completed, Bulloch fancied going to Thailand. Norris was keen to see his mother and sister in England. Circumstances had prevented him from returning to his native Stockport, and apart from John Bulloch, his mother and sister were the only people he felt for. But first, there was a job to be done – a man they must kill.

Bulloch and Norris waited patiently. The window table of a

small café gave them an excellent field of vision. They could watch the street and cover the whole café, observing both the passers-by and the clientele scattered around the room. Bulloch and Norris had taken the same table several nights running, awaiting the appearance of their target, a middle-aged man living with his mistress in an apartment at 220 rue d'Gare, an address to which he had only recently moved. When contracting the two killers, their principal had identified the address of the wanted man. He had also supplied, along with a full description and photograph, the fact that he visited the Café Royal several times a week. It was thought that he had organised the shooting of Saddam's son, Uday Hussein, leaving him with 14 bullets in his body and the need for spinal surgery.

Bulloch's plan to kill the man was simple. Having conducted a discreet reconnoitre of the area and taken a good look at the apartments, they discovered that the lobby had tight security; a permanent concierge and two security cameras. This had prevented them from simply shooting the man as he left his home. Using a street map of Paris, they followed the obvious route to the café, with the purpose of selecting a more secluded killing area. The one they both favoured was a small, narrow archway that provided a shortcut between the apartments and the café. The archway ran directly under the building forming a tunnel ten metres long directly opposite the apartment block. It was a logical shortcut, reducing the walking distance to the café by almost 300 metres. On further investigation, they discovered a single light in the centre of the domed roof that provided illumination for pedestrians. Norris also noticed a single, recessed doorway half way along one wall of the archway. This led into one of the buildings but on checking, Norris found that the door was littered with age-old cobwebs and had, therefore, not been used for a very long time.

By maintaining surveillance, they twice observed the target walking the route during his frequent visits to the café. That night they had gone for the kill, Norris shooting out the tunnel light using the Welrod, silently plunging the archway into darkness as they lay in wait for their prey. Unfortunately, on this occasion the target had not shown himself.

While they sat in the café and waited for another opportunity, Bulloch explained to Norris about the Colombian contract that had been offered to them. It was his recommendation that they do the job immediately upon finishing their current assignment in Paris. The delay in the target presenting himself was getting to Bulloch. The thought of waiting around in Paris for the target to show was beginning to piss him off. He voiced his opinion to Norris. 'If the Colombians want some guy hit, I say let's do it. The money's good and the job is a piece of cake. I thought we could stay on in South America afterwards and soak up a bit of Latin sunshine – get a couple of girls.' He knew the latter idea would help persuade Norris.

'How come they don't kill him themselves?' Norris wondered, playing with his half-empty beer glass. 'I was always led to believe the Colombians have enough fire-power to slot anyone.'

'The guy in question is an American DEA agent. They don't want any of their own guys fingered for the job, that's why they want us to do it. We're not known over there,' answered Bulloch, looking at his watch.

It had just gone 10 o'clock when Bulloch dropped his feet

from the chair on which he had draped them and tossed the British newspaper he had been reading onto the table. He looked around the café. The place was very quiet. Only a low murmur of conversation emerged from the back part of the room where Madame was discussing with some local customers the horrors of finding one of the waitresses in bed with her husband and what she intended to do about it.

Outside the evening sky darkened further as the moon was diffused behind some light clouds. It was then that Bulloch noticed the two people. He sat upright as they crossed the street and watched as they entered the café, removing their coats before seating themselves at a table. The Madame stopped her chatter and walked over, inquiring with an uncaring smile as to their pleasure.

Norris had instantly caught the change in Bulloch's posture and followed his gaze. The couple was easy to spot for, despite being dressed in western clothes, he was obviously an Arab. His face was olive brown and his head covered with thick, black hair, charred at the edges by the silver of age. He was laughing at the woman, his full lips parting to reveal a set of pearl-white teeth, while his dark eyes sparkled. This was their target. Bulloch, who spoke reasonable French, ordered two more beers then settled down to wait. When at last the Arab called for his bill, Bulloch motioned to Norris.

'Let's get the raghead bastard,' he said under his breath, standing up to leave. 'Pay for the drinks and follow them out.'

'Roger that,' replied Norris.

'Don't switch your radio on until you get outside. I'll give you a call when I'm at the other end of the archway.' With that, Bulloch left the café.

Steve Norris watched and waited. He saw Bulloch cross

the road and disappear around the corner of the building opposite. He made to leave and, as he did so, both the Arab and the woman stood up. Norris watched the couple put on their coats. They were walking in Bulloch's footsteps. Norris took his time paying the bill before he followed the couple at a discreet distance.

'The archway is clear, and the street all quiet this side,' Bulloch's whispered voice resonated in the tiny earpiece in Norris's ear.

'Roger that,' said Norris, speaking into the small microphone concealed beneath his shirt. 'Fifty metres from the archway. Closing up. Clear behind.'

By the time the couple had reached the archway, Norris was no more than three metres behind them. As he entered the gloom, his hand fastened on the handle of the silenced Welrod inside his jacket. Again, Bulloch's voice echoed through his earpiece.

'Still clear. Go for the shot.'

Despite the darkness of the archway, the couple's silhouette was sharply defined by the street lights at the opposite end. Norris stopped, carefully poising. Standing with his feet slightly apart, he gripped the heavy pistol with both hands. Taking aim, he squeezed the trigger with a steady but rapid motion. Six shots spat out in quick succession. Four went into the man, and two into the woman. The noise of the Welrod was little more than a muffled 'putting' sound, indistinct and almost inaudible. Norris saw the man fall to the ground his arm still gripping the woman, dragging her down with him as he fell. He ran forward, stopping to stand astride the couple. Neither moved. Quickly bending over the man, he placed the lengthy pistol against the man's neck and pumped the remaining two rounds into his victim.

Something stirred close by in the darkness and Norris sensed a presence.

Turning swiftly he saw the faint outline of two people lurking in the murkiness of the recessed doorway, then a woman screamed.

'Shit!' howled Norris, raising the pistol and holding it a few inches from the woman's gaping mouth. He pulled the trigger. Nothing happened. The magazine was empty. At the sight of the gun, the woman stopped screaming. For a brief second the whole scene froze.

'Move, Steve! Move!' Bulloch's voice was loud in his earpiece. 'We have company!' Bulloch's words registered, jarring Norris into action. He ran out into the street and seconds later he flashed past Bulloch in full stride.

'Let's get the fuck out of here!' he shouted over his shoulder. Bulloch ran to catch him. 'There were two fucking lovers in the doorway – why didn't you spot them?'

'Sorry, mate. Didn't see 'em. They must have been very quiet when I walked through – pitch black in there.' Bulloch's excuse sounded feeble. 'Slow down. Don't attract attention.'

They gradually slowed to a brisk walk, bringing their breathing under control. Behind them, they could hear the woman. She was screaming again. Seconds later her cries were joined by several others, all adding to the commotion. Some 200 metres away from the scene they turned the corner and found themselves in a much busier street. There was a constant flow of traffic and more people walked the pavements, making it easier for them to blend into the crowd. They slowed to a normal walking pace.

'Have you still got the gun?'

'Yes,' retorted Norris, still peeved at Bulloch's blunder. 'I think we'll be okay. I'll hang on to it.'

'No. You know the rules. There's no point in taking a chance,' said Bulloch looking across the street. 'Quick, over there.' Bulloch dodged the traffic in an effort to cross the road, with Norris hot on his heels. 'In here,' he said, pushing his way through a dilapidated gate that led, Bulloch presumed, into a small park. It turned out to be a disused graveyard, confined on three sides by a high stone wall. Many of the headstones had fallen to be hidden by the uncut grass, while those monuments that remained standing were old and moss-covered, crumbling with age. Everywhere the weeds grew unabated while ancient trees lofted above, blotting the moonlight into darkened shadows. 'This will do. Find a hiding place over there and wrap it up.'

'Give me a minute,' Norris pulled a small, green plastic bag from his pocket. Removing the pistol from inside his jacket, he placed it in the bag and closed the bag's airtight zipper.

'Right, this is as good as anywhere. Get rid of it; I'll keep watch,' said Bulloch. Norris walked across the grass before disappearing behind a large bush some 20 metres away. Less than a minute later he was back.

'That should serve as a temporary measure,' said Bulloch. 'I doubt if anybody's going to find it too soon. You can come back and pick it up tomorrow.'

'Good. Now let's get the fuck out of here. I don't know about you, but I say you owe me a drink. Let's find ourselves a bar.'

'Good idea.' said Bulloch. He led the way back into the street. They paced along the pavement for another 300 metres before they found a small bar. 'In here,' commanded Bulloch.

'This'll do.' Entering, both men sat at the all-but-empty bar and ordered two beers. Outside they could hear the wail of sirens. A minute later, a police car shot past heading in the direction of the shooting. Taking their time over their drink and talking in whispers, Norris asked what had gone wrong.

'I really didn't see them. They could have been shagging and not wanting anyone to see they – whatever – I missed them. Sorry.'

'Forget it,' said Norris, taking another mouthful of beer. 'At least the Arab is dead. I took out the girl for good measure. She may have recognised us from the café. I would have shot the other two as well but I emptied my gun into the target.'

'You did right, mate. We get paid to take out the target – nothing else matters.' Ten minutes went by before Bulloch thought it safe for them to make their way back to their hotel. They left the bar and walked back into the street. It had begun to rain. About 50 metres down the pavement, they stopped at the traffic lights and waited to cross the road. As the lights changed several cars came to a halt, allowing the pedestrians to cross. Bulloch and Norris were halfway across the road when the doors to one of the cars opened and several men jumped out. It was the sound of slamming doors that made Norris glance back over his shoulder. He saw three men weaving their way through the traffic – then he recognised the woman sitting in the back of one of the cars. She was screaming and pointing towards him and Bulloch. Without doubt, it was the woman from the archway. Instinctively Bulloch assessed their predicament. He noticed that Steve was about to run and quickly cautioned him. 'Police! The fucking bitch must have recognised us. Keep going – no running.' They were almost on the opposite pavement, pushing their way past several other pedestrians. The desire to run was overwhelming but to do so would have been a clear admission of guilt. Behind them they could hear the sound of running feet and men shouting. Bulloch risked a glance back – the men had drawn their weapons. Out of the corner of his mouth, he whispered to Norris, 'Stay calm, Steve – just bluff it out.' Next moment the three men grabbed them, their momentum forcing Bulloch and Norris face first against the glass of a large restaurant window. Speaking rapidly in French, one man flashed a metal badge while another frisked them both for weapons. 'CRS police,' muttered Bulloch, his face squashed against the glass just inches from Norris. 'How the fuck did they find us?'

'The woman in the car at the lights. She was the one in the alley,' whispered Norris. 'The police must've been taking her back to the station just as we crossed the road.'

'Fuck! Talk about bad luck compromise!' hissed Bulloch.

Moments later they were handcuffed and bundled into a windowless van. They were driven to a local police station and locked in a cell. Sitting close together during the short journey, Bulloch and Norris rationalised their story. It would be easy to make out they were tourists and plead no knowledge of the shooting. The way they saw it, problems would only arise if it were discovered that their passports were false. But things did not progress well. Both the man and the woman who had been under the archway positively identified Norris. Shortly after, the Madame from the café was brought in. She confirmed that both men had been recent regular visitors, saying that they had left more or less at the same time as the victim. By mid-morning the next day, a search had produced the hidden Welrod and, although Norris had used gloves, the fact that it was a British-made weapon did little to improve their predicament. In the end, the French authorities decided to lodge them for safety in a cell at Paris's La Sante prison, while they awaited a full report from Interpol.

CHAPTER

5

England,
July 28, 1997

Harmsham Park, in West Sussex, sits proudly in an ancient deer park overlooking the Sussex Downs. Built in 1577 by Sir Thomas Cameron, head of a Sussex family of mercers, the building was constructed on land which, at one time, had belonged to Westminster Abbey. In 1601 Thomas Cameron, who had held naval commands under Drake and Hawkins, sold the property to Sir Archibald Scott as a hunting lodge. Over the generations, it passed down through his descendants whose few modifications to the original building were both discreet and sympathetic. It was an unusual house, its lofty gables built of solid masonry and topped by six large, ornate chimney stacks, making it a home of fine features and great elegance. The mansion was not overly large: four reception rooms, nine bedrooms, five bathrooms and, to the rear, a large covered swimming pool.

Sir Gilbert Scott, the current occupier, rose from his desk

in the library. This was his favourite room, and one he utilised as his office. Since resigning from the British security services he had created, and now controlled, his own company – Phantom Securities. He had chosen the name Phantom as a mark of respect for Churchill's wartime special forces unit of the same name, the unit of which his uncle had been a member. Despite the rather awkward matter of his resignation, there were those in the service who still supported him. Some of the company's most lucrative contracts were arranged through the government, which much preferred a civilian organisation to handle its more sensitive work, thus remaining on safe political ground in the event of a crisis. Such contracts gave Sir Gilbert inside knowledge of government operations and access to some very influential people, both of which meant power. The telephone call he had just received, however, had not come from the usual source. The caller, Sir Robert Trescott, was an old and trusted friend. He was also deputy head of the security services.

Sir Gilbert stood just inside the gateway of the Memorial Gardens at the south-east corner of Green Park. He staggered a little against the force of the wind while adjusting his collar to fend off the threatening rain. Despite the weather he stood resolute, his mind occupied by pressing thoughts. What did they want of him? It had been eight long years since he had left the service. His mind focused with complete clarity on that distressing day. He had been forced to resign; even now the memory still pained him. His mood changed suddenly to one of anticipation and exhilaration. The message had been perfectly clear; we need your help. As if on cue a voice barked out his name.

'Gilbert! Thank you for meeting me. Sorry I'm a little late. This bloody weather – English summer, eh? Come, let's walk.' They turned in unison as if performing a perfect military manoeuvre. Keeping in step, they walked the tarmac path that crossed the eastern end of the park. Trescott waited a few moments before continuing. 'Gilbert, we have a problem and after serious discussion your name was put forward to help us solve it.'

'And the nature of this problem?'

'Diana, Princess of Wales. We want you to keep an eye on her.'

'But surely that's what your department is there for?'

'Yes, this is true and we do have her under full surveillance, but her more recent actions require a more intrusive reaction and unfortunately we, the department, cannot be seen responding so. The solution is simple – set-up an operation which runs parallel to our own, but make the shadow operation totally deniable.'

'Why me?'

'Who else is better qualified? You know the workings of the department. And you've carried out similar operations during your time with the security services.' This mention of the past caused both men to stop and face each other. 'Regardless of the past, your name is still spoken with distinction in some quarters.' With this, he turned his head back towards the way they had walked.

Sir Gilbert followed the man's gaze down to the magnificent building that was Buckingham Palace. A feeling of warmth slowly rose from his stomach and filtered up to lodge in his throat. He swallowed. 'How may I serve?' The formality of his words pronounced both his commitment and unswerving loyalty.

'All stations, this is Zero. What's the state of play?'

'Zero from Echo-three, 11.15. Tangos one, two and three now on the beach. Normal routine. Nothing to report.' The man sat in the shade provided by the fly bridge of the small boat looking through the camera eyepiece. 'Fucking marvellous, here we are in paradise and what are we doing? Sweating our butts off while that lot enjoy themselves. Look, there he goes again, better record it. "11.23, Tango-two riding jet-ski with Tango-one on the pillion." I'll take another shot.' The man bent slightly, pressing his right eye to the camera, and swept the huge lens across the still water until he picked up the couple on the jet-ski. He stabilised the camera as the image filled the viewfinder. 'Gotcha.'

'Zero, this is Echo-two, 16.55. We have a newcomer.'

'How do you mean, Echo-two?'

'Well, this guy has just turned up on the boat. At first we thought he was a deck hand or something but he embraced Tango-four and was introduced to the Tangos one, two and three. Over.'

'Roger that, Echo-two. Can you transmit an image?'

'Did it two minutes ago. Come back to me if it's important.'

'Roger that, Echo-two. Out to you. Romeo-one, are you receiving?'

'Romeo-one, that's a roger. We will have the problem sorted in about 30 minutes, making the final connections to the villa now. The satellite link is locked down and stable. Is the loop your end operational?'

'Affirmative, Romeo-one. Waiting to receive.'

'Romeo-one out.'

'All units, this is Zero. We have just received a transmit from Echo-two. Image identified as Dodi Al Fayed. Repeat, Mohamed Al Fayed's son. Now will someone tell me how he suddenly appeared on the boat without getting noticed? Get it together, people. Dodi Al Fayed now designated Tango-eight. Repeat, Dodi Al Fayed now designated Tango-eight.'

'Zero, this is Sierra-five. We confirm that Tango-eight arrived around 14.00 and was seen getting out of a vehicle with an unknown female. Both went aboard the *Sakara*, which is moored on Al Fayed's private jetty. We thought they were crew members. We have a good close-up. Stand by for transmit.'

'Sierra-five, roger that. Wait. Out.'

'All units, this is Zero. Female identified as Kelly Fisher, designation Tango-nine. Get it together, people! Zero out.'

'They were picked up at the airport and taken to the harbour in St Laurent-du-Var whereby they boarded the *Jonikal*. There is a full breakdown of the yacht in a separate file. Briefly, Al Fayed purchased the yacht just a few days ago. It is a 195 footer and has a crew of 16. We are going through the crew members now to see if any of them could be of use.

'The sailing took around five hours and we picked them up again at St Tropez. Al Fayed has a very large compound there, including a private beach. At this stage we are only able to intercept some of the calls, most of which are made using mobile phones. We have now located the relay and can access it at any time.

'During the first few days the assessment team could detect nothing out of the ordinary based on the surveillance information. Two calls were made alerting the press as to the royal presence, one from the *Jonikal* and the other from the compound. There is now a permanent press presence both onshore and out at sea. We have taken advantage of this and moved in some better equipment.

'Mohamed Al Fayed's son, Dodi, together with his American girlfriend, Kelly Fisher, arrived on the afternoon of the 14th. The woman was confined to one of the other Al Fayed boats and was not introduced to the royal party. The assessment team indicates that a great deal of effort was expended and neither of the two women realised that the other was present. Fisher eventually left a few days later.

'Changes started to appear when the Princess of Wales and Dodi Al Fayed shared a private dinner together. Ever since they have been very close. The assessment team defines a sudden change in both targets.'

'Are they sharing the same bed?'

'Not at this stage. However, on the 24th Diana was back in Paris staying at the Ritz Hotel where she and Dodi Al Fayed shared the Imperial Suite. We have a full report of their conversations and phone calls, the main point of interest being that they plan to holiday onboard the *Jonikal* – this time alone.'

'Thank you, Collins – a splendid job. Have you made an appointment for me to talk to the princess before she departs for Bosnia?'

'Yes, sir. She has agreed to see you on August the 7th.'

Sir Robert Trescott sat mulling over the surveillance material that had reached his desk earlier that morning. He did not particularly like black operations but on this occasion he had no option but to sanction further action. The princess had to be brought under control. Gilbert Scott was the ideal choice to head the Sovereign Committee, added to which most of the men now working for Phantom Securities had at some stage been government employees.

Rewinding the tapes, Trescott replaced the film and text in a red fabric bag, similar to the type used for office mail. This one, however, had several added features, one of which was a self-destruct mechanism in the event that it should fall into the wrong hands. When he had finished, he called one of his security couriers. 'Deliver this, please. You will require today's codeword, and make sure you get his personal signature – give it to no one else.'

The butler entered, informing Sir Gilbert of the courier's arrival, fussing over the fact that he was not allowed to sign for the package. Having received a phone call from Trescott some two hours earlier, Sir Gilbert ignored the lackey's whining, gave the codeword and personally signed for the security bag. Returning to the library, he locked himself in and, like Trescott, analysed the tapes and text. Trescott's men had done an excellent job. The cameras had been well placed, and the picture quality was exceptionally good. His own teams would have to pull out all the stops to match this. As he browsed, he pondered over the scenes he was witnessing – here was the mother of the future King cavorting with a playboy. Moreover, he was a Muslim. Such openly displayed antics were a Godsend for the gutter press. While the holiday with the Al Fayed family had been offensive, this latest meeting confirmed their worst fears. Trescott's plan to form the Sovereign Committee had been a wise and prompt decision, for time was not on their side. If Diana continued to develop this relationship they would have no option other than to implement Operation Royal Blood. To that end Trescott had asked Sir Gilbert to organise a meeting of the Sovereign Committee for later that evening.

The car swept up the winding driveway in haste, forcing small stones to spit out from under its wheels. With a final crunch it came to an abrupt stop, settling in a small cloud of dust. As if by some hidden signal, the butler appeared in the large open doorway and strode down the steps in time to hold open the vehicle door.

'Good evening, sir. They are waiting for you in the library. I am afraid they have already started.' Trescott grunted at the butler's implied rebuke and made his way into the house. He nodded his apologies as he entered the room and took his seat. Sir Gilbert was on his feet, in full flow.

'I spent most of this morning going over the conversations and pictures that were taken over the weekend. Whether or not Mohamed Al Fayed orchestrated this union between his son and the Princess of Wales is now immaterial. This past weekend has clearly revealed to us that something must be done to check this latest entanglement!' Sir Gilbert spat out the words, ejecting them as if they were some evil taste in his mouth. 'This, gentlemen, is the mother of our future King. If not stopped, she will do irreversible damage to our Monarchy. Despite the best efforts of our security services we can no longer control or conceal her actions.' He stood before them and apart from the odd intonation of accord, they remained silent, waiting in anticipation. Looking at their faces, Sir Gilbert searched for the slightest sign of weakness. On finding none, he continued. 'For the past year she has been enthralled by several other Muslims. To be blunt, and I quote a report in one newspaper, "I'm never going to date an Englishman again. They are such inadequates." '

To emphasise his point, Sir Gilbert turned to pick up several newspapers and hold them aloft. Each carried front page photographs of Diana and her two sons together with members of the Al Fayed family. Sir Gilbert let them slip from his hands, releasing them as if they were filth. He was silent, letting his words weave their repugnance in the minds of those before him. Sir Gilbert's face was a reddening flush and small beads of sweat erupted across his forehead. He brushed back the fine strands of grey hair that covered his balding head, signalling an end to his verbal tirade.

'What are we going to do?' the Hon. Alexander Kesterton held the half-empty brandy glass with both hands, as if afraid it might escape.

'If I might answer that, Gilbert,' Robert Trescott stood to address them. 'I have requested an appointment with the Princess of Wales under the pretext of my department's concern about her safety while travelling abroad. She will no longer be allowed to take the boys with her, thus she is not entitled to royal protection. During my visit I will bluntly confront her about the relationship and highlight some of the hazards such an affair could produce. I have also arranged for our surveillance team to cover her every movement with the express instructions that no one is to take any overt action. We will watch her and where possible harass her. If possible, get her to make mistakes.'

'Thank you, Robert,' said Sir Gilbert. 'As for the rest of you gentlemen I want no stone unturned. Discredit both

Mohamed Al Fayed and his son. They both have a colourful past, so let's make some headlines of our own.' Sir Gilbert had seen a brief crease touch Trescott's brow and understood his concern. 'Don't worry, Robert. The media made Diana, ultimately they can destroy her, too. The more we can feed them, the easier will be our task.'

'Yesterday I paid a visit to Diana, Princess of Wales,' Sir Robert Trescott stood before the hastily-assembled meeting of the Sovereign Committee, his face pale and drawn. 'It was not a cordial meeting and the conversation became rather heated. At first I highlighted the importance of her forthcoming visit to Bosnia, praising her anti-landmine campaign, but the topic soon came round to Al Fayed. In brief, I tried to emphasise the tremendous damage she was doing, not just to the monarchy but also to Britain. She could not agree, arguing that the House of Windsor no longer had any hold over her. Then she informed me that she was in love with Dodi Al Fayed.'

Murmurs of disapproval rumbled round the room as the committee members turned to each other to express their distaste.

Trescott held up his hand, quashing any further interruptions before he continued. 'I had the feeling she was testing me and looking for a reaction. Shocked as I was, I pleaded with her not too make any rash decisions. Although she might not be in accord with the Royal Family, it would be imprudent not to prepare the British people. Her answer was simple – if she wanted to marry Al Fayed she would; if she wanted his child then she would have it; she did not need anyone's permission.' Trescott paused. There was a solemn silence as he surveyed the hardened faces of the committee. They all realised what now had to be done. 'Other than those present, I have not informed anyone about the real purpose of my visit, neither are there any records indicating the same. In light of my conversation with the Princess of Wales and based upon the evidence we have accumulated over the past few days, I have reluctantly asked Gilbert to set in motion Operation Royal Blood – Gilbert.'

Sir Gilbert rose to his feet. 'Operation Royal Blood calls for us to provide a contingency plan whereby Diana, Princess of Wales can be terminated. We cannot allow them to marry, or for that matter, even contemplate marriage. To allow them to do so would force this nation to question the very role of our Monarchy. Our traditional society, which we all hold so dear, will be gone forever.' Sir Gilbert bowed his head gravely before asking for a show of hands. 'Are we in agreement, gentlemen? To a man, or not at all.' With some satisfaction he watched as, one by one, the hands came up – some held thick Havana cigars, while others gripped cut-glass balloons of fine brandy – but they were unanimous.

'May one inquire,' the Honourable Alexander Kesterton's voice was lazy with arrogance, 'how do you intend to dispose of the woman?' It was a question begged by all.

'The detailed plan has not yet been finalised, but to all intents and purposes, her death will present itself through natural causes, Sir Gilbert replied. 'However, to help us in this unpleasant task, John's department in Whitehall has furnished us with a little help. If you would kindly explain, John.' Sir Gilbert seated himself while Sir John Turlingham took the floor.

'It would seem that two ex-SAS men, both wanted for

murder and desertion, have been detained in France. Their identity has not, so far, been confirmed which gives us time to intervene. Their names came up through Interpol when the French arrested two men near the murder scene of an exiled Iraqi diplomat. We do know that they were travelling on forged passports and the French have asked the Home Office to officially identify the men. Once it was brought to my attention who these men actually were, I realised their possible potential in aiding this committee. After briefly discussing the situation with Gilbert, I saw to it that the French request was delayed in order that we should assess their capabilities.'

'Thank you, John,' said Sir Gilbert, standing once more. 'I intend to visit the men and make them a proposition. If they agree to our terms, and given their profession and current circumstance I think they will, it will be a simple matter to have the men released due to mistaken identity. John's office has supplied a full dossier on both men and from their records I would say they are ideally suited. SAS trained, men who could get close without being identified, men who can be discreet.'

'Can they be trusted? How much will they know about the Committee?' Kesterton asked, looking more than a little concerned.

'As I have already stated, these men are wanted in connection with serious war crimes and desertion during the Gulf War. From what John tells me, since that time they have become professional assassins, leaving a trail of corpses across Europe and the Middle East. If they do not work for us, they will simply rot in jail. For security purposes, I will be the only one they will ever meet. The Sovereign Committee will never be mentioned and you will not be implicated, either in name or deed.'

The following day, armed with a full dossier on both men's capabilities, Sir Gilbert flew to France. Partly to occupy his mind, but also to refresh his memory, he read through the dossiers once more during the flight. When he had finished he placed the papers securely in his briefcase. 'Where do such men come from?' he wondered. 'Was the entire SAS capable of acting like this, or are these two just stray wolves?' The notes read more like case histories of patients from a high security hospital than career histories of professional soldiers. Still, the men suited his needs admirably, yet inwardly he cautioned himself to proceed with care.

Through Turlingham's efforts, Sir Gilbert's visit to Paris was deliberately kept low-key, although he was collected at Charles de Gaulle airport by an official limousine complete with police escort. He was taken, as requested, directly to La Sante prison in the capital's suburb. After a brief interview with the governor of the prison, he was escorted by two prison officers to a small room. A third officer, who had been standing outside the door, smartened to attention and saluted as he approached. Then, turning to unlock the door, he allowed Sir Gilbert to enter. The room was not large, its spartan fittings consisting of nothing more than a table and three chairs. On the far side of the table, sitting in the chairs opposite, were two men. Sir Gilbert detected the strong stench of urine and tobacco smoke that served to suppress an even more unpleasant, much older, musty smell.

'Nice place,' he muttered, turning to his escort and changing to fluent French. 'Thank you. I should like to speak in private. I shall not be more than twenty minutes. When I am finished, or should the need arise, I shall call out.' The door closed behind him.

Both Bulloch and Norris watched in silence as the older man sat down facing them.

'Good morning, gentlemen. You seem to be in a spot of trouble,' Sir Gilbert said, placing his briefcase on the table and looking up at them. The larger of the two men, whom he guessed was Bulloch, held his gaze. The eyes were bright, like some animal checking for danger, the head, with its close-cropped hair, lifted a little as if sniffing the air.

'What's all this then?' asked Bulloch. 'You a bloody lawyer or something?' His voice sounded a little nervous.

Sir Gilbert did not reply. He simply opened the briefcase, letting the catches flip with two loud clicks. He raised the lid slowly, lifting out the men's personal files, before deliberately turning the open case to face the two men. The smaller, stockier man, pushed back his chair and stood up. 'Fuck me!' exclaimed Norris. 'Got to be a hundred grand there.'

Although Bulloch's eyes took in the money, he remained silent. Only his expression changed. He still felt nervous, but instantly recognised the money for what it was – a signal. Their circumstances were clearly about to change. 'I take it you're offering us this money?'

'This and a great deal more, plus the promise of freedom. If you are interested, I have come to procure your services.' Sir Gilbert studied both their faces and quickly realised that if any deal was to be struck it would be with Bulloch.

'Who are you? How do we know this is not a set-up?' Bulloch demanded.

'You are John Bulloch. Born, Cardiff in 1954. You joined the army, 1st Battalion the Parachute Regiment, then volunteered for the SAS where you were accepted in 1976. You were promoted to sergeant in 1982 but were demoted to corporal due to fighting. During the Gulf War, you and Norris were accused of shooting an American liaison officer – a Captain Wesley – and of war crimes against the Iraqis. You illegally tortured and killed three young Iraqi soldiers. In the past six years, the British security services have monitored over a dozen assassinations in the Middle East, most of which bear your hallmark. Shall I go on?' Sir Gilbert felt pleased with himself.

'Where did you get all this . . .?' Norris started to ask.

'Shut it, Steve. Let me handle this,' snapped Bulloch, his eyes never leaving Sir Gilbert. 'So you've done your homework. What do you want from us?'

'I have need of two men such as you. I have a problem which I cannot solve, and it may turn out that the only solution is murder.'

'Why us? If you're from the government, why use us? You have your own K Section, why not use them?' Bulloch stared directly at Sir Gilbert. Just for an instant, he saw the grey-blue eyes waver. 'You're not from the government are you? This is something private?' Bulloch sat back, his cheeks stretched in a taunting grin.

'How very astute of you,' Sir Gilbert recovered his composure. 'You are correct in your assumption. I do not work for the British Government. My allegiance is similar, but my authority comes from a different domain. Although, make no mistake, I do have jurisdiction over your lives. Besides, any action by K requires at least a quorum of four cabinet ministers and I don't think they all share my views. That is why I am making you this offer. The person you have to deal with is a very prominent figure – very prominent indeed.' Sir Gilbert played on his words, hoping that Bulloch could not resist the challenge.

'For the right money, we will slot the whole fucking government for you. So cut the shit and tell us who the target is – the Prime Minister?' said Bulloch, half guessing, looking to Norris for backup.

'Yeah, we took out that bloody African Prime Minister. You know who paid us? His brother. Now he's the Prime Minister. So if you want to move up the ladder, just tell us who's getting in your way and me and John'll fix it for you.' Feeling more confident, Norris stretched out to feel the money in the briefcase. As he did so, Sir Gilbert slammed the lid down hard, trapping his hand. Bulloch was on his feet immediately. Reaching over the table he grabbed at Sir Gilbert's sleeve, while Norris hurriedly removed his fingers from the briefcase.

'Who the fuck do you think you're dealing with?' demanded Bulloch, his right fist coming up ready to strike.

'Remember where you are! Touch me and you will both rot in prison for the rest of your lives.' Sir Gilbert snarled, pulling away from Bulloch's grip. 'Your futures are now in my hands and you will soon learn that I am not to be trifled with. If you want out, and new identities – if you want enough money to retire on – you will do as I say.' His voice was stern enough to make Bulloch release his hold, yet not so loud as to summon the guard. Bulloch sat down, while Sir Gilbert remained standing, his words clear and concise. 'This is not a game. The target you have to eliminate is Diana, Princess of Wales.'

There was silence for a moment, until Steve Norris, who could contain himself no longer, burst forth. 'Fuck me, Lady Di!'

'As you may be aware, the princess is presently involved with an Egyptian by the name of Dodi Al Fayed. Unlike her other relationships, this one is serious; we believe she intends to marry. That is why I want you two to formulate a plan that will terminate the relationship permanently.'

After a moment's silence, Steve Norris turned to look the man straight in the face. 'I remember when we took part in her training, the time her and Charlie came to Hereford. I was the one that snatched her out of the room, while the rest of the team shot up the targets,' Norris grinned. 'I had my arm around her waist gripping her from behind. My hand was on her boob the whole time. You remember, John?'

'I remember,' said Bulloch, watching the look of disdain that had crept over Sir Gilbert's face as he listened to Steve's story.

'Then who better?' said Sir Gilbert. 'The security on Diana since her divorce from Charles has slackened somewhat. That should help. As ex-members of the SAS, you have excellent knowledge of the security procedures covering the Royal Family, and should therefore be able to find a way in which to eradicate her. It is only when she is with the children that her former maximum security status is implemented. At most other times she is vulnerable. That said, the method of her demise must be made to look natural.'

'Why not just to shoot her?' suggested Norris.

'No!' Sir Gilbert snapped. 'The princess must die without suspicion being pointed at anyone other than herself.' He paused again. 'Throughout our royal history, kings, queens and princes have all plotted to kill or overthrow one another, but I fear in this day and age, the public will not tolerate such behaviour. There would be investigations, trials and culprits. The method I am looking for must be subtle. Her death will shock the world, so it must be made to be acceptable. In light of the information with which you will be supplied, combined with you own expert skills, I am sure we can find a solution.' Sir Gilbert paused momentarily before continuing. 'The royals are constantly under threat, and there have been many security scares over the years. I have chosen you two because you know the system. Find me a chink in her armour, but do it outside of Britain. France, if possible.'

'And if we say no?' asked Bulloch.

'Then you will rot here, and these files will be handed over to the French authorities. However, if you need time to think, so be it. You might not be aware of how slow the French judicial system is.' Sir Gilbert looked vacantly at the squalid room, then moved to close the briefcase. Bulloch stopped him. He had no doubt that Sir Gilbert was a formidable person. He obviously had the resources and the connections which allowed him to by-pass official channels and reach them in a French jail. The man had reserve, confidence and more than a little arrogance; all the attributes of real power. It suddenly dawned on Bulloch that maybe he and Norris were simply being used by the British government to carry out their dirty work. 'Whatever,' thought Bulloch, 'anything was better than spending forever in a French jail.'

'We have a deal. Now how do we get out of this shit-hole?'

'I will make the necessary arrangements. You should be free within the hour. Say nothing to anyone. You will be given everything you need plus full instructions which will be handed to you on your way out – *follow them to the letter.* The courier will also take you to the airport and provide you with a contact number. Anything you need while you are in London will be supplied. I will furnish you with comprehensive material on the Princess of Wales. When you have come up with a solution, you can contact me. Any questions?'

'How long do we have?' inquired Bulloch.

'I estimate three weeks at best. However, the sooner you come up with a workable plan the better,' Sir Gilbert stood and knocked for the guard. As the door opened he turned. 'I must remind you both, if you try anything foolish, K section will track you down, and you will be terminated.' He exited and the door slammed shut behind him. For a moment both men sat close-mouthed, listening as the footsteps receded down the corridor.

'Steve, our luck just changed,' declared Bulloch.

Despite what Sir Gilbert had promised, it was almost six in the evening before they were finally released. The courier handed over the briefcase Sir Gilbert had been carrying, together with their personal belongings which, in the course of the murder investigation, had been removed from their hotel. They were then driven to the airport whereupon they were given new British passports and tickets for the first available flight to London. During the short flight, Norris could not resist opening the case. 'All this and more just to waste some toffee-nosed fucking tart!' In addition to the money, there was an envelope tucked in the inner wallet of the lid. He gave it to Bulloch. It contained a single card giving an address in Battersea, together with a set of what were presumably door keys. Norris, in the meantime was busy counting the money. The briefcase contained £100,000 in £50 notes.

'We really fell on our feet this time, John,' said Norris, a faraway look coming over his face. 'You remember the story I told you? When I got myself a handful of her tit? Well the truth is, when I finally dragged her into the corridor and let go of the bitch, she turned and gave me a real dirty look . . . like I was a piece of shit or something. I'll show her this time.'

By ten o'clock that evening, the taxi they had taken from Heathrow dropped them off next to Oddbins, the off-licence on the south side of Battersea Bridge.

'This looks like the place,' said Norris, studying the smart apartment block opposite. Then, nodding his head towards the off-licence, he added, 'What say we grab a couple of bottles while we're here?'

'Why not?' replied Bulloch.

The apartment, they discovered, was on the third floor. 'Fuck me,' said Norris, looking around at the extravagant fixtures. 'This is a bit of all right.' Bulloch grunted, dropping his case before having a proper look. 'Beats a French prison.' Several doorways led off the small hallway they had just entered and a large open arch led directly into the lounge. He strode casually through the arch, surveying the surroundings. Norris came close behind, the bottles in the carrier bag clinking together as he tossed them onto the settee. The apartment had been expensively decorated and lavishly furnished but it showed little sign of use.

'This must be a "safe-house",' commented Bulloch as he walked to the large patio window and looked down over the Thames. Despite the weather, the city looked illuminated and alive. For a moment he watched the night lights twinkle on the muddy waters. He turned just as Norris was coming from the kitchen clutching two glasses. As he put them on the table, Bulloch noticed two boxes. He picked one up to discover that they were brand new mobile phones.

'I take it these are for us,' he said, turning one over in his hand. 'Presumably, this is how he is going to keep in touch.'

'Safer than using a land line, John,' Norris put the two glasses down and took one of the bottles from the carrier bag. He proceeded to pour two large Scotches. 'You want to go out and eat, or what?'

'No. I'm not hungry. In fact, I could do with a shower and get a good night's sleep. I still have the stink of that fucking prison on me.' Bulloch picked up one of the glasses, and made his way back to the hallway whereupon he opened one of the doors. As expected, the bedroom was equally well fitted, with the bed freshly made. 'I'll take this one, Steve,' he said, picking up his suitcase from the hall and tossing it into the bedroom.

'Fair enough with me,' answered Norris, picking up the remote and switching on the television. 'Nice pad. A safe-house you reckon?'

'I don't know,' replied Bulloch shouting from the bedroom. 'Either that or this is where his lordship brings his tarts.'

'If you ask me, I think the man's a poofter,' laughed Norris, flicking through the channels.

'Whatever. Just keep the sound down will you? As soon as I've showered, I'm going to get my head down.' With that, Bulloch shut the bathroom door behind him.

Next morning, feeling refreshed, they walked down Battersea Bridge Road, where they found a small breakfast bar. 'I could eat a scabby horse between two bread vans,' said Norris ordering the mammoth breakfast. They were halfway through their meal, when Bulloch's mobile phone rang.

'Yes.'

'You have a package arriving in thirty minutes. Understood?'

'Yes.' The line was disconnected and Bulloch put the

phone down next to his plate. 'Finish up, Steve, we're expecting a package.' But Norris refused to be hurried and would not leave until he had consumed every morsel of his breakfast. Consequently, when they arrived back at the flat, the courier was waiting.

'I need to see your passports,' said the leather-clad courier. Bulloch nodded, indicating for the man to follow them up the stairs. Once they had identified themselves to his satisfaction, the man handed them a large wallet for which he required a signature. When he had gone, Bulloch took the package into the lounge and placed it on the table. It had a security tag which he broke before unzipping the package. Reaching inside he took out the contents and laid them on the table.

Three large internal mail envelopes contained almost a hundred pages of typed text. There was a large street map of Paris and a large-scale map of the Mediterranean. Both were marked by small, numbered stick-on paper dots; a legend stuck to the side of each map, indicated what each dot represented. Eager to be in on the act, Norris picked up the several video tapes which had been in the package and stacked them by the television. He started to flip through a large envelope full of photographs. In all, the material represented the surveillance summary on Diana since her holiday with the Al Fayed's some four weeks previously.

'Find some tape and stick this on the wall, Steve,' said Bulloch.

'What?' replied Norris, absentmindedly thumbing through the fist full of photographs he was holding. 'Have you seen these? To think that I, Steve Norris, have actually held one of those tits.'

'I'm pleased for you. Now stop your bragging, we have

work to do. Stick this fucking map on the wall will you? Let's get this show on the road.'

Bulloch had always taken his work seriously and now he was anxious to please their new master. He set about preparing a plan. The information was extensive and Bulloch studied everything minutely, occasionally stopping to make notes on a small pad. In essence, Sir Gilbert had supplied them with detailed itineraries of Diana's daily movements, the time they had breakfast, restaurants they visited, what transport they used, etc. There were photographs of Diana going about her daily life, but mostly they showed her with her new male companion, Dodi Al Fayed. For identification, each picture was clearly marked on the back with the accompanying subjects' names.

'This information is outstanding, John. Someone has done an excellent job. How on earth did they get a shot like this?' Norris held up a photograph depicting the princess wearing a swimsuit, sitting in a chair on board a boat. 'The paparazzi could never get shots like this. These pictures were taken by real professionals. You would need a lot of manpower and virtually unlimited funds to purchase the surveillance equipment required to get pictures of this quality.'

'There's only one organisation that I know of with that capability – E4 surveillance unit. No one else has the money or the expertise,' replied Bulloch. 'Now let's see if we can identify some kind of pattern to all this, something that will give us an edge.'

Norris and Bulloch took their time filtering through the information, and the hours passed quickly. For the next three days, apart from going to the breakfast bar or visiting the pub for an evening meal, they worked non-stop. Bulloch, with his slow, methodical pace, used the large street map of Paris, carefully retracing Diana's steps, trying to make some sense of her movements, hoping to establish a pattern. He especially studied those incidents where she had forsaken her security and ventured out alone. He separated the information into various piles and subdivided these piles into individual events covering Diana's life. By late evening of the third day, the lounge floor was strewn with paper, yet nothing had presented itself as an opportunity for murder.

'I don't know about you, Steve, but I've had enough for one day; what say we get something to eat and down a couple of beers? Tomorrow we'll categorise all this stuff and concentrate on her more recent movements. I have an idea we might be able to take out the boat next time she and Al Fayed are on board – send them all to the bottom of the Med.' Bulloch stood, stretching. The room felt stuffy. He walked to the patio window, slid open the door and stepped out onto the small balcony. The summer breeze had a cool edge to it, threatening rain again, and to clear his head he inhaled deeply. He gripped the balcony and looked out over the Thames. Down to his right the tarmac span of Battersea Bridge was busy with home-bound commuters. Absentmindedly, he wondered of what their days had consisted, and he realised that he despised them. They were inert, with dull lives, scared shitless of getting a parking fine or losing their jobs. At least he and Steve had the guts to kill, to live life on their own terms. Bulloch was still daydreaming when Norris came up beside him. He had become obsessed with the pictures of Diana, even now he was holding several photographs.

'Look at this, John,' he said, pointing to a photograph. It depicted Diana wearing a protective vest, complete with helmet and visor.

'What's that?' asked Bulloch, still mesmerised by the flow of humanity below.

'I was just saying, what an idiot she must be, to go visiting all these landmine victims.'

'What do you mean?' Bulloch stepped back into the lounge, closing the window behind him. He shivered suddenly, listening half-heartedly as Steve rambled on.

'I mean she's a typical dumb blonde. Fancy walking in a minefield just to prove a point? Two ounces of explosive – BOOM – and there go your legs. Did I ever tell you I shagged a girl with no legs once? Lost them in a car crash. Pity,' reflected Norris, 'she was a great shag.'

'They're all great shags to you. Come on, let's get a beer and something to eat.'

It was two o'clock in the morning when Bulloch awoke. He had tossed and turned for the past hour. He could hear Steve snoring loudly in the next room, yet it was not that which had awoken him. Something nagged in the back of his mind, a nagging that would not leave him alone. He rose, fetched a glass of water from the kitchen and went to stand before the spacious window as he had done earlier. Save for a few cars and the odd pedestrian, the bridge was now deserted. Further downriver, the bright lights which decorated Albert Bridge sparkled on the ebony surface of the Thames. For a moment his hand rested on the door handle as he considered letting the fresh night air fill his lungs, but he resisted the temptation. He admitted to himself that he was getting nowhere with this assignment and although Steve was always there for support, Bulloch knew that the plan would ultimately fall on his shoulders.

Outside, the rain had started again. It came in sudden gushes. Waves of heavy, wind-driven droplets beat against the window. As his view of the river became obscured, Bulloch raised his glass and swallowed the remaining water. Down on the bridge, he noticed the headlights of a car weave from side to side, as if the driver had lost control. 'The wind must be strong,' Bulloch thought to himself. 'Either that or the driver's pissed.'

A cacophony of rapid thoughts crashed through his mind; he shook his head trying to unravel the jumble and find a clear equation. Car swerving on the bridge – right spot – car crash – *'Two ounces of explosive – BOOM'*. Steve's words pierced the mist of his mind and he had the beginning of an answer! Bulloch needed to talk, to clarify his thoughts. In four swift paces he crossed the lounge and burst into Steve's room. His hand hit the light switch, turning darkness into day. Engrossed with his budding idea, he had not been thinking. Bulloch stopped abruptly, standing very still in the doorway.

Although sound asleep, the noise of the door opening and the bright light triggered an automatic reaction within Norris – and he was quick. The right hand slipped smoothly from under the pillow. It was holding a pistol. Bulloch remained perfectly still until, through sleep fogged eyes, Norris recognised him.

'Jesus Christ, John? You know better than to burst in on me like that! I could have blown you away!' Norris put the pistol down and brushed the sleep from his eyes. 'What time is it?'

Bulloch looked down at his friend lying on the bed and smiled. 'Never mind the time. Listen to me, I think we could be in business. I know how we're going to get her!'

'How?' Norris sat up. Alerted by the enthusiasm in Bulloch's voice, he became fully awake.

'A straightforward road accident.'

Norris shook his head as if he had not heard correctly. 'Big deal,' he looked at Bulloch as if his idea were totally insane, then, swinging his feet off the bed, he headed for the lounge. 'How the fucking hell are you going to do that without anyone noticing?' he voiced over his shoulder before disappearing into the kitchen. 'You can't guarantee the kill just by crashing the car. You'd have to blow the fucker to bits. Doesn't look like much of an accident then, does it? You want a beer?'

'No, thanks. Now listen, just think about it,' said Bulloch, as he dropped to his knees and searched excitedly through the piles of paper scattered around the room. Norris returned holding a bottle of beer and, flopping on the settee, observed Bulloch's frantic search with weary interest.

'What are you looking for? How can . . .?' he broke off mid-sentence as Bulloch stood up, grinning, thrusting a photograph under Steve's nose. The picture was fairly recent and showed a speeding black Mercedes, supposedly containing Diana, being chased by photographers on motorcycles.

'We know what makes her run,' smiled Bulloch. 'Al Fayed can't put that many vehicles at her disposal. All we need to know is which one she will be travelling in on a given day. Our employers are bound to have someone inside Al Fayed's organisation who will be able to supply information. They couldn't have got all this surveillance material without someone on the payroll.

'The route is not all that important, we simply follow and choose our spot at random. You remember how we got rid of

Gerard Mullan in Northern Ireland? We fitted that device they use on the anti-terrorist team, and blinded the bastard with an ambush light fitted to the back of our car. We followed that bastard for days before the ideal opportunity came up.'

'You're right. I had forgotten about that. We ran him into a sharp bend just before a bridge. He was decapitated,' Norris smiled. 'You think you can make it work in Paris, John?'

'Yeah. Providing we can find the guy who came up with the ambush light and the other gadget. What the hell was his name?

Norris stared into space, searching his memory. 'The light was made by some guy from Cannock. He also designed a kind of radio-controlled bomb for stopping a motor. He called it the Blockbuster – and the man's name was Jarvis.'

'I knew I could count on you to remember,' laughed Bulloch, jealous of his friend's exceptional memory. 'I was on a demolition course at the time and we did several field trials with the Blockbuster device. Providing the transmitter was close enough it could slow a vehicle from forty miles an hour to just twenty in less than a hundred metres. Detonating the Blockbuster would then stop the target dead in its tracks. What I'm thinking is we wind up the paparazzi buzzing around Diana and get them to harass her. If we can get their car to accelerate, blind the driver and then blow the engine we have the perfect accident. We'll recce the routes they use around Paris and choose a number of locations. We simply stay with Diana's car until we reach a point that will cause maximum damage.'

'So you really think we can get close to one of her cars?' asked Norris.

'Why not? The paparazzi do. What are two more faces, especially when they're hidden by crash helmets?' asked

Bulloch. 'Sure, we need to refine the plan to make it look natural. Shit, even if she doesn't die straight away, we can be on hand to make sure that she does. It worked well in Northern Ireland. Why not in Paris?'

Norris took another mouthful of his beer, looking at Bulloch as he did so. He had long since come to recognise John's cunning and creativity. True, he could be ruthless and was able to kill without thought, but he was also a meticulous planner. If John believed that this was a good idea, he would go along. 'Where do we start?'

Bulloch smiled, pleased with himself. 'First we get some sleep. Then, tomorrow morning, I want you to find out all you can about the type of vehicle we may be up against – how they are serviced, where they are garaged, who has access, the lot. Include those of Al Fayed, both here and in France. I want to know what happens if they become damaged or involved in an accident. Find out anything that will be helpful.'

'What are you going to do?'

'Me? First thing tomorrow morning, I'm going to see a man about making me a Blockbuster and an ambush light.'

They breakfasted next morning as usual, but were totally immersed in their new project. Before they left the apartment, Bulloch used one of the mobile phones Sir Gilbert had provided, ringing the contact number he had been given. He kept his request precisely to the point. Having given all the details he and Norris could recall of the whereabouts of the Cannock-based engineer who had developed the Blockbuster device, he requested a car. When Sir Gilbert inquired the reason for the information, Bulloch fobbed him off, saying it was purely research, not wishing to commit his plan until he was sure that it was certain of success.

When they returned from breakfast, Norris took a taxi into town. Bulloch sifted through the batch of papers covering Diana's transportation. It had gone eleven before the doorbell rang. It was the same courier, only this time the man was dressed in an expensive pin-striped suit. He handed over a thin envelope, then gave Bulloch the keys to a car. 'It's the dark blue 306 XSi. I've parked downstairs, in the apartment's allotted space in the garage.'

'Thanks,' said Bulloch, taking the keys before closing the door in the man's face. He opened the envelope and read through the enclosed file. It took no more than two minutes to register the information; Sir Gilbert's resources were extremely good. The man they sought was Oliver Jarvis, a 47-year-old, self-employed engineer. He still lived in Cannock. It listed a few personal details, together with the man's address and telephone number. Picking up the mobile phone, Bulloch punched in the number and waited. After several rings, a female voice answered.

'I would like to speak to Oliver Jarvis, please.'

'He's not here at the moment, but he should be back around midday. Would you like to leave your number, and I will get him to call you back?'

'No. If I can be sure that he will be there this afternoon, I will drive up and speak to him personally. My name is Rogers and, if he's not too busy, I have some work for him,' Bulloch replied.

'Oliver will be here this afternoon. What time shall I say you will be arriving, Mr Rogers?'

'Expect me about three, but allow half an hour either way. Could you give me directions once I reach Cannock?' He jotted down the directions as the woman dictated them, slipping them into his pocket, and left the apartment. He walked down the steps that led to the underground garage and found the Peugeot 306 parked where the courier had left it. The late morning traffic was light and 30 minutes later he was driving up the M40 at a steady 80 miles an hour. The details the woman had given him proved accurate and three hours after leaving London, Bulloch found himself travelling in undulating countryside. At last he came to a small side road that ran uphill into a large, wooded copse behind which stood Jarvis's house.

The house was built of red brick, and sat back from the narrow road, nestling under the shade of two large oak trees. Bulloch parked the car next to a battered and ageing Land Rover and walked up the gravel drive.

'So what can I do for you?' asked Oliver Jarvis, stepping back from the doorway, allowing Bulloch to enter the kitchen. Jarvis was a tall, awkward-looking man, a careless dresser, who talked with a rough, abrupt manner. Bulloch noted the man was somewhat animated, his large hands moved quickly, yet with a certain deftness, smoothly skilful, almost as if they were independent accessories. Bulloch took Jarvis's outstretched hand and shook it vigorously, putting on a display of greeting some long-lost colleague. The skin felt rough, indicating the hands of a craftsman; in this case, an inventor of weapons. In his field, Oliver Jarvis was both artist and engineer. His labour of late had been developing explosive devices for use in the film industry but such work was infrequent, making money tight. His wife had mentioned the possibility of work, but as he confronted Bulloch in the open doorway, some hidden sense warned of impending disaster. Hiding his fears behind a smile, Jarvis offered Bulloch a chair at the kitchen table.

'Can I get you a drink of anything?' he asked, once Bulloch was seated.

'No, thanks. I'm fine.'

'So do I know you, then?' Jarvis inquired. 'Your face looks kind of familiar.'

'John Rogers – I was with the SAS in Hereford. You provided us with a prototype of your Blockbuster. At the time of the trials I personally found it very impressive. I believe the regiment still uses it.'

'So are you still with the regiment?'

'No. I left some time ago. I'm into private security work now, just like the rest of the boys. At present, I'm working down in South America, protecting shipments of gold. We've had several armoured vehicles hijacked lately and we're looking for a way of preventing this. I remembered the device you invented and thought it could be an option for totally immobilising a vehicle if it was in the process of being stolen.'

'The original type you're talking about is outdated now. Besides, you need an explosives permit for those. If it's just the electronics you're looking for, then there's no real problem. I've been working on several new devices that would allow for more extensive remote control over a moving vehicle, increase acceleration, disable the brakes, inflate the airbags etc. The trouble is, no one wants them; I still have a couple of my prototypes knocking around somewhere.' Jarvis's voice started to show a keen edge. What the hell? Who cares why the guy wanted them? If it meant earning a few hundred pounds, he was willing to sell his working prototypes.

Bulloch did not miss the eagerness; he had already taken stock of the man's situation. Times looked hard. The house was neat and clean, if somewhat cluttered. Though an open door, Bulloch observed what was obviously the lounge, an odd-looking wooden statue stood beside the fireplace above which hung a large, daubed painting of a nude woman. Jarvis clearly had a lot of spare time. They chatted about the SAS for several minutes before Bulloch outlined his real needs. 'What I really want is something simple, something that will guarantee the vehicle will crash while leaving no trace of its presence. Can you do that?'

Oliver Jarvis looked at Bulloch for a long time. In the cosiness of his own kitchen, he suddenly felt afraid. Despite the outward appearance, the man sitting opposite was very dangerous. The initial warmth had gone from their conversation, and the dialogue had turned to business. Jarvis could not recall Rogers from the days of testing his device in Hereford, but that had been some 15 years ago. What the man was asking for was not secret, but it was highly sensitive. The SAS and the security services had used the older-type Blockbuster in training but as far as he knew it had never been used operationally. His contracts with the government had run out five years ago when a German company had stolen his idea and improved upon it. He was just a one-man band and unable to compete, or take legal action. Within his means he had continued to experiment, modifying the advanced electronics used by modern cars, interfering with the fuel flow, timing and braking systems. In theory, speeding up a car for a short distance would be possible and, depending on the type of car, he could also suppress the brakes as well as cut all power to the electrical systems. Still, he wasn't going to tell Bulloch that. He detected money in this, and life had been difficult lately. He looked at the man sitting opposite. 'Yeah, in theory I could make such a device for you. It will depend on the vehicle type. Armoured vans, you say?'

Bulloch realised the first flaw in his interpretation of what the device was to be used for. He decided he would have to confide a little in Jarvis. 'We use a range of vehicles at the moment. They're either Range Rovers or armoured Mercedes.'

'VIP vehicles?' Even as he said it, Jarvis guessed that the device was being designed to kill a human. Still, most ex-SAS were doing some kind of dirty work. Why should he complain? He didn't have to hit the trigger – but his price had just gone up.

There was little need to lie any more. Both men knew what they were talking about. 'I'm not sure of the model, but the device should look like part of the vehicle. If explosives are required I will supply my own in-country. I trust PE-4 will suffice? So, will you do it?' Bulloch deliberately avoided saying which country, although he was fairly sure that Jarvis had guessed the real purpose behind his request.

Oliver Jarvis looked at Bulloch. 'If you're talking Range Rover or Mercedes I can't see a problem, they are both heavy vehicles. However, you should be aware that these cars now incorporate excellent safety features in the event of a crash.'

'I am aware of that that,' Bulloch replied absent-mindedly, his mind lost in thought. 'Interfering with the electronics or engine management systems would require access to the vehicle and a good knowledge of onboard computers – all that takes time – so keep it simple.'

Jarvis nodded several times, reiterating Bulloch's demands, 'Easy to fit, undetectable, yet guaranteed to cause an accident. I'll need to experiment and it's going to cost. Do you want to track the vehicle? I can supply you with a very good GPS and GSM system.'

'That would be handy, but keep it straightforward' said Bulloch. 'I'd prefer you to find a solution that is common to the more exclusive range of Mercedes.' He waited while Jarvis scribbled a few notes on a scrap of paper. 'There is also a device know as an ambush light. I want you to make me something similar. One that can be fitted into the rear of a motorbike.'

'Type of bike?'

'Kawasaki ZX600.' Again Bulloch waited while Jarvis made a note, then he issued a word of caution. 'I take it you will keep our little venture private? I always think privacy is worth paying for.' He paused to let the meaning sink in. 'Shall we say £5,000 in advance, and another £10,000 when the job is finished?' His voice conveyed sufficient meaning for Oliver Jarvis to understand. £15,000 was a lot of money, money he badly needed.

'Am I to take it that the device on the bike needs to be fitted covertly with a simultaneous trigger for light and to initiate the disabling device?' All pretence had now gone.

'Precisely,' replied Bulloch, pulling an envelope from his inside jacket pocket

'What the eye don't see, the heart don't grieve over,' said Jarvis, taking the envelope. He flicked through the notes without really counting them. He didn't have to; he knew it would contain exactly £5,000. 'Give me a week.' The deal was done.

'No longer,' warned Bulloch, standing. 'I'll phone you in seven days time, at which stage I want to collect them. Agreed?'

'Agreed,' said Jarvis. 'How do I get in touch?'

Bulloch had already started for the door. Neither man offered to shake hands on the way out. 'You don't. I will contact you.'

It was almost seven o'clock in the evening by the time Bulloch returned to the apartment. Norris was waiting for him. 'Any joy?' Norris inquired, as Bulloch dropped carelessly into the couch.

'Yes, but he'll need a week, and we need to identify the exact vehicle. Still, if he can do what he claims, I think we have the answer. Now, do me a favour and get me a beer, mate. Then you can tell me how you got on.' Bulloch kicked off his shoes and, resting his feet on the ornate marble table, he relaxed into the softness of the cushions.

'Well, I managed to find out quite a bit,' Norris shouted from the kitchen. 'Got several good mechanical guides for Mercedes.' Norris came back into the lounge clutching two beers. 'There you go,' he handed Bulloch one of the bottles before flopping into the couch opposite. 'I also have a whole lot of technical stuff on modern car electronics.' Norris paused, indicating the pile of books resting on the table by Bulloch's feet. 'Changing the subject, while I was at a loose end, I checked with our answering service. There were two coded messages from our South American friends. Basically, he is asking if we can still do the Colombian job.'

Bulloch took another pull from the bottle and thought for a minute. 'After the fuck-up in Paris, I have half a mind to cancel it. Besides, this job has priority.'

'I know that,' said Norris, 'but it's only a straightforward head shot. I can handle the Colombian job on my own. One week and I'll be back. With me out of the way it will give you time to work out the details on the Diana hit.'

Norris's keenness to impress his friend was obvious. He was looking for a chance to prove that he could be trusted alone. 'You sure?' queried Bulloch. 'It might be best if we cancelled it.'

'Piece of piss,' replied Norris. 'Besides, we have our reputation to think of.'

Bulloch relented. 'You're right. I'll speak to Bogota tomorrow and make the arrangements. Now let's go and get something to eat, I'm starving.'

'What was Mr Rogers like, dear?' Oliver Jarvis's wife inquired as she entered the kitchen. She had suffered one of her migraines and had taken to her bed during his visit.

'Oh, just an old friend from the SAS in Hereford. He wants me to make him something,' Jarvis replied, focusing on the part-assembled circuitry in the small workshop adjoining the rear of the house.

'Oh, that's nice,' she cooed back.

'Yeah, isn't it just?' mumbled Jarvis, looking down at the bundle of £50 notes in front of him. 'It's very nice.'

Jarvis started to work. Disabling a car in the manner specified posed many problems. As each problem arose, his brain searched for an answer, and he was suddenly aware that the task had become a challenge. He was sure that Rogers (if that was his real name) was up to no good, yet the thought did not bother him. Secretly, he enjoyed the undertaking, speculation as to the use for his devices did not concern him. Here was a chance to develop and use his creative abilities, something he had not had for a long time. Besides, he thought to himself, he could buy most of what he wanted from a small firm in East London for a fraction of the cost was charging. He worked methodically, checking and testing each small detail. He was oblivious to time or his other needs. It was almost midnight when his wife came into the workshop dressed ready for bed.

'Have you seen the time, Oliver. Aren't you coming to bed?

'In a minute, sweetheart, in a minute. Just let me finish this. You go on ahead, dear. I promise I won't be long.'

Despite his promise, it was four o'clock in the morning by the time he had finished. 'Now all I need is the model of the vehicle and a spare electronic control and I shall have myself another £10,000,' Oliver Jarvis thought happily to himself before switching off the workshop lights. He made his way upstairs to bed. Undressing quietly, so as not to disturb his wife, he crawled beneath the duvet and closed his eyes. Despite the late hour, sleep would not come. For some time he just lay there, his mind pondering over Bulloch's required use for his work. It was almost dawn before he finally fell asleep.

A day later, Bulloch drove Norris to Heathrow airport. They had woken early, flight BA295 to Miami was scheduled for departure at 10 o'clock, and Bulloch wanted to miss the morning traffic. While Norris dressed, Bulloch wrote down last-minute instructions, shouting them out at the same time. 'I've arranged for you to fly from Miami on Colombian Airlines. You pick the tickets up at the transfer desk. Our principal will meet you in Bogota. He will take you to the hotel where he will supply you with the weapon – it's the new Heckler & Koch sniper rifle. The target is an American DEA agent planted within the cartel. He was in so deep it was only by luck that they discovered him. He slips away to meet his contact once a week and that's when they want this done. Let them know we know. One shot is all you'll get,' warned Bulloch. 'Get in, do the job, and get out.'

'No problem, don't worry,' said Norris, strolling through the bedroom door into the lounge. 'Have you ever known me to miss? How do I look?'

Norris was dressed in a trim, dark suit. He strutted in front of the mirror and adjusted his tie. 'Very nice. Very nice indeed,' he answered his own reflection.

Bulloch laughed, 'The suit looks great, but do you always have to wear that fucking tie?'

'What's wrong with it? It's a good tie,' he said, centering the knot between the wings of the crisp, white collar. 'It makes me feel as if I still belong to the regiment.'

Bulloch rose and handed him the slip of paper. 'Contact names and places, just in case you forget. Come on, we don't want you to miss the plane.'

CHAPTER

6

Colombia,
August 16, 1997

Caleb Wesley loved the jungle, and when the powers that be
decided that a special force was needed to train the
Colombian Army and to help fight the Colombian drugs
cartel, he had volunteered. Promoted to rank of major, Cal
had flown into Bogota, where the senior DEA administrator
had briefed him on the situation, assigning him to a military
base in the small mountain town of Buga. Cal used all his
jungle skills to teach his new recruits. He started with the
basics. They learned fieldcraft and weapon handling, tactics
and drills, and they learnt well. After two months, he
considered them good enough to start patrolling the
surrounding jungle terrain, an area which had, until now, been
dominated by drug-running rebels.

On August 16 1997, his operations were suspended when
an aircraft en route from Miami to Bogota crashed in the
nearby Andes Mountains. All 189 passengers and crew were

killed. The weather had not been good, and the aircraft had been diverted to Cali. It was thought that the pilot misprogrammed the aircraft's autopilot, instructing it to go to a way-point they had already passed. When this was realised, his attempts to put them back on the correct course led them directly into the mountains. It was only when the ground proximity warning system suddenly started screaming, that the pilot and co-pilot realised the seriousness of the situation. Seven seconds later the huge aircraft ploughed into the jungle.

The Colombian government reacted quickly, setting up a rescue operation and despatching both troops and police to secure the area and recover the bodies. It was at this stage that they realised they had a major problem. The aircraft had come down in rebel-held territory. Fierce fighting erupted around the crash site and four soldiers were killed. Cal's freshly trained troops, being the nearest military unit, were ordered in to protect the crash site and support the rescue effort. It took two days of heavy fighting before Cal and his men managed to secure a wide enough perimeter. Even then, the rebels continued taking periodical pot shots as the soldiers and recovery teams continued to carry out their gruesome work. With the rebels forced back into the jungle, the situation became tolerable, allowing the bodies to be collected.

Corpses were taken to a large military tent that had been erected at the edge of the crash site. Here they were bagged and tagged. During daylight hours three helicopters, working in relays, transported them to Buga, where a post-mortem reception area had been organised.

By day three, over half of the bodies had been reclaimed and shipped to the temporary mortuary, which occupied the gymnasium at the northern end of the town's sports field. As the helicopters brought the bodies in from the crash site, so the rescue organisation in Buga processed the remains.

His men having secured the perimeter, Cal sat on a fallen tree overlooking the devastation. An M16/203, combined automatic rifle and grenade thrower, lay across his knees. His jungle uniform stank with a strange mixture of old sweat and decay. Such was life in the jungle. He lifted his head away from his own body. He smelt the air, sniffing the sweet odour of bloating bodies – he needed a bath. The crash site covered a huge area; strewn with mutilated grey metal that lay in total contrast to the vivid green mass that made up the surrounding jungle. The aircraft had bulldozed a path some 300 metres long, snapping trees like matchsticks. The tail section had broken off on first impact while the rest slowly disintegrated all along the mountain-top. Cal watched as two soldiers passed by carrying a grey, heavyweight bag. They entered a large tent that had been erected near the edge of the disaster area and added their burden to the neat line of similar bags. Personal items and luggage were also being collected and stacked in a large net ready to be lifted down to the town by helicopter.

With idle curiosity, Cal walked into the tent where he noticed that some of the partially dismembered bodies had not yet been bagged. He reflected on the horrific destruction caused to the human body during an air crash. Most of the passengers had been Colombians and would be repatriated, their relatives openly dissuaded from viewing the remains, identification relying instead on photographs taken by the pathologist. A reasonable precaution, thought Cal as he forced himself to look at the naked body of a little girl. Her golden hair lay wet and matted around what was left of her head. The only items of clothing that remained attached were her socks – the young body completely exposed by the blast which had ripped through the plane on impact. On the ground next to her lay a man in a similar state. He had been placed in a body bag but the zip appeared to be broken. Cal bent down, pulling the plastic covers together in an effort to cover the exposed features. The grey mask that had been the man's face stared up at him, unseeing. All that remained of his clothes was his neck tie. With the shirt gone it looked more like a noose. Stupefied by the carnage, Cal stood to turn away . . . then a sudden blast of memory shocked his mind causing him to stop dead. A cold shiver took him.

The tie, there was something about the man's tie.

Quickly he turned, kneeling down to grab at the material. At the same time, his eyes levelled on the man's face. The tie was dark blue, patterned with small, embroidered winged daggers. Unmistakably, the official tie of the British SAS – and the face was unmistakably that of Steve Norris.

Cal found that his body was suddenly trembling, as if somehow he had been caught in an act of stealing. Nervously, he glanced around the tent, checking to see if anyone was watching. He calmed himself. He reasoned. What the hell? He was an American officer heading up the rescue team. No one would question his behaviour. Bending down, he read the number 00148 on the body tag. Cal noted the number then replaced the card and searched further. As his hand slid over the plastic body bag in which Norris lay, he noted the odd rectangle shaped bulge below the chest. With a swift movement Cal lowered the zip, pulling back the flaps to discover a small money belt secured about the man's waist. It contained both the man's wallet and passport. The passport was British, in the name of James Moore, yet the photograph was that of Norris. Strangely enough, despite the date showing it as three years old, the document looked brand new. Cal checked the wallet; it contained over three thousand dollars in cash, together with a little over six hundred pounds Sterling, but there were no credit cards. Tucked under one of the inner flaps were several bits of paper, mostly receipts. He palmed them, crushing the paper into a ball before slipping it into his pocket. Replacing the wallet and passport into the waist pouch, he discovered a buff coloured envelope. It was thick, and at first Cal thought it simply contained more money, but using his two fingers he fished out several photographs. For a moment he simply stared then, in one swift movement, Cal slipped the envelope inside his jacket. Turning, partly to check that he had not been observed, he stood up and shouted in Spanish to two soldiers who were now busy bagging bodies.

'This one needs a new bag. The zip is broken. Remember, all the luggage must be separated and placed in the net.' Cal made a sham of being annoyed, then swiftly left the tent and walked outside amid the wreckage. Two minutes later, he was sitting in one of the few aircraft seats that had survived the crash. It was located in what remained of the cabin, which was still attached to the port wing. For the moment it sufficed to shield Cal from prying eyes. Not wanting to be disturbed, he waited, listening. The jungle around him rustled with life, yet there was little sound, only the clatter of metal on metal, as the soldiers turned over pieces of wreckage searching for more dead. Cal pulled out the crumpled receipts he had found in Norris's wallet. One was for money conversion at Heathrow, another from a store in central London, while the third appeared to be from a liquor store called Oddbins. The fourth was a single sheet of notepaper. On it was written the name of a hotel in Bogota, below which were two other names, one of which had been circled with a pen. He would check on them later, he thought, slipping them all back into his pocket. Withdrawing the envelope he examined the photographs. They were an odd mixture. Some, Cal observed, bordered on being pornographic, but without exception he recognised that all had been taken during a surveillance operation. Of this he had no doubt, all the tell-tail signs were there. 'So Bulloch and Norris haven't changed their spots,' Cal thought wryly, whereupon his grin faded as he recognised the woman. He brought the pictures closer, studying them intently. The woman was undoubtedly the British princess, Diana.

Unsure at first what he had actually found, Cal sat pondering. Then another thought gripped him. If Norris was here, there was a possibility that Bulloch had also been on the aircraft! Putting the photographs back into the envelope, he placed them securely in his inside pocket. There would be time to study all this later, for the moment there was a job to be done. He had just started to pick his way through the fragments of the wreck when bursts of gunfire zipped through the air. Cal dived for cover, rolling behind a large section of crumpled wing. Several more shots rang out before he was able to make a wild rush for the jungle perimeter and reasonable safety.

'Why the hell have they come back?' demanded Cal, dropping down on the forest floor next to the Colombian colonel. 'Is anyone hurt?'

'One of the soldiers who was out in the open, searching for luggage, was hit in the leg but it is not serious. I have radioed down and told them to hold the choppers. In turn they tell me we have a new problem. Several bodies are still missing, Caleb. One of them is an 18-year-old son of an American businessman. The boy's father has arrived in Buga with a personal search party of friends and relatives, all of whom intend to come up to the crash site and search for the boy. The police have pointed out the dangers of being shot by rebels, but this has done little to deter them. The man is quite determined to recover his son's remains.'

'That's the most idiotic idea I have ever heard. Radio down and tell the police to confine them to their hotel. In the meantime,' snarled Cal, 'I'm going to take care of the bastards out there once and for all.'

'You want me to form a patrol?'

'No. I estimate there are only a handful. I will work better on my own. We can't let them carry on sniping at us. Do you have any idea where they are coming from, Colonel?'

'Sir, I believe they have made their rebel camp in an old village. It lies about three kilometres to the north of here.' The Colombian colonel indicated a point beyond the wreckage. 'There is a small track that runs from over there.'

Ten minutes later, Cal was ready for battle. The colonel tried in vain to dissuade him from going. 'Good God, Caleb. We are almost finished here. Don't go and get your ass shot off.'

'Don't worry about me, I'm wearing my lucky bullet-proof vest. Besides, if I don't go, and those American civilians decide to go looking for their missing son, it's going to get a lot messier around here. If I don't come back in 24 hours, come looking for me.' With that Cal shouldered the small pack and, gripping his rifle, picked his way through the wreckage before disappearing into the jungle. He headed north for about two kilometres when he came across a small clearing. Moving back some five metres he lay down on the wet surface of the jungle and started to construct a small hide.

The rain continued to fall on the jungle canopy. The heavy drops of water splattering on the broad-leafed foliage, creating a cold, soothing rhythm that made the mind wander. Cal had been cold before – and wet. Neither bothered him. Finding Norris's body, however, refreshed his memory and his mind slipped back to the Gulf War. It had been a horrifying ordeal – a miracle he had survived – and his body had healed. His father had flown in from *USS Bunker Hill* by helicopter, landing directly outside the field hospital just an hour after the rescue team dropped Cal off. Together with several high-ranking officers, they visited him, sitting in silence while they listened to his amazing story. He explained in great detail his treatment at the hands of Bulloch and Norris; how they had left him for dead.

When he explained about his interrogation, only his father could hold Cal's eyes. Although the High Command was horrified, such incidents were best hushed up and kept from the media. They assured Cal that both the CIA and MI6 would conduct a major search for the two renegades. Now, six years on, fate had seen fit for him to cross paths with his killers once again. When he finished here, Cal had already decided to search the rest of the passenger list for any sign of Bulloch. He was still contemplating the mystery of finding Norris, and the photographs, when a dull voice echoed clearly above the dripping rain, snapping Cal back to the present.

For a short while he lay without moving. Then he grasped the automatic weapon, checked the safety and, like a snake shedding its skin, slipped from the hide. The voices were no more than 20 metres to his left, and getting louder. Cal shadowed the sounds, moving silently through the thick jungle vegetation. The rain hid his movement as he slid from clump to clump, feeling the leaves wet against his body. Occasionally, he stopped to listen, glancing both left and right, before continuing after the men. Anxious to catch sight of his foe, the words of his Indian instructor from his jungle training days filtered through his thoughts. 'Look through the jungle, not at it.' There they were.

The men had stopped. His gaze pierced the dripping foliage, and focused on several men. Two sat on a rotting log, two more stood nearby. As the tropical storm blew over, the last of the wind and sharp rain cut his face, bringing with it the smell of tobacco smoke. Like some prehistoric animal, Cal filled his nostrils as he watched the movement of the men before him. For a fleeting moment, he realised the danger in which he had placed himself. His nerve steeled as the muscles in his right arm tightened. He raised the weapon to his shoulder. With a swaying movement of his upper body, he cleared his line of fire. As he did so, he realised that all four men were standing. It was not a good shot. Dropping silently, Cal took cover behind a large bush. He watched the men walk towards him.

'You can't argue with men like this,' the warning words filled his brain. 'Kill them before they kill you.'

Their voices close now, he heard the crackle of their boots as they crushed the forest floor. He caught the swish of the plant life as they brushed along the narrow path. Cal's eyes focused directly at the lead man, now no more than three metres from him. He recognised the moment to kill. The man's foot landed almost on him, it was a military boot.

Looking up, Cal saw the upper body was covered with a poncho, the head hung low under its hood. For one brief instant their eyes met. Then the weapon in Cal's hand kicked for several short seconds, sending a full magazine into the patrol of men.

The thunderous rattle stopped, echoing away, as the silence of dripping rain returned. Three of the men were down, but the fourth was missing. While Cal registered this, he hit the button beside the trigger guard, dropping the magazine to the floor and instantly replaced it with a full one. There was a double clicking sound as the cocking handle fed a fresh round into the empty chamber. He edged forward. As he did so, two of the men moved, emitting low-pitched groans. Cal fired two deliberate short bursts, and the men were still. Instinct told him to move. He crawled several metres to his left, dropping into the root flanges of a large tree. He listened. There was no sound. He moved again; four metres; six metres. Then he saw him. Like a raptor playing in his own back garden, the man had waited in ambush for Cal to expose himself. Cal had no time to use the weapon – the man was on him, wielding a metre-long machete. The rush forced Cal back, with the man bearing down upon him. He blocked the first slash with his weapon, but the man was flailing wildly with the long blade. He stared into the fierce black eyes, and Cal felt real fear. In that instant, Cal raised his foot hitting the man mid-stomach. At the same time he felt the slap of the machete hit his shoulder. He felt the metal cut his flesh and he screamed when it hit the bone. With one mighty effort, Cal heaved and kicked the man from his body. He staggered and fell, landing on his backside, but he still held the blade. Cal knew the cut had gone deep. His right hand grasped impulsively at the area of the wound. Then he felt the small Gerber knife clipped to his left breast pocket. The motion was instinctive; pulling the one-piece steel blade from its scabbard, Cal swung his arm out in a snapping motion. His attacker had started to get up, raising the machete for the final kill. The steel blade was nothing more than a shadowy blur as it left Cal's hand and pierced the man's throat a little left of centre. The man was still coming . . . or was he falling? Desperately Cal slapped at the man's arm holding the machete. It was partially successful, but again he felt the steel slice sideways into his flesh. The man fell on top of him, before rolling off to one side. In an instant Cal was on him, grabbing for the protruding knife and pushing it further into the man's throat. He realised that his opponent was dead. Cal sat back on the rebel's body, panting. He felt weak and sick.

The storm had returned and with it the rain. The large trees creaked in the darkness as Cal came to. He was back at the hide, but he had no recollection of how he had got there. He felt weak from the loss of blood and knew that he would not remain conscious for very long. In a desperate effort he reached for the medical pack attached to the back of his belt. Emptying the contents on the wet earth, he found a large military field dressing and ripped it open with his teeth. Then with agonising effort, he slipped it inside his shirt, pushing it up over the wound. He struggled for several minutes, screaming with the terrible pain. Finally, he managed to get the dressing in position. At least that would stem the bleeding. Next he reached for small plastic bottle and once more he ripped off the top with his teeth. Putting the container to his lips he swallowed four of the DF118 painkillers. With his left arm totally numb, he could not find the strength to put away the medical kit. Instead, he tucked it loose inside his jacket. As he struggled to crawl back into his hide, the darkness was already fogging his brain. Cal fell forward. He was unconscious.

Awakening in the darkness, the pain in his shoulder had stiffened the whole left side of his body. With an effort, he forced the pain from his mind and listened. The rain had stopped and there was silence, broken only by the distant barking of some jungle animal and the fluttering stir of a bird nesting high up in the canopy. The moon was barred behind the thick leaves but here and there small beams of light fell to the forest floor. He stood, trying hard not to move his upper body, then set off down the track towards the crash site.

For almost two hours he stumbled down the track, slowly realising that the jungle had played a cruel trick on him, somehow leading him past the crashed plane. The track merged with a small, winding dirt road. Calling on the last of his reserves, he staggered on. It was another hour before he spotted the lights emanating from the town below. After a further 20 minutes, the dirt track connected with the main road that ran into Buga. Shortly after, Cal came across a police road block. At first they thought him a rebel, but Cal's curt military Spanish convinced them otherwise and they agreed to give him a ride to the sports centre where he could get medical aid.

'Doc, I need to call my father in London. What facilities have we here?' Cal asked as the doctor treated his shoulder wound.

'Well, if you go past the refrigerated trucks and into the compound, you'll find the office of the US Consul. They have a Satcom unit installed. But your best bet is to use a GSM mobile phone. I do and it works perfectly. If it's really important, we have two global satellite units, which allow us world-wide voice, fax and data communications – very high tech. But first we have to finish patching you up. Lucky you were wearing a protective vest, otherwise that cut could have taken your arm off.'

'Would you believe, it's the second time it's saved my life? How are we doing on the body count, Doc?' Cal asked, keeping an eye on the human effort going on around him. Near the entrance, recovered bodies still held in plastic bags were awaiting their turn to be processed. The doctor noted Cal's interest and nodded.

'Not a pretty sight is it? We've recovered most of the bodies, two thirds of them were Colombians. The rest are mainly American citizens. First thing we do is strip the bodies. Their clothing and possessions are taken away for documentation, a gruesome task carried out by the Colombian police, supervised by the FBI. Where possible, we take fingerprints before a post-mortem is carried out. At this stage, the bodies are photographed with a Polaroid camera and we pin the pictures to a board in the waiting room for relatives to identify their kin. Those that are recognised go through a Judiciary, confirming identification. At this stage the bodies are released to the family. Those that are not recognised, or were alien to the country, are taken to the embalming area prior to storage.'

'One hell of a job you've got, Doc. Now tell me, what happened to the British guy?'

The doctor looked up from his work, his face full of surprise. There had been no mention of the single British subject found on the aircraft and the body had passed through processing less than six hours ago, at which time the man he was treating had been getting his shoulder chopped off by rebels.

'How did you know about him?' he asked, eyeing the young American with renewed interest.

'I recognised the man,' said Cal, careful not to say how. 'We served in the military together.' He fumbled with his good arm, and withdrew a dirty slip of paper from his inside shirt pocket and showed it to the doctor. 'Here, I took his body bag number. I would be grateful if you could let me know what's going to happen to the body.' When the doctor had finished, he got up from the chair, giving his wounded shoulder a small circular shrug. 'Thanks, Doc, that feels a lot better. Now, how about that phone call?'

'Don't forget there's a time difference between here and the United Kingdom,' said the doctor, showing Cal the small telephone unit. It was no larger than a laptop computer, yet it could be operated anywhere in the world. Cal hunted through his pockets and produced a small electronic organiser. He searched through the telephone numbers. Picking up the handset, he took his time tapping in the digits. He waited for a few moments and then he heard a voice.

'American Embassy. How can I help you?'

'Good morning, I would like to speak to the Defence Attaché's office, please.'

'May I ask who's calling, please?'

'My name is Major Caleb Wesley. My father is Dan Wesley. I understand he is attached to Defence Attaché's office.'

'One moment, sir, trying to connect you.'

Cal waited, listening for several seconds before he heard a woman's voice. 'Hello, Major Wesley, my name's Susan

Greenwood. I'm afraid your father is not here at the moment. Can I take a message for him?'

The voice sounded soft, with a suggestion of a foreign accent. 'I need to speak to my father. I'm stuck in the Colombian jungle at the moment, near the aircraft crash site. I presume it's made the news over there.' Not knowing who Susan Greenwood was, he decided not to expand upon his reason for calling and cut the conversation short. 'Any idea what time my father will be back in the office?'

'Give him two hours and try again.'

'Okay. Thanks a lot. Tell him I'll call back in two hours.' Cal put down the handset.

'Any luck?' asked the doctor, looking at Cal's worried face.

'No, he's not there at the moment. Okay if I try again in a couple of hours?' He was about to walk away when the bright flash of a camera going off stopped him. 'Doc, do you take pictures of all the deceased?'

'Yes, we do. It's a lot kinder than letting the relatives view the remains. We also keep a copy for our own records. They're over there on the table, but if you intend looking at them, do me a favour – leave them tidy.'

'Thanks,' said Cal, leaving the doctor to get on with his work.

It took Cal ten minutes to check through the files that lay on the table. None of the pictures looked remotely like Bulloch. The air in the gymnasium was heavy with the smell of embalming fluid. It smelt of death. He walked from the building, making his way into the compound, and headed for the office that housed the Colombian Army Headquarters. He spoke briefly to the officer in charge and, after giving an accurate report of the incident with the rebels, finished with his recommendation that any large portions of the aircraft should be blown up to prevent the looting of spare parts. Finally, he called his immediate superior in Bogota requesting four weeks' sick leave because of his shoulder injury. They granted the leave, asking if they should book him on a flight back to the United States. They also requested a written report be sent to the office prior to his leaving.

Cal sat at one of the tables in the military office and was busy writing out his report when the British doctor who had treated him pulled up a chair.

'Hi, Doc, you taking a break?'

'No,' replied the doctor. 'I was looking for you. That British passenger you mentioned, your old military friend, we have a claim on him.'

'Who?' asked Cal, unable to keep the excitement from his voice.

'His brother in London. He wants the body shipped to Stockport. That's near Manchester in the north of England. He has also put in a request with the insurance company for the belongings.'

'When will you ship the body?' asked Cal.

'Most of the British team here will be flying back by private charter. The way things are going, I would say that'll be around the end of the week. As there's only one body to be repatriated to the United Kingdom, I would imagine his casket will fly back with us.'

Two hours later, Cal dialled the American Embassy once more. After a few moments, he managed to get through to his father. 'Hello, Dad? That you?'

'Hi, Caleb. Greenwood told me you'd called. How's the job going in Colombia?'

'I'm in a town called Buga, near where the aircraft went down. It's one hell of a mess. To top it all, it crashed right in the middle of rebel-held territory, which caused a lot of problems for the rescue services. The rebels obviously thought they were going to get some rich pickings from the dead. Anyway, we've taken care of it.'

'What's your involvement there Cal? Are you okay?'

'The Colombian unit I was training just happened to be the nearest military outfit when the aircraft went down. It cost me a slight wound to the shoulder,' Cal said, keeping his voice even, 'but nothing that won't heal.'

'Are you sure you're okay, Cal?' His father's voice sounded full of concern. 'Why don't you get yourself a normal job, boy?'

Cal laughed, 'Can you see me in an office, Dad? Don't worry, I'm fine, I'm fine. Listen, Dad, this is important. I need you to do me a favour. You remember back in the Gulf War when I told you about the two Brits that shot me?' Cal paused for a moment. 'Well, I've found one of them. He was on the aircraft.' Cal went on, explaining how he had spotted the SAS tie and of his certainty that this was Norris. Finally he mentioned the pictures. 'Dad, I'm a little confused. When I searched his body I found an envelope stuffed full of compromising pictures. The woman looks remarkably like Princess Diana. You know, the British Princess.'

The American Army had appointed Dan Wesley to his present post to utilise his unrivalled negotiating skills. Too old for active service, the Pentagon fielded him as a sounding board, searching the sincerity of the men who were once his country's enemy; Warsaw Pact countries now wishing to join NATO. It was a business that needed integrity, the fabric from which Dan Wesley was made. So while he knew little of his son's work within Delta Force, he knew Caleb would never discredit himself by making up the tale he had just told, not even in jest. The boy was telling the truth, or at least what he believed to be the truth. In the silence that followed, Cal continued. 'The problem is, Dad, what have I got here? What was Norris doing in Colombia? Apart from the photographs, all I found was the address of a hotel in Bogota, together with two names, and some telephone numbers on a piece of paper. I'll fax them to you later. They may be something or they may be nothing. What really worries me are the pictures of Princess Diana. Someone has been watching her very closely. I have to tell you some are very compromising, by that I mean they could seriously tarnish her image.'

'Okay, Cal. Now you listen. Fax nothing – the world has too many ears and eyes. Give me the names on the paper and I will do a little digging. And keep this to yourself until we have a clearer picture of what we are dealing with here.'

Cal read off the names, before adding, 'There's more, Dad. The doctor here informs me that there's been a request for Norris's body to be repatriated back to the United Kingdom. A British team that specialises in sorting out this sort of mess was employed by the aircraft insurers. They have a charter flight returning in a few days' time. They'll be bringing Norris's body back with them. The paperwork will show Norris as James Moore – that was the name on his passport. I've been granted four weeks' sick leave, but I must report to Washington. Then I intend to come to England. If, for some reason, I don't make it there in time, can you have the body followed? I need to know where it goes, and I need to know who picks it up. My bet is this so-called brother of his is his partner, Bulloch.'

'I think you're getting a bit ahead of yourself, Cal,' the concern was back in his father's voice.

'Dad, I want Bulloch. You above all people must understand.'

'I understand, Cal. Leave it to me. Let me know when you will be arriving in England. I will arrange to have you collected.'

'You got it. I have to tidy up here first but I'm hoping to be there for the weekend, the same time as Norris's body. If not, I need to know where the corpse is taken and who turns up at the funeral. Got it?'

'I understand. Anything else?'

'No, I'll be in touch later. Oh, and thanks, Dad.'

'Bye, son. You take care of yourself now, do you hear?' Cal's father replaced the receiver, and sat quietly pondering for a while. Then, picking up the handset once more, he dialled an internal number. 'Susan, would you come in here for a moment? I've got a little job for you.'

CHAPTER
7

London,
August 21, 1997

Naked, standing with his feet apart, arms outstretched, resting on fingertips, he leaned against the tiled wall of the shower, standing as if he were a prisoner under interrogation. He had remained in this position for the past 20 minutes, letting the warm jet of water beat against his head. It ran through his short-cropped hair, tiny rivulets trickling down the muscular curves of his physique, cleansing both body and soul. Slowly, as the water rehydrated his flesh, the throb in his head started to recede. His soul would take longer to heal. He could not believe that Steve was dead.

He had been so engrossed in his work; studying Paris street maps; evaluating possible killing grounds; identifying potential problems; planning different escape routes; he had not read a newspaper or watched the television in days. Details of the crash had eluded him. Three days after Steve had flown to Colombia there was still no word from him. In the end,

Bulloch had phoned their principal in Bogota. It was only then that he learned of the disaster. A call to the airline confirmed his worst fears. Yes, he would like his brother's body repatriated – Stockport in the north of England. No, he would leave it to them to organise a funeral service. Yes, they could contact him on the following number. Bulloch had no thoughts for security when he passed on the number of his mobile phone. His friend, his only friend, was dead.

For the rest of that day he walked the streets of London in a total stupor. Unable to comprehend, or come to grips with the fact that his best friend, his only friend, was dead. Vivid thoughts of Steve jumped and pummelled his brain, leaving him helpless, unable to concentrate. He wandered from bar to bar, staggering the streets, raving wildly at anyone who got in his way. Angry and drunk, a single cord of reasoning made him climb into a taxi and make his way back to the apartment. As always, the taxi dropped him off near the off-licence. Its bright lights beckoned Bulloch inside like a moth drawn to a flame. Incapable of coherent speech, he simply grabbed two bottles of Scotch and threw a £50 note onto the counter. He left without waiting for his change, staggering across the road. He climbed the stairs to the flat. From that moment he remembered nothing, seeking only to drown any conscious thoughts with alcohol. For two days his mind drifted, always ebbing between thoughts of Steve and drunken oblivion. 'Me an' you, Steve – always me an' you.' Bulloch slurred his words. At times his face would smile, as the kaleidoscope images of Steve painted his drink-sodden brain. He recalled the evening they had first become friends.

Passing through the rigorous selection process together, both had joined the ranks of the elite SAS. Being very much the new boys of the regiment, they had spent much of their free time together. Through companionship, they discovered their mutual liking for certain pleasures, one of which was fighting. One evening, shortly after their arrival in Hereford, several local boys, much the worse for drink, had seen fit to pick on Steve Norris as he made his way back to camp. Although giving a good account of himself, he was heavily outnumbered and on the point of going down. That was until Bulloch arrived on the scene. Wading in like some berserker, he inflicted enough violence to keep three of the attackers hospitalised for several weeks. Since that time, he and Steve had become inseparable. At first, many in the SAS thought their relationship bordered on being homosexual, but nothing could have been further from the truth. Their affinity stemmed from their shared understanding of each other's desires and weaknesses – namely, violence and sex.

For almost 48 hours, Bulloch remained comatose. Occasionally, his eyes would open as once more he searched for the drink. Lying on the settee, raised on one elbow, his hand would grope aimlessly about his prostrate body. When at last, through blurred vision, he located the whisky bottle he put it to his lips and drank deeply. The recollection continued.

Steve had been there for him when he found his wife having an affair with the exchange sergeant from America. They had beaten both to a pulp, wrecking the army quarters in the process. Held in custody, he and Steve had narrowly avoided being thrown out of the SAS. Their saving grace, as their commanding officer put it, was that the government had paid good money to hone their military skills. He was right, the SAS had created an insatiable killing machine. If there was killing to be done, he and Steve were always first in line. 'You should have seen us in the Falklands war – we would sneak right into the Argentinean headquarters and grab a prisoner. They said we was crazy, but we proved our worth time after time.' Bulloch blurted to the empty room. Now Steve was gone. Bulloch's babbling voice extolled their friendship; but they had been more than friends, more than brothers. Without Steve, Bulloch was alone in the world. He slept.

When at last the dawn sky washed into the room, flooding light onto the settee where he lay, his eyes opened. The anger was still in him, like some hurting void it made him feel empty. Someone had taken away half his life. They had taken what he could never replace – the bond of a real friendship. He rose into a sitting position, looking blindly around the room. The maps of Paris and the Mediterranean still clung to the wall by one corner. In his drunken stupor he had failed in his attempt to pull them down. Gone were the neat piles of paper and photographs, transformed into a mass of litter which covered the entire floor. Slowly, as sanity returned, he smelt the stench emanating from his crotch, mixing with the reek of whisky, which he had dribbled down his shirt. He had stood, stripped off his clothes, and staggered to the bathroom, to let the shower cleanse him.

Now, as his head cleared, he started to think once more. With Steve gone, he had only his work. He would use it, making it his anchor for the lonely weeks ahead.

Later that day, he contacted the airline, checking on the arrangements for the body to be shipped back to Britain. He then prepared himself to phone Steve's mother. He had never spoken to the woman before and he would warn her to be silent; persuade her to let him discreetly handle the funeral arrangements. This he would do for Steve, knowing that he held his mother in great affection. Taking care of his mother had been Norris's last request to Bulloch on many an occasion.

'If anything was to happen to me – you look after me mum. Give her my share of the money. She may not want it, 'cos I think my sister has turned her against me, but try anyway. One other thing, I buried an ammo box full of 'goodies' in the back garden. It's at the rear of the shed. It's stuff I nicked from the regiment. I'd hate for the old dear to get caught with it. Besides, it will come in handy for you.'

'Stupid bastard,' The memory of Steve's words sharpened the sadness in Bulloch's heart but a promise was a promise, Steve would have done the same for him. He made plans to visit Stockport. That done he telephoned Sir Gilbert.

'I need to see you – Norris is dead.'

'Dead? What do you mean dead? Has something gone wrong?' Sir Gilbert's voice sounded anxious.

'He was killed in an air crash in Colombia. It had nothing to do with your operation.'

'What on earth was he doing in Colombia?'

'It's a long story, I'll explain later. Now listen, I think I have the answer to your problem, and it's not something we can discuss on the phone.'

'I will meet you at the apartment first thing tomorrow morning.' The phone went dead.

Bulloch tidied the room, repairing the destruction his drinking bout had caused. He would need to re-model his plan, trying to fill the vacuum created by Steve's death, but he was confident that he could handle it. By late evening, the headache was gone and he felt more human, but the desire to drink again slowly devoured his willpower. He resisted until ten in the evening. Then, pouring himself one large Scotch, he went to bed.

'This had better be good,' Sir Gilbert growled, as Bulloch let him in. 'What on earth was Norris doing in Colombia?' Without waiting for an answer, he walked to the centre of the lounge, noting the mess of paper strewn around the floor. Bulloch's effort to clean up did not meet with Sir Gilbert's notion of neatness. 'Do you know how much effort has been put into collating those files? What the hell is wrong with you?' Rage surfaced, but with a violent effort, Sir Gilbert controlled himself, his stormy outburst defused by the fierce expression in Bulloch's eyes. This was not a good time to provoke the man. Unable to hold Bulloch's stare, he wheeled to face the window, relieving his mind by uttering a few angry words at the calm world outside. There was a moment's silence before he turned to face Bulloch once more. With a sigh, the older man shook his head and began afresh. 'I'm not as unreasonable as you might think,' he said, in a composed tone. 'I know well enough, that you and Norris were friends and I imagine, in your profession, close friends are hard to come by.' Sir Gilbert took a seat. 'Now tell me what happened.'

Bulloch explained with the simple truth while Sir Gilbert listened without interruption. He explained how the Colombian job had been offered long before the Diana hit had appeared on the scene and how professional conduct required that they complete it. He ended the conversation with, 'Steve was a brilliant shot – he wanted to do it. Had it not been for the air crash he would have returned and you would have been none the wiser.'

'I see,' remarked Sir Gilbert, 'and what of your professional commitment to my operation?'

'I'm just coming to that. Do you want a drink?'

'No, thank you, but you go ahead if it makes you feel better.'

Bulloch took the half-empty bottle from the table and poured himself a large Scotch. Sitting down, he gulped half of it before looking at Sir Gilbert. 'I've come up with a plan that should satisfy your needs. Now that Steve's gone, I want more than ever to carry on. It's not the money, it's . . .' he broke off, unable to explain himself.

Sir Gilbert waited for several moments, mulling over the situation, assessing whether Bulloch alone was capable of carrying out the operation. He would listen to what the man had to say. 'I am glad to see there is no reluctance on your behalf to carry on with the operation. Despite the loss of Norris, I am inclined to put a certain amount of faith in your ability to cope with the situation. Now give me your thoughts on the matter. What is this plan of yours?'

Bulloch raised the glass to his lips and took another swallow, knowing his proposed idea would be viewed with some scepticism. 'I'm going to involve her in a car accident in which both she and Al Fayed will die.' He waited for Sir Gilbert's reaction. It was swift in coming.

'An accident? Is that the best you can come up with?' The older man jumped up, moved about the room, stopping here and there in a tentative manner, as if about to say something, yet unable to find the words. 'To be honest, I have people who can cause accidents. I was anticipating something a little more innovative!'

'Let me explain,' tempered Bulloch in a calm voice. 'Hear me out. I never do anything without planning it first. If you don't like the idea, then fine, but at least listen.' Bulloch paused, waiting while Sir Gilbert returned to his seat. 'We need a plan that is flexible, one that can work the instant an opportunity arises, a plan that will withstand instant media scrutiny . . . in essence, a real accident.

'Some years ago we topped a bomb-maker in Northern Ireland. His name was Gerard Mullan. On the surface Mullan was an ordinary schoolteacher, squeaky clean; but we knew different. We had just dispatched one bomb maker with a 'home goal', making it look like he was blown to bits while assembling one of his own devices, so it was deemed that Mullan should die in a road accident. Surveillance came up with a list of the target's usual routes. The SAS chose a number of sites where an accident could take place. Two of the cars were fitted with ambush lights converted to look like a rear spotlight. A small explosive device used by the anti-terrorist team was attached to the engine of the target's car. We followed the target for several days. One evening, the target was travelling alone from Portadown to Londonderry. As he approached the Shanalongford Bridge a blinding flash destroyed his vision. At the same time, the car's engine was wrecked. The result was quite devastating, Mullan was totally decapitated.' Bulloch paused, picking up a set of photographs that lay on the floor.

'If I assume correctly, surveillance on this scale is being conducted by E4 and, given the information you have so far provided, I would hazard a guess that you also have someone inside Al Fayed's organisation?'

Sir Gilbert had followed Bulloch's every word and began to see how the man's mind was working. He nodded his confirmation.

Bulloch continued. 'Although I intend to blind the driver I do not propose to blow the engine. Instead, I want your technical department to attach some explosive bolts to any vehicles allocated to the target while she is staying in Paris. These will cause the driver's-side wheel to collapse. Providing it's going at more than about 60 mph this will put the car into an anticlockwise spin. I have also arranged for an ambush light to be made that can be fitted to the rear of a Kawasaki ZX600 motorbike. This will be initiated simultaneously . . .'

Sir Gilbert raised his hands, stopping Bulloch's flow. 'I know about such equipment – so that's why you went to see Jarvis? How can you be sure that this new device will disable the vehicle?'

'I can't, other than Jarvis assures me that it will do the job. The plan also relies on you supplying me with advance information about the target's movements and getting the paparazzi to increase their harassment. It's not complex. The plan is very straightforward. It will look like an accident.'

Sir Gilbert started to look for flaws in the plan 'If the device utilises some form of explosive, surely this will be detectable afterwards?'

'Jarvis will make four similar devices which I will fill with a very small amount of PE-4. The device we are talking about will look like part of the car and while the explosive is detectable, most of the device will have been disintegrated and scattered among the wreckage. But to be on the safe side, I am sure your technical department could organise a clean up afterwards,' Bulloch paused, smiling at Sir Gilbert, 'just like we did in Northern Ireland. Likewise, once the job is completed they can remove the unused devices from the other vehicles.'

Sir Gilbert sat quietly for a moment; Bulloch had already answered most of his questions. Although several elements needed to be put in place, the plan had been well conceived. Above all, he had a feeling that Bulloch could pull it off.

'When will Jarvis be ready?'

'In a few days. I'll contact you the moment I have the hardware. I estimate that the Ritz Hotel in Paris can put about four cars at the target's disposal. As far as your technical team is concerned, tell them they're fitting tracking devices to help the surveillance boys keep tabs on Diana.'

Sir Gilbert pondered Bulloch's strategy. He had thought the whole thing through. 'Go on.'

'The target is now back in the Mediterranean and will not return to Paris before the end of the month.' Bulloch moved to stand by the map of Paris. 'This gives me time to recce all the main routes and select a number of possible accident sites. Given that you supply me with a continuous update on the target's movements, I can choose the exact location to crash their vehicle. Journalists constantly surround the couple. One more man on a motorbike will not be out of place. I am an expert rider and the machine I have chosen will outrun any car. I need just 30 seconds warning to get in front of them on any chosen route. That's why I need a constant tracking report, although your surveillance people need not even be aware of my presence. Once the accident has happened, I will be closest and, therefore, first at the scene. It will all look like a simple accident, no one other than you and I need ever know any different.'

Sir Gilbert sat quietly, reflecting on Bulloch's words. He stared at the man sitting opposite; a killer, yes, but also cunning. The more Bulloch explained, the more he realised the amount of research the man had done. If he could pull this off, the general public would associate the princess's death with media harassment, something to which they were already reconciled. The latest surveillance report had indicated that Diana was planning a repeat performance of her boating holiday with Al Fayed. Sir Gilbert found himself asking questions.

'What if she is not killed?'

Bulloch walked over to a small side table and picked up a black leather glove. As his hand slid easily into the glove, he turned towards Sir Gilbert. 'We have one of two choices.' With lightening speed Bulloch half twisted, driving his fist into the wall. A dull rumbling sound echoed through the room as bits of fractured plaster fell to the floor. 'If there is time I can administer a fatal blow to her heart.' He pulled off the glove and let it fall onto the coffee table. It landed with a heavy thud. 'Power glove . . . delivers a deadly blow.'

The abrupt action had not been expected. It shook Sir Gilbert who found himself staring at the damaged wall. His voice remained icily calm, 'And if you don't have time?'

'Then at least I will have placed her in a situation where you will have the opportunity to administer some other remedy. Either at the accident site, during the ambulance ride or at the hospital. That will be your problem.'

The man was right, Sir Gilbert reasoned. At the very least the princess would be hospitalised. He would need to think about that. He turned his attention back to Bulloch. 'This must take place before the 1st of September, the Princess of Wales must not be allowed to return to Britain.'

'I know Paris like the back of my hand. Steve and I have done several jobs in the city. Your people are still tailing Diana?'

'She has been under complete surveillance since she first started seeing Al Fayed. We have done all in our power to discredit the man, drag up his past, accuse him of being drug dependant – all to no avail. We have no option but to terminate them both.' Sir Gilbert was quiet, studying the face of the man before him. There was no doubt Bulloch believed he could pull it off. 'Tell me about this man Jarvis.'

Bulloch went on to explain about his visit to Oliver Jarvis and how the man had accepted the £5,000. 'Jarvis may be a one-man band, but he has developed several devices for the SAS.'

'So what is your next move?'

'The devices will be ready soon. I intend to pick them up on my way back from Steve's funeral. After that I think I should move to Paris – somewhere near to Al Fayed's headquarters at the Ritz.'

Sir Gilbert sat very still, his mind trying hard to form some linear pattern to the jumble of his thoughts. In his earlier years, when he had served with MI5, he had been party to several intricate assassination plots but they paled to insignificance compared to the one Bulloch proposed. Yet the simplicity of the plan intrigued him and, in fairness, if Bulloch could pull it off, only a few people would ever know the whole truth, and that was all-important.

Sir Gilbert stood, preparing to leave. 'I underestimated you. You may possibly have found the perfect answer to our problem. I will have your boffin's handiwork picked up from you the moment it is ready. I will also make arrangements for you to fly to France. You will not have direct contact with the surveillance unit, but I can arrange for a radio allowing you to listen in on their conversation – that way you will know every movement made by the princess.'

'So, I take it we go ahead?' invited Bulloch.

'Yes, the operation will proceed,' Sir Gilbert turned to leave but stopped in the doorway. 'Is it absolutely necessary for you to attend Norris's funeral? I mean, isn't there a danger that you will be recognised?'

'No. Steve's body was shipped back using the false name supplied on the passport. His mother and sister are the only ones who know his real identity. I have spoken to them. They will say nothing. Besides, I won't be going to the funeral. I have other reasons for going to Stockport.' Bulloch went on to explain about his promise to Steve and about removing his secret cache.

'I never realised members of the SAS were so far-sighted.'

'What did you expect? The government spends a fortune training us to kill. If it's for the country, anything goes, but when you leave the regiment, no one wants to know you. That's why most of the guys hide away the odd bit of ammunition or explosive. You just never know when you're going to need it.'

'I understand. What about Jarvis? Can you guarantee his silence?'

'If that's what you want,' replied Bulloch, who had already made his mind up to kill the man.

'I think it would be best,' Sir Gilbert closed the door behind him.

Bulloch walked back into the lounge and poured himself another Scotch. 'Here's to you, Steve.' He threw the Scotch down his throat in one swallow.

Mid-afternoon on Friday, the mobile phone beeped, warning of an incoming call. It was the funeral director, Frank Lewis &

Sons, phoning Mr Rogers to let him know that his brother's body would be arriving back in England the following day. Arrangements had been made to transport the casket directly to their premises in Stockport.

'Have you made arrangements for the cremation?'

'Yes, sir. The service takes place at Stockport Crematorium, 2.00 pm this coming Monday, that's the 25th of August. It's a little rushed but we find it's better in such cases. I trust you will be attending, sir?'

'Just mother, my sister and myself. I will inform them of the place and time.'

'Thank you, sir,' the voice changed in tone slightly as the caller changed the subject. 'Repatriation of the body is charged to the airline insurance company, sir, but there is the matter of payment for the funeral itself. If that can be arranged before . . .'

Bulloch cut the man short. 'I will be in Stockport on Sunday, around midday, at which time I will pay in cash. You are open on a Sunday?'

'Yes, sir. By nature ours is a 24-hour business.'

'Fine.' Pressing the clear button, Bulloch tossed the phone carelessly onto the settee, and continued with his plans.

He rang Jarvis, who confirmed that the devices would be ready Monday evening, adding that they seemed to be working perfectly. Finally, Bulloch went shopping and purchased a roll of shrink-wrap, a commercial cousin of household cling-film but with far stronger properties. It was used to secure boxes on a fork-lift pallet.

Saturday was a bad day. With nothing to do, Steve's ghost continued to haunt him. He tried to occupy his mind by going over the plan. When this failed, he walked the embankment, keeping to the riverside footpath. Passing through Battersea Park, he made his way back over the river into Chelsea. By four in the afternoon, he seriously needed a drink, but managed to hold off by ordering a large meal at a restaurant off Sloane Square. By seven o'clock he was back at the apartment, having consumed several pints of beer and half a bottle of Scotch. In a drunken stupor, he climbed into bed. By tomorrow his head would clear and he would have work to keep him occupied.

By ten o'clock next morning he had already turned off the M1 at junction 28, heading for Matlock, travelling northbound on the A6 to Stockport. Bulloch felt strange. For some reason he didn't relish the thought of seeing Steve's mother. The way she had expressed herself during their brief phone conversation made him feel as if he was responsible for Steve's death. He drove for another hour, passing through the district of High Green, three miles south of Stockport, when he caught sight of the Bay Horse hotel. Steve's voice echoed through his daydreaming, causing him to stop and turn the car round. 'Great pub, the Bay Horse. Me mum's place has only got two bedrooms, so I used to stay there when I went home on leave. You can drink in the bar all night.'

Bulloch drove into the pub car park, and stopped. Reaching into his pocket he pulled out the piece of paper on which he had written Steve's address, and sat pondering for a moment. He had no idea which way to go, but he guessed that the house was close. Getting out of the car, he decided to get himself a bed for the night. The place turned out to be more of a restaurant than a pub, with a small six-bedroom hotel attached to the one end. Inside the main entrance was a small reception area, situated between the restaurant and the public bar. The whole place looked to have been recently refurbished, polished oak and brass fittings mocked the old-world charms of bygone years. Still, the place looked bright and friendly. He approached the reception area, where a woman in her mid-thirties stood waiting, and inquired after a room.

'Just for the night, sir?'

'Better make it two. I'll let you know if there's any change.'

She handed him a card, silently requesting that he fill it in. 'Thank you, sir. Would you care to book a table for dinner this evening?'

'Why not?' Bulloch smiled, putting on his friendly face. 'I was wondering, could you tell me – is there a street called Andrews Close near here?'

'Oh, yes, that's not far away. Go back down the A6 for about half a mile, turn left by the telephone box and Andrews Close is second on the left.' She handed Bulloch a key. 'There you are, room number 4. Through the door and up the stairs.'

'Thank you.' Grabbing his bags, Bulloch followed her instructions. Number four had a large, old-fashioned bed taking up half the room, with bedroom furniture of a similar age placed around the walls. It looked clean and comfortable. He dropped his suitcase onto the bed, unzipped the lid and took out a large, buff coloured envelope. He returned to the bar and ordered a plate of sandwiches and a beer for his lunch.

After lunch it was back to the car and off to Stockport where Bulloch went to locate the undertakers, Frank Lewis & Sons. Their offices were housed in a large, Victorian building which had long since been converted to a funeral parlour. Maintaining the pretence of being Norris's brother, he completed the necessary arrangements for the cremation and paid the bill. In the event that there should be some delay, he informed the undertaker that he was staying at the Bay Horse. Before driving back towards the hotel, he followed the receptionist's directions and went in search of Norris's home.

Andrews Close was a small cul-de-sac in which most of the properties were bungalows. He had no problem finding No 16, although there was nothing special to separate the bungalow from the other homes in the street. In Bulloch's eyes they were all identical; their gardens neat and tidy, most with an average sized car parked in the driveway. Stopping in the quiet street, he sat for a moment contemplating the story he was going to tell. He wanted to find some explanation for his and Steve's actions, but nothing came to mind. At last he decided to give them the time of the funeral service, leave the money and go. He owed them nothing; it was only out of friendship to Steve that he had come at all. He had not received a warm welcome when he had phoned Steve's mother. At first the woman's voice had been cold and distant when he had described the circumstance of her son's death, outlining his plans to have the body shipped to Stockport for burial. Towards the end, Bulloch could hear the woman sobbing, she needed comfort but it was not in him to speak words of sympathy. He finished by saying that due to Steve's work, it would be best not to say anything to anyone, and that he would take care of the funeral arrangements.

Picking up the buff envelope that he had taken earlier from his suitcase, Bulloch made his way up the neat drive towards the front door. He had not expected a warm welcome, although the open hostility displayed by Steve's sister made him angry.

'I know who you are,' snapped the middle-aged woman.

'Why don't you just leave us alone? I've a good mind to call the police. You've no idea the hell my mother and I went through after the Gulf War – all those people asking questions. They watched this house for months hoping to catch him.' Temper turned to tears and she raised her hands covering her face. 'They told us what you and my brother did to those poor men, they . . .'

'Don't, Jane, please,' the mother implored. 'Steve's dead now. It's all over.' Watching her daughter's outburst, she stepped forward, letting the weeping face fall onto her breast, before wrapping her arms around the sobbing body. She mouthed soothing words, talking in hushed whispers.

Bulloch wanted to walk out, but controlled the urge. He had made Steve a promise. They despised him. While the mother had remained silent, Steve's sister had vented her anger on him since he first entered the house. He made a vain attempt to explain his feelings. 'You have no idea about war. Steve was my friend. Whatever you might think of him, he was closer to me than a real brother. I made him a promise – if he were to die, I would see him taken home. That's just what I'm doing.' The conversation was not going well; he had shouted too loudly. He would leave soon. He spoke to Steve's mother. 'The cremation is at two o'clock tomorrow. For obvious reasons, I will not be there. I only came here because Steve asked me to give you this.' Bulloch placed the large envelope he had been clutching, on the table.

'What is it?' asked the old woman, looking at the packet with renewed fear.

'It was Steve's. He wanted you to have it. Letting go of her daughter, she opened the envelope and peered inside. There was a period of utter silence, during which time both women gaped at the money. Quietly closing the envelope over the bundles of £50 notes, she looked up at Bulloch.

'Take it away,' she muttered in a low voice. 'We will go to Steve's funeral but we don't need your blood money. Now go, please, and I swear we will say nothing of seeing you.' Bulloch stepped back, the violent emotion in the old woman's voice and her rejection of the money unsettled him. Grabbing the packet from her hands, he made to leave. He turned in the doorway and saw that the two women were holding each other once more.

'Despite what you think of Steve, he always talked about you. In his own way, he loved you.' In the awkward interval that ensued, the old woman's body gave a heaving sob. Tears dripped down her cheeks in rhythm with those of her daughter. Bulloch left and returned to the hotel.

CHAPTER
8

London,
August 24, 1997

While Bulloch had been driving to Stockport, the plane bringing Caleb Wesley to London arrived at Heathrow Airport. As his father had promised, he was met and driven directly to the American Embassy. This was his first visit to London and as the car wove its way through the late morning traffic, its well-polished surface flashing in the sunlight, he suddenly felt excited. The car slowed as they came parallel to Grosvenor Square. He had not seen his father for over a year and, although he never understood why, his stomach was always gripped by butterflies every time they met. It was a strange mixture of excitement and fondness, born from the love that Cal felt for his father.

Despite the London traffic, an hour after leaving the airport, the car pulled up near the steps of the American Embassy. It was a modern, five floored, flat roofed, grey concrete block raised on low pyramid steps.

'There's something solid about it,' thought Cal, looking up at the large building crested by the American flag. He was immediately struck by the number of people queuing, most of whom, the driver informed him, were seeking American visas.

'Colonel Wesley has booked you in at the Marriott, I have to park there. I'll take your case to the lobby.'

'I need this one,' Cal grabbed his briefcase, thanking the driver before walking up the steps towards the main entrance. By the glass doors at the top, a doorman blocked his path. Using his passport and military identification, Cal explained who he was, and the doorman let him pass. Inside he gave his name to the receptionist and waited, taking in the quiet bustle of the busy embassy. Moments later, he saw an immaculately dressed Marine coming down the corridor, his boots clipping smartly on the marble tiles. He stopped by the counter and spoke briefly to the receptionist. She indicated with a nod of her head to where Cal was standing.

'Excuse me, sir. You are Caleb Wesley?' inquired the Marine, in a brisk voice.

'Yes.'

'Would you like to follow me, please?' said the Marine, maintaining his military style. Cal did as asked and followed the clockwork Marine down the corridor. Finally, they came to a room marked 'Intelligence & Security'.

'There you go, sir.'

'Thank you,' said Cal, stepping closer to knock at the door before opening it. His father was halfway across the room, the smile on his face radiant. 'Hi, Dad,' said Cal, opening his arms to his father's bearhug.

'Good to see you, Cal – really good to see you.'

Despite his age, Dan Wesley was still a big man. Even now,

he stood a good inch taller than Cal. As they held one another, his big arms closed like a vice around his son. Cal winced and pulled back.

'Whoa, Dad – take it easy!'

'What is it, son?' Parental concern studied Cal's face.

'Nothing, Dad. My shoulder. I told you about it on the phone. Some turkey tried to chop me up with a machete.'

'Sorry. I forgot about that. Hurt bad? I thought you said it was just a scratch.'

'Let's just say it's a big scratch that's slowly getting better,' Cal laughed, trying to ease his father's concern.

'Come on, sit down. You want coffee?' While his father went to a small side table and poured two cups of coffee, Cal chose one of the two chairs that were positioned facing the ornate desk.

'There you go. That'll make you feel better.' He handed Cal the cup before walking around the desk and enveloping himself in a big leather armchair. 'Okay son, let's have it from the top.'

'First, Dad, I need to know, did you manage to follow Norris's coffin?'

'Yes, we did. It went very much as you said. The body was returned to the family in Stockport, that's a town just south of Manchester. It was collected and signed for at customs by a local undertaker. Nothing unusual. Anyway, Susan Greenwood will fill you in on the details later. I want you to tell me what's happening or, more to the point, what you think is happening.'

'As I said, we were in the area, training recruits for a new unit the Colombians are setting up. It was my job to teach them jungle tactics. The whole thing is part of the American programme to shut down drugs production in the area. When the aircraft went down we just happened to be the nearest military unit. We suspended operations to deal with the problem. I was at the crash site, walking down a line of bodies that were waiting to be airlifted down to the town of Buga, when I noticed this guy's tie. That's when I found Norris's face sticking out of a body bag. I was really confused, it was one hell of a shock, I can tell you. On checking I found a money belt. It held a lot of cash but no credit cards and an envelope.

'Around this time, the rebels came back in force, and something needed to be done. I decided enough was enough and went after them. I got this for my troubles.' Cal hitched his thumb towards his left shoulder. 'For some reason they were determined to drive us off. Maybe they didn't like people crashing into their drug production facilities, or maybe they just wanted to rob the bodies. Whether it was money or drugs, I'm not sure, but they made a determined attempt. They killed four Colombian soldiers during the crossfire and wounded several others. The rescue services just couldn't operate,' Cal dropped his head a little, smiling as he did so. 'That's when I decided to go after them and even up the score. When it was over, I managed to find a jungle track that eventually led me down into Buga. It was the nearest town to the crash site, where the Colombians had set up a temporary mortuary in the sports hall. I managed to stumble into a road block and the police eventually took me to the gymnasium. Once there, I had a choice of at least five good doctors. One of them, a British doctor, patched me up real good. By this time most of the bodies had been recovered, and everyone was busy with post-mortem and identifying the bodies.' Cal stopped long enough to take a mouthful of coffee.

'Go on,' said his father listening intently.

'I got permission to go and have another look at Norris, just to confirm that it was him. Next, I checked through the photographs of the dead to see if Bulloch had been on the flight, but I came up blank. In any event, all I can say is that Norris was on that plane, and that he was carrying these.' Cal tossed the bundle of photographs on to the desk, fanning them out on the neat white blotter in front of his father. 'As you can see, it's always the same woman. All the cameras have an internal timing device, but if you look closely the clocks differ, which means several types of cameras were used. Someone has written on the back what I take to be a serial number starting with the prefix SC.'

Dan Wesley sat in silence while he minutely inspected each photograph. Several times he raised his head to look at his son, but still said nothing. Finally, he placed the photographs in front of him, neatly stacking them as if they were playing cards. 'You telling me this guy Norris had these pictures on him?'

'That's what I'm telling you, Dad. I also know that Bulloch and Norris deserted together. There were rumours that they had become hit men, working in the Middle East. I do know they were inseparable. If there is a chance that Norris's coffin will lead me to Bulloch, then I have to take it.'

'Wait one moment,' said his father, picking up the telephone. 'Would you come in now, Susan?' Replacing the handset, Dan Wesley sat looking at the young man seated before him. His boy had grown into a fine man. Sharon would have been proud of him. He had the Wesley family jaw, and that prominent blade of a nose which all contributed to

Caleb's rangy good looks. Dan knew his son to be a patient man and he had a quick mind. If Cal had any fault, it was his stubbornness. He would not call him an academic; through school and college he had tried hard to achieve good grades, but if he struggled in the classroom, then he excelled on the playing field. The man before him was strong and independent, the boyish good looks marred only by the white scar that formed the shape of a star, just above his right eye. 'Yes,' Dan Wesley thought to himself, 'he does have a right to find the man who tried to kill him . . . and I will do all in my power to help him.'

The door to his father's office opened. Cal turned his head, unsure as to what form Susan Greenwood would take. In the event, he was pleasantly surprised. She drifted into his vision smartly dressed in a slim, charcoal suit, a white silk blouse beneath the jacket was open enough to expose a modest amount of noticeable cleavage. Cal stood while his father made the introductions. He took the offered hand, feeling the strength in her butterfly fingers.

'It's very nice to meet you, Caleb. I've heard so much about you from your father.' Her voice was soft with a slight hint of accent.

For the first time in ages, Cal was stuck for words. He smiled then, realised he was still holding her hand, and let it drop quickly.

'Hi,' was all his mouth could utter.

'Sit down, please, Susan.'

Cal watched, transfixed, as she seated herself in the empty chair next to his. She sat straight, her legs crossed, a note pad resting on her knee as if she was about to take dictation. Her head turned towards Cal. Although hidden behind shell-framed glasses, he sensed the scrutiny of her cool look. With a major effort, he lifted his eyes from her calf muscles, and concentrated on the woman. She was in her mid-twenties, with a slender face, a tiny pink-lipped mouth, button nose, all topped by dark green eyes. Her jet-black hair fell halfway down her back in the old Spanish style. She was simply stunning.

Dan Wesley coughed loudly to regain their attention. 'Susan here is on loan from our French Embassy. Okay, Susan, tell it to Cal just like you told it to me.'

Heeding his father's gesture, Cal shifted in his seat, but not before he had seen the corners of Susan's eyes crinkle and a wry smile flit across her lips. He felt she was somehow challenging him.

'First off,' her voice was clear, 'I ran a check on the names you gave me. One is a well-known paymaster for the Cartel. We checked the Colombian hotel and he was registered there – so was a James Moore, alias your Steve Norris. This would indicate to us that your man Norris was on his way to do some business in Colombia. The other name, the one circled, belongs to one of our guys. He's a DEA undercover agent and he's in deep. From what you have given us, we think the Cartel have tumbled him, and intend to wipe him out. To be on the safe side, we have informed Washington. As for your man Norris, the body was collected by a bona fide funeral parlour and taken to their offices in Stockport. I made enquires, and it would seem you are in luck. The funeral takes place tomorrow. Here's the address of the funeral parlour and the crematorium where the service will take place.' Susan Greenwood handed Cal a sheet of paper. There was silence for a moment, then Greenwood asked, 'Is that all, sir?'

'Yes, thank you, Susan. No wait. Take a look at these.' He picked up the pile of photographs and handed them to Greenwood. 'These were found on Norris.'

Save for the shuffling sound made as Susan Greenwood leafed through the pictures, the silence prevailed. When she had finished, she placed them back on the table.

'This is definitely the Princess of Wales – professional work. A government agency took these, no doubt about it. Who's this?' she asked, holding up the odd Polaroid picture.

'That's a photograph of Norris taken after they had cleaned him up. I was hoping it might lead me to Bulloch.'

'Fascinating stuff,' said Susan. 'Have you any idea what this is all about?'

'No, but I intend to find out. Now that I know the funeral's not until tomorrow, it gives me the perfect opportunity to see if Bulloch turns up. I don't think he'll miss it; he and Norris were very close. However, I'm beginning to find it just as intriguing why Norris should have these photographs of Princess Diana. If Bulloch shows up, maybe he can shed some light on all this. Now, who's going to pay for lunch?' asked Cal, hoping that Susan Greenwood would join them.

'I'm afraid I can't make it today, Cal. I already have luncheon with the Ambassador on a Sunday, but you two feel free.' Dan Wesley dropped his head, half-pretending to look at his diary. Spotting the opening his father had made for him, Cal looked at Susan Greenwood, hopefully. But she had also seen through the thinly veiled attempt to saddle her with Cal for lunch.

'Oh, I am so sorry, Caleb, but I don't normally eat mid-day,' the smile on her face widened as she watched his shoulders droop a little and the look of disappointment bathe his face, 'but as it's you, I'll make an exception. What do you like to eat?'

'Anything,' said Cal standing, and moving a little closer. Just the smell of Susan Greenwood gave Cal a lift, making his head swim as if he had drunk some magic draught. He felt his blood thicken as it flowed through his body.

Cal's father intervened for the second time, 'I've booked you in at the Marriott, Caleb, I'm also staying there, room 307. It's not far from here. Maybe Susan will be kind enough to show you.'

'Thanks, Dad. I'll catch up with you later this evening.' With that, Cal turned to Susan. 'Shall we?'

The summer sunshine seemed even brighter as Cal walked down the embassy steps with a beautiful woman by his side. They talked, keeping the conversation light, both agreeing to call each other 'Suzie' or 'Cal'. Passing the picturesque gardens of Grosvenor Square, she pointed out the statues of Dwight Eisenhower and Franklin Roosevelt, their uncovered heads polished by a thousand rains. Despite the traffic, Cal could hear birds singing, and all at once he was happy. They crossed the road and continued down Brook Street until at last Susan indicated a restaurant.

'How do you fancy a nice Greek salad?'

'I'm game for anything – lead the way,' replied Cal.

The restaurant was busy, both with lunchtime customers and waiters flitting between the tables, trays of food and drink balanced on upturned fingers. Susan wove her way through the chattering throng, making her way to a seating area where the mid-day sunlight filtered through a large glass-panelled roof, drenching the room with brightness and warmth. A passing waiter waved them to an empty table, dropping off two menus as he did so.

'This is very nice,' remarked Cal, looking around the restaurant.

'I come here from time to time. The food is simple, but it's tasty.'

'In that case you can order for me,' replied Cal. 'So tell me, how long have you been working with my father?'

'For almost six months now. As you may have gathered, I am a research specialist. Normally I am employed at the American Embassy in Paris. My mother was French. She met my father while she was on holiday in Boston. They fell in love and I came along shortly after. I live in Paris and commute during the week to work with your father. Our department is trying to assess the personal profiles of various senior military commanders of the old Warsaw Pact countries, those which now wish to join NATO. It's a boring job really, but London is such a wonderful place, there is always so much to see and do. You really must take in a couple of shows while you are here.'

'That's nice of you to offer, but how come you're not spending the weekend in Paris? Couldn't resist meeting me, huh?' laughed Cal.

Susan grinned. 'I let myself walk into that one. Let's just say I have the greatest respect for your father and, yes, I was interested to see what his offspring looked like. But back to business,' Susan changed the subject. 'What do you intend to do with Bulloch when you find him?'

'To be honest,' answered Cal, 'I don't rightly know. I suppose the simplest thing would be to find out where he is living and have him arrested. At least then he would be in jail, where he could do no further harm.'

With an involuntary move, Susan reached out with her hand, letting her fingers tenderly touch the white splash of scar tissue above Cal's right eye. 'Your father told me about your narrow escape during Desert Storm. You are very lucky to be alive.'

From the moment she had heard Cal was coming to London, she had been strangely excited. At first she had put it down to simple curiosity but there was something distinctly different about the tall, muscular man sitting across the table from her. It was a combination of his concise speech, and those observant eyes that questioned everything within their range, as if he was constantly searching for answers. 'He would make the perfect spy,' she thought foolishly to herself. He loved his country with a passion, yet could honour truth with practical necessity. Lifting her head slightly, she looked into the depth of his eyes. 'Careful, girl,' her heart warned, 'get to know him a little better first.' One thing was for sure, Caleb Wesley was certainly going to change her life. The waiter arrived to take their order.

Throughout lunch they continued to enjoy the warmth of each other's company. Cal discovered that Susan was an only child, the daughter of a most affectionate and indulgent father who had put her through college. Like Cal, her mother had died when she was young and, although her father had worked wonders during her upbringing, it had fallen a little short of a mother's love. Nevertheless, he had honoured his wife's memory by completing his daughter's education in France.

'How are you getting to Stockport tomorrow?' asked Susan as they left the restaurant, retracing their steps to the Embassy.

'I was hoping to hire a car at the hotel, unless you have a better idea.'

'No, but if you do, park it in the NCP car park at the back of the Marriott,' she hunted around in her shoulder bag. 'Here you go,' Susan handed Cal a pass. 'The Embassy reserves several parking spaces there but they're hardly ever used. You'll save yourself a fortune.'

Leaving Susan at the Embassy steps, Cal walked the short distance to the hotel and checked in to his room. Thirty minutes later, he was back in the lobby, handing over his credit card before signing for the hire car. 'It's a red Vauxhall Vectra GLS, registration P437 HHW,' said the Avis rep, arranging to have the car parked in the embassy lot and for the keys to be left at reception. Cal used the rest of the afternoon for shopping, buying essentials he would need, before making his way to Stockport.

Before returning to the hotel, Cal went to the car park and checked out the hire car. The road map he had requested lay on the passenger seat. Satisfied that everything was in order for an early start the following morning, he went back to his room, showered and met up with his father for dinner.

Later that evening, as Cal sat with his father in the Marriott's palacious bar, their conversation drifted back to family life. When that was exhausted, the subject returned to Cal's discovery and to figuring out why Norris should be carrying explicit photographs of the Princess of Wales. Cal knew little of his father's work, other than that he worked for Military Intelligence. Although still in good shape, Cal noticed his father had gained a few pounds – too much time sitting behind a desk. Dan Wesley noted the direction of his son's gaze and fended off any pending derogatory comment.

'Yes, I know,' he said patting his stomach, 'but there was a time when I could have shown you a clean pair of heels, boy.'

Cal laughed. 'You'd die of a heart attack if you tried nowadays.'

'Trouble is, son, they work me too hard. Ever since I left active service they have found me one liaison job after the other. In the Gulf, Schwartzkopf sent me to patch up the rocky relations between the Army and Navy, now they got me talking to a bunch of generals, trying to work out if they're capable of working within the structure of NATO.'

'Where does Susan Greenwood fit into all this? She tells me she's just a researcher from the Paris office helping you out,' said Cal, hoping to learn more about the woman.

'If that's what she told you, then that's what she does,' Dan Wesley looked thoughtfully at his son. 'I did note she came back to her office with a spring to her step. You showing interest there, son? 'Bout time you settled down.'

'She's nice. I like her. Now if you'll excuse me.' Cal emptied his glass, setting it firmly on the table before standing. 'If you don't mind, it's been a long day. I'm going to turn in. I'll leave early in the morning, so I won't see you until I get back.'

'Any idea when that will be?'

'Not sure. I may stay in Manchester overnight, but don't be surprised if I should suddenly turn up late tomorrow night.' Cal stretched a little, massaging his injured shoulder.

'Just remember, Caleb. This is England, not the United States. Don't go getting yourself into trouble before you know all the facts; no embarrassing situations.' Dan Wesley warned. His face then softened a little. 'Also, remember that you're not on your own. I'm here to help.'

'Thanks, Dad, I appreciate that.'

It was still dark when he set off, and the streets were devoid of heavy traffic. Cal manoeuvred the car around Hyde Park and up Edgware Road, heading for the M1 motorway, making steady progress all the way towards Manchester. Three hours after leaving London, he made his way onto the A6 which, according to the map, led him to Stockport. By nine o'clock the traffic became heavier, a situation compounded by a series of road works, and it was almost 10.30 before he eventually located the crematorium. It was situated on the side of the main A6, separated from the busy road by a low stone wall topped with ornate railings. At the first opportunity, Cal turned the car around, parking directly opposite the crematorium. He got out of the car to take a good look. Happy that he would have no trouble finding the place later that afternoon, he drove off in search of the undertakers who had collected Norris's body. They were located only a short distance from the crematorium. The converted Victorian house faced the main road, making it easy to find. Parking the car, Cal made his way into the building with the idea of checking the funeral arrangements. The offices of Frank Lewis & Sons were austere, solemn and also deserted. Cal shouted, 'Hello,' then waited a few moments. Eventually, he heard noises and a lank, bleached-faced man appeared.

'How may I help you, sir?' Cal was surprised to see that the man actually bowed his head a little, in mock submission.

'You've a funeral this afternoon at the crematorium. A Mr Moore.' Cal used the name he had found in Norris's passport.

'We have several cremations this afternoon, sir,' the man's attitude changed when he realised Cal's inquiry did not relate to new business. He stooped over a large ledger that lay open on the desk. 'Here we are, sir – the belated Mr. Moore. Will you be attending?'

'I don't have time to go to the service,' Cal said, thinking quickly. 'I just wanted to send the family some flowers. I wonder, do you have their address?'

'Certainly. One moment, please.' This time the man seated himself at the solitary desk, pushing the ledger away before flipping through the pages of a diary. 'Here you are; Number Seven, Andrews Close, High Lane.' The man muttered out loud, writing the address on the back of a business card. 'There you go, sir.' He handed the card to Cal. 'A most distressing circumstance. I have always considered air travel so safe. They told me at the airport that he was the only British passenger on board. Tragic.'

Cal muttered agreement. Thanking the man, he made to leave. As he reached the door, the man spoke again. 'You may wish to speak to his brother, he's the one who made all the arrangements. I believe he's staying at the Bay Horse.'

'The Bay Horse?' queried Cal, barely able to believe his luck.

'Yes, sir. It's a mainly a restaurant, but has a small hotel attached – straight down the A6 for about three miles. On the right, you can't miss it.'

With confused excitement, Cal hastened back to the car. The realisation that Bulloch might be no more than three miles away made him apprehensive. He deliberated whether he should confront his adversary or whether he should call the police. Heeding his father's words, he decided to wait, at least until he confirmed if Norris's brother really was Bulloch. In any case, Cal felt sure that Bulloch would show up at the funeral later that afternoon. It was best not to expose himself. If he lost Bulloch now, he might never get the chance to find him again. As if to settle the matter, his stomach grumbled, warning him that he had not eaten since yesterday. It was almost lunchtime, and from what the man said, the Bay Horse was just a few miles down the road. 'Worth a look,' he said to himself, driving off.

Prior to entering the hotel, Cal bought a daily newspaper and, settling down with a bottle of beer, he took stock of the place. He was tempted to ask at reception about who was in residence but that was risky. Presumably Bulloch would be travelling under yet another false name, anyway. Instead, he sat reading the newspaper, pretending to be engrossed while casually watching customers as they arrived through what seemed to be the only entrance. He had selected a table near the window in the small bar that separated the main restaurant from the hotel section, and from there he could observe the reception area. For a while he became engrossed in the newspaper, during which period the lunchtime trade began to fill the tables. He wondered if Bulloch had changed much over the past six years and whether he would recognise him from the mental image he retained.

By 1.30 pm the place was quite crowded, but there was no sign of Bulloch. Cal risked having another beer, determined to stay at the hotel until two o'clock, at which time he intended leaving for the crematorium, hopefully there to spot Bulloch. Suddenly, the door that led to the hotel section opened. Cal glanced up, looking over the top of the newspaper. He was about to drop his head and continue reading, when he recognised Bulloch. It was more the man's stature than his features that he first recognised. His tall, bulky frame towered above the gathering of lunchtime drinkers. He was casually dressed, wearing a dark sports jacket and slacks. With a dozen paces, Bulloch crossed to the small reception, placing what looked like a key on the small counter. Turning, he left via the main door. In a flash, Cal was on his feet, intending to follow Bulloch, hoping to detain his enemy. By the time he had reached the reception area, Bulloch was already through the main door, heading for the car park. Cal stopped. Instinct cautioned him; would it not be better to find out what Bulloch was up to? In that moment of indecision, his eyes fell on the room key that Bulloch had dropped at the unmanned reception. With one swift movement he turned and placed the newspaper he was holding over the key. His fingers touched it, cupping it into his palm. He stood for a second longer, surreptitiously checking to see if he had been spotted. The barmaid, who normally dealt with reception, was busy serving a drink and had not noticed. Neither, it seemed, had anyone else. Cal turned and strode back to the table where he had been sitting, the key clutched in his hand. Outwardly calm, his mind was racing. This was an opportunity not to be missed. Twisting his head, he peered through the window. There were several people outside in the car park, none of whom were Bulloch. Cal forced himself to wait for a full two minutes. Standing once more, he walked towards the inner door from which Bulloch had emerged and entered. The door led to a small passageway and a narrow flight of stairs. Cal climbed swiftly, taking the steps two at a time. The steps opened into a short landing. The key tag indicated room number four. He glanced at the doors in front of him. Number four was to the right. Swiftly he placed the key in the lock and opened the door. Stepping inside, he closed it securely behind him. Cal halted, taking in a deep breath. He could not believe his luck. Suddenly his muscles tensed – what if Bulloch returned?

Cal would confront him. He didn't give a shit any more. He had found the man who had left him for dead. He glanced round the room. It was neat and tidy. The bed had been made, but there was an impression where a body had lain on top of the cover, along with a dent in the pillow. Cal checked for luggage. A small suitcase had been dumped near the foot of the bed. He opened it, quickly flipping through the soiled clothes. Finding nothing of interest, he checked the old-fashioned wardrobe. A pair of slacks and a sports jacket were the only items hanging there. Meticulously, he went through all the pockets and found nothing. 'This has got to be Bulloch, no one else would be this careful,' Cal muttered to himself. He moved to the waste bin. Again, it was empty. 'Damn.' There was nothing at all. He went to the bathroom. Apart from the hotel toiletry, there was just a man's washing and shaving gear, all contained in a neat, black Samsonite travel bag. 'Nothing.' Cal dropped to the press-up position, checking under the bed. Still nothing. Standing, his eyes passed over the room one last time. He checked his watch and decided it was time to go to the funeral. He made to leave and was two paces from the door when a small green light caught his eye. On the floor by the side of the bed, half hidden by the trouser press, stood a mobile phone in its charger.

'Bingo!' said Cal.

Bending down, he picked up the phone, taking a moment to examine it. Then, pressing the 'ON' button, he waited. It gave a little 'burp' and displayed a message. Despite being only half-charged, when Cal pressed the 'SEND' button a list of the last calls appeared in the window. He moved to the dresser and used the pen and pad supplied by the hotel carefully to jot down the numbers. He was surprised to see that several of them were repeated. He continued to key the function buttons until he managed to call up the mobile unit's own number. Carefully switching off the phone, he replaced it in its charger, and left the room. Walking back down the narrow stairs, he passed through the inner door and back into the bar. Again, no one paid any particular attention. Cal kept going, walked up to the small reception desk, which was still unmanned, and calmly placed the key on the counter. With a child-like sense of complete elation, he turned and left the hotel. Getting in the car, Cal checked his watch; it had just gone two o'clock. He drove back towards Stockport and the crematorium.

Parking on the busy road was not easy. Eventually, Cal pulled into a small side street some 300 metres from the Crematorium. He took his camera and made his way to the railed entrance. His decision to search Bulloch's room had made him miss the start of the service, and the opportunity to see who had actually gone into the small chapel. He walked past the building and saw that the hearse had already arrived. One other car stood beside it, the drivers chatting idly. He was tempted to go into the chapel and confront Bulloch, convinced he was inside. His father's words bade him to be prudent. Cal decided to wait.

He had no idea how long the service would last, but he estimated that it would be less than an hour. The hearse had driven off, leaving just one car. At last a vicar appeared in the large, ornate doorway, his robes flowing in the breeze. Next came an elderly woman, supported by a second whose age, Cal guessed, was mid-30s. He assumed the women were Norris's mother and sister. Both got into the waiting car, which then drove off.

There was no sign of Bulloch or anyone else for that matter. Quickly, Cal entered the railed courtyard that separated the crematorium from the main road. The door to the chapel was open and he walked into the quiet sanctuary. The odd smell of incense was pungent in the air. 'Can I help you?' The chaplain had been standing to one side, both hands cupping a pile of hymn books.

'Yes,' said Cal, somewhat startled by the man. 'I seem to have missed the service, I was hoping to speak to Mr Moore's brother.'

'Then I am afraid you are disappointed on this occasion. Only his mother and sister were present at the service. They left a few moments ago. There was no brother. I always find it so sad when . . .' Cal did not hear any more. He had missed Bulloch. Running to the car, he drove quickly back to the hotel.

'The man in number four, could you tell me his name please?' Cal turned up the American accent. 'I know it's irregular but when I was here earlier I thought I recognised him as an old army buddy – I just had to come back and check.'

'Oh, you should have asked earlier. Mr Rogers checked out ten minutes ago.'

Cal awoke to the persistent banging on his door. Still half asleep, he stumbled out of bed. 'I'm coming, I'm coming,' he said, opening the door to find his father standing in the hallway.

'Good morning, son. I was just on my way to the office and thought I'd check to see how you got on in Stockport. Did you find Bulloch?'

Cal stretched for a moment before answering. 'Yeah, I found him; he was staying at a hotel close to Norris's home.' Cal explained what happened, how he had 'borrowed' the key. 'It was an opportunity too good to miss. I decided searching his room was better than following him. I wrongly assumed he would go to the funeral. I arrived late and the service was halfway through. I waited to the end, but there was no sign of Bulloch. He had never been there. I went back to the hotel, hoping to catch him there, but while I was away, he'd already checked out.'

'So you've lost him completely. Have you any idea where he went?'

'Not a clue. There was no point in chasing him, I had no idea what type of car he was driving, or which direction he was heading. The only thing I could do was locate Norris's mother and watch the house. The road was a dead end, but I hung around watching the house for several hours. There was nothing.' Cal hesitated. 'Look, Dad, I'm one hundred per cent sure it's him. I searched his bedroom and it was totally clean. Who else but a man on the run lives like that? The only thing I found was his mobile phone. He had left it charging. I was able to access the last nine numbers, and the phone unit's own number. Again, your help would be appreciated.'

'Give them to me. I have several meetings this morning but I am sure Susan Greenwood will help. You get showered, then come on over. We can see what she has come up with and discuss what best to do next.'

'Too many cobwebs,' Cal muttered to himself when his father had left. What he needed was some fresh air.

A brisk 15 minutes later, dressed in his jogging suit, Cal crossed the busy road, making his way into Hyde Park. He ran for over an hour, clearing his mind of Bulloch and Norris, letting the sweat purge his body. The steady rhythm of his feet criss-crossed the labyrinth of paths that patterned London's most famous park . . . a place of tranquillity and beauty amid the roaring bustle of city traffic.

Returning to the hotel, he had just entered the shower when the constant ringing of the telephone forced him to answer it. Wrapping a towel round his waist he stumbled from the bathroom, leaving wet foot marks across the carpet. Grabbing the phone abruptly, he was about to snap when he heard Susan's voice. He sat down on the bed.

'Good morning,' she said, placing enough emphasis on the 'morning' to make it sound taunting. 'I've been trying to call you for the past half hour, don't you think it's time you got out of bed? If you come to the embassy, I might have some news that will intrigue you.'

'You're going to let me take you to dinner!'

'That wasn't what I had in mind, but we might discuss that as well. What I really meant to say was that I have come up with some interesting stuff on your friend Bulloch.'

'What is it?' Cal demanded.

'Not over the phone, come to the embassy as soon as you can.'

'I've just been for a run, and was taking a shower when you called. Give me 15 minutes,' Cal heard the line go dead and replaced the phone. Heading back to the shower, his spirits lifted at the thought of seeing Susan.

With a feeling of anticipation Cal entered his father's office, closing the door behind him. Susan was already seated, talking to his father. They both looked up as Cal approached. He declined the offer of coffee and took the seat next to Susan.

'What's happening? You two look as if you have just discovered a Russian spy in our midst,' Cal said jokingly.

'Close,' replied Susan. 'While you were away, I did a little checking using the photograph you left me of Norris – amazing stuff. When I ran a check on Norris, or James Moore as he called himself, this is what I found. Both he and Bulloch were on an Interpol inquiry bulletin a couple of weeks back,' Susan handed Cal three sheets of paper clipped together. 'We always keep a copy. Can you confirm that this is Bulloch, and Norris?

Cal looked at the head and shoulder shots of the two men. Although this was a photocopy of the original there was no mistaking the two men. He nodded, noting the names the two men had adopted and added, 'Rogers, the woman at the hotel called him Mr Rogers.' He pointed at the name beneath Bulloch's picture.

'I rang Paris and questioned the Interpol officer involved. He informed me that Scotland Yard had informed the British Home Office, who in turn sent out a man to check on the two suspects. For some reason there was a delay, but the man who eventually went to Paris and confirmed that the two men were innocent . . . was Sir Gilbert Scott.'

The way Susan said it, Cal thought he should know the name. 'Who the hell is Sir Gilbert Scott?'

Dan Wesley echoed his son's words, with contrary definition. 'The Sir Gilbert Scott?'

'The very same,' The rest of Susan's conversation was addressed mainly to Cal. 'I also checked out the phone numbers. There are two to Harmsham Park in West Sussex. That's Sir Gilbert's home. There's one to Colombia, which matched the hotel number found on Norris and one to the emergency number given out by the airline. Two to an address in Cannock and finally three to Stockport – the undertaker and Norris's mother.'

Cal had the feeling that his father and Susan had already discussed the findings and that small alarm bells were beginning to go off. 'Most of the calls make sense,' Cal reasoned. 'He contacts Colombia and learns of the air crash, then he rings the emergency number and confirms Norris is dead. He needs to contact an undertaker and inform the next of kin. Now, would someone like to tell me how this Sir Gilbert Scott enters the picture? Could Bulloch be working for him?'

'It's a possibility. The mobile phone checks out to Phantom Security, the company that operates out of Harmsham Park. Sir Gilbert owns it.' Susan looked at the old man. 'I'm still working on the Cannock number. The guy's name is Jarvis but there is no obvious reason for Bulloch to call him.'

'If Sir Gilbert is involved, you need to tread very carefully,' Dan Wesley looked troubled. 'I want you to stay on this full time, Susan. Find anything that might throw some light on the subject and pull the file on Sir Gilbert. Let Caleb read it.' He stood and walked towards the door. 'Best keep this to ourselves for the time being.'

For the past twenty minutes Cal had sat engrossed, reading the file Susan had given him, while she busied herself popping in and out of the office. When he had finished he put the file on Susan's desk. 'Who is this guy, James Bond? I'm impressed.'

'He was considered one of the best field agents the British

had during the '60s and early '70s. He could have gone to the top. Then, out of the blue, it was found that he had been making secret financial deals in the Middle East. Nothing that involved the nation's security but the countries involved were not friendly. In the end, he resigned. What you will not find in the file is the fact that Harmsham Park is still used for debriefing high level defectors, or more recently for the less publicised attempts to initiate peace talks. That is why the place has armed guards. I had a discreet word with a friend of mine at the Home Office. It would appear that Sir Gilbert has cancelled the forthcoming talks between several factions in the Northern Ireland troubles. Sir Robert Trescott, who is deputy head of the security services, gave "a more pressing matter" as the reason.'

'It might be worth taking a look at Harmsham Park.'

'Not a chance,' warned Susan. 'Your father would not allow it. What evidence have we got other than the phone calls? In any case, all it points to is some British undercover operation where the Princess of Wales might be involved, and they might be using Bulloch's services. The British security services have done far worse than hire people like him and surveillance on the princess is logical. No. The Ambassador would not sanction it.'

'I'm not asking him to. Neither am I going to tell him. I came here with the express purpose of finding Bulloch. If that means doing a little breaking and entering, then so be it. I'll take the responsibility.'

Susan Greenwood stood staring at the man before her, his anger contorting his face. She wanted to say, 'It's impossible,' but it would be no use. She had been right in her first assessment; Caleb Wesley was very much his own man. 'Might

I suggest we leave it for the moment? I need to do a little more checking.' Susan moved closer standing directly in front of him, their bodies almost touching. 'I can meet you tonight. We can discuss it over dinner.' The small lips pouted just enough, and her head tilted back.

She had caught him unawares. Cal smiled, 'Okay, meet you at eight in the hotel bar. Not a word to my father.'

At the time when Cal had spotted Bulloch leaving the Bay Horse Hotel, he had wrongly assumed that he would be going to the funeral. Bulloch, however, had other plans. He had not driven far. Without the women's knowledge he returned to Norris's home. He parked the car were he could observe the road junction to the cul-de-sac and waited. Ten minutes later, a black car drove out of Andrew's Close, turning towards the A6. Norris's mother and sister were sitting in the back.

While Norris's mother and sister sat in the all-but-empty chapel at the crematorium, Bulloch entered the side gate that led to the rear of their home. Passing down the side of the bungalow, he followed the garden path to where a small shed sat in one corner. Glancing around, making sure he was not being observed, he removed the small hook-and-eye catch, and opened the door. The shed smelled of must, years old garden material, piled in cluttered heaps, covered the whole floor. Stepping inside, Bulloch hunted through the muddle before picking up a spade. Moving outside, to the rear of the hut, he found the concealed space formed by the back of the shed and the garden fence. Various bits of junk and compost had been piled on top of three single paving slabs. Bulloch worked for several minutes, removing enough garbage to clear the first and second slab. Then, using the spade, he prised up the centre slab. Resting it against the fence, he looked down at the worm-etched earth that lay beneath it. He started to dig. The soil was wet and clay-like; it stuck to the spade but, after removing 10 to 15 centimetres of dirt, he hit something solid. Kneeling down, Bulloch continued to scrape away the loose earth, exposing a metal box. Quickly pulling it out, he laid it to one side. He refilled the hole and replaced the flagstone, concealing his handiwork by restacking some of the junk. Taking a carrier bag from his pocket, he picked up the metal box, and placed it inside. He took great care to leave everything as before, returned to his car and drove back to the hotel. Ten minutes later he had checked out and was heading south towards Macclesfield. Joining the M6 at Sandbach, he drove towards Cannock, intent upon collecting the devices from Jarvis.

It was early evening and still light as he parked the car. Jarvis's house looked old and dirty. In the garden, several pieces of plastic sacking danced in the evening breeze. 'What a shit hole,' Bulloch thought, walking towards the back of the house. An old glass conservatory covered the rear entrance. The conservatory door stood open. Bulloch entered and stepped up to the back door. He looked around, satisfied that no one had noticed his arrival, before finally knocking on the door. He heard footsteps and moments later the door was opened by a woman. She was in her mid-40s with a gentle, if somewhat strained face.

Bulloch hesitated, 'I'm looking for Oliver. My name is Rogers.'

'Please come in. He told me you were coming. I'm Oliver's wife, Shirley,' she stepped back, allowing Bulloch to enter the small kitchen before closing the door behind them. 'He's in his workshop. I'll show you the way.'

Bulloch followed her from the kitchen through a short, dark corridor before stepping into the small, well-lit workshop. The room was clean, if somewhat cluttered. Oliver Jarvis sat propped in a battered old director's chair flanked between two small tables, the tops of which were scattered with every conceivable type of electronic gadget. He was watching a television monitor, so absorbed that he failed to notice their presence.

'Oliver, Mr Rogers is here.'

Jarvis made no effort to look up, but waved his arm a little indicating a stool. Bulloch took a seat. The woman excused herself, disappearing back towards the kitchen.

'With you in a moment,' said Jarvis, his eyes flicking between the monitor and a small device he held in his hand. Bulloch said nothing but continued watching, trying to evaluate the physical strength of the man. The thin arm was bare from the elbow down, the muscle long since wasted, the veins protruding below the surface skin like burrowing serpents. Jarvis would not pose a problem.

'There, that just about does it.' At last the man turned in his seat, facing Bulloch. 'Did you bring the money?'

Bulloch half-opened the briefcase, resting it on his lap, and took out a bundle of notes.

'£10,000,' he placed it carefully on the workbench between them, leaving his hand over the bundle, a clear indication for Jarvis to produce his part of the bargain.

'I have modified the ambush light so that it fits into the rear light of a ZX600. It would be better if I fitted it to the machine.' There was silence for a moment while Jarvis waited for some form of acknowledgement. It was not forthcoming, so he continued. 'You need to replace the original housing with this lamp, refitting the wires as normal. That will ensure the lights function perfectly at night. This cable,' Jarvis held it up so that Bulloch could clearly identify it, 'you should tape to your bike's frame, fitting this switch onto the handlebars. I've deliberately made the switch big so that you can easily use it while wearing motor cycle gloves. There is a simple split pin fitted through the switch to prevent accidental firing. It's a little crude but will suffice. The power supply will be taken directly from the battery. If the police stop you everything will look normal.

'The tracking unit can be covertly or magnetically installed in a few seconds. It is set in motion by a simple telephone call. Once triggered, it will then activate itself contacting a pre-programmed number which will allow monitoring of any device, cameras, audio etcetera.

'As for the other device,' Jarvis picked up what looked like a threaded bolt the likes of which were to be found in any car engine, 'this will do the job you want.' He handed Bulloch a photocopied sheet. 'I took this from the manual. You will see that I have identified the two bolts in question. You need to remove either one of the two original bolts and insert this one. Although this may weaken the original joint it should make little difference to the car's performance in the short term, say a month or so. The receiver is hidden in the bolt head and I have incorporated a miniature detonator.' Jarvis turned the bolt up so that Bulloch could observe the threaded end. 'You will see that I have drilled out the centre of the thread, leaving just enough metal for you to safety screw it into place. You need to stuff the hole with explosive so that it backs up on to the detonator. I estimate it will take 10 grams.'

Jarvis handed the bolt to Bulloch and indicated a large brown envelope sitting on one of his side tables. 'I have made three sets altogether, two that are common for the top model Mercedes and one for a Range Rover. Follow the step-by-step instructions and you won't have any problems. The explosive bolts can be initiated either by the tracking device, or when you activate the ambush light – a coded signal will be sent to the bolt. It has a range of about 75 metres. The driver will blind when the bolt blows; the left steering joint will be severed sending the car spinning in an anticlockwise direction causing it to roll over and . . . ' Jarvis stopped talking as his wife re-entered the room.

'If you don't mind, I'm going to have a bath then go to bed, dear. I don't feel very well. Nice to have met you, Mr Rogers.' She left the room once more. Bulloch watched her go. It would be easier to kill her upstairs. He had already planned how to kill Jarvis. He was just waiting for the right moment.

Jarvis, misreading Bulloch's intentions, apologised for his wife. 'You must forgive her, she suffers from migraine.' He continued his briefing. 'I have incorporated a four-digit security code preventing any unauthorised users calling the system. So to summarise, you can you track any vehicle and listen in on their conversation. Then, should it be necessary, you can manipulate the electronics or trigger a second remote device that will immobilise the vehicle. Providing you can get your hands on the digital mapping for the area of operation you can do all this from a laptop computer from anywhere in the world.' Jarvis paused to let the value of his work be absorbed. 'Now, are there any other questions you would like to ask?'

'No,' replied Bulloch, deliberately opening his briefcase

and taking out the roll of shrink-wrap film. 'I'll wrap them in this for safety. Maybe you should count the money.' Jarvis, whose eyes had hardly left the bundle, reached out to pick up the money. Bulloch positioned himself behind Jarvis's chair, unravelling about a metre of film as he did so. It made a weird, rubbing noise. In one deft movement, Bulloch casually lifted the film over the top of Jarvis, pulling it tight against the man's chest. Jarvis let out a cry. 'What the fuck do you think you're doing?'

Ignoring the man's words, Bulloch swiftly unwrapped the role, spinning it rapidly, pinning his victim's chest to the chair. He moved with the deftness of a man who had done such work before. The film whirred noisily in protest at being unwrapped so quickly. Jarvis began to struggle. Unable to move, he shouted, although not very loud. Content that Jarvis's body was securely fastened to the seat, Bulloch started to cover his head. He covered the mouth and nose with several layers, making sure the man could not breathe. Once he had finished, he pulled the chair to the centre of the workshop, where Jarvis's futile efforts to free himself would not damage the devices. Jarvis started to twitch, kicking out with his legs, rocking his head from side to side. The effort was in vain. Walking casually round the chair, Bulloch stood facing the dying man, studying his victim as if he were some kind of experiment. The facial features protruded. The mouth was slightly apart, the tongue probing hopelessly at the film, the nose squashed flat, as if the face were pushing against glass. With a final struggle, his eyes opened pleading. Slowly, life left the dying man.

It took almost three minutes for Oliver Jarvis to die, although Bulloch waited for five, just to be sure. While he waited, he collected the money which had fallen and scattered on the floor during the struggle. Once gathered, he placed it into his briefcase together with the devices. He examined the room. Satisfied, he left Jarvis's body and went in search of his wife. As he reached the kitchen, Bulloch could hear the sound of water draining away, the woman had finished her bath. Reaching inside his jacket pocket he produced an old-fashioned cut-throat razor and proceeded to climb the stairs. He moved slowly, listening for sounds of the woman. The noise of running water still guided his steps as he reached the landing. The bathroom door was a little to his left and lay half-open. He could clearly see the woman bending over, busy cleaning the bath. He moved forward. A loose floorboard creaked, the woman turned, her head snapping up at the sight of Bulloch.

'I need the toilet,' Bulloch's face looked apologetic.

Embarrassed at the intrusion, the woman placed both hands on the collar of her housecoat, pulling it tight together. She made a move to slip past Bulloch . . . and he struck. Seizing the woman, his left hand fastened over her mouth. With one swift movement the weight of his body forced her to twist around. Then, pushing her in front of him, he forced her to bend over the bath. In an effort to stop herself falling, Shirley Jarvis reached out with her right arm. It was the reaction Bulloch wanted. His right hand slashed down, the open razor fleeting over her wrist. Blood spurted instantly, splashing the tiles in a crimson jet. Letting the razor drop, Bulloch seized the injured arm, holding it over the bath. The woman's knees gave way, as his weight and frame pinned her to the side of the bath. For what seemed like an age she knelt, unable to move. His left hand forced her head so tight against his chest that she could not breathe. Horror-stricken eyes rolled down to see the bright trickle of blood bloating in spurts from the cut. It ran in small rivulets down into her palm, dripping progressively into the bath. She struggled in vain against his grip. In the end, there was no pain. She closed her eyes. Softly the shadow of life flowed from her body. Her mind misty, neither asleep nor awake, feeling only the desire to rest, Shirley Jarvis lost consciousness.

Bulloch waited for her body to go limp before releasing her to flop over the edge of the bath. Picking up the razor he placed it in her left hand, pressing her fingers tight around it, then he let it fall. The whole thing had taken no more than two minutes. With care he removed the blooded gloves, placing them in his pocket before making his way downstairs. 'With luck, they'll think that she killed Jarvis, before topping herself. What the fuck,' thought Bulloch to himself, 'I don't give a fuck what they think. They can never connect me.' Picking up the briefcase, he left the building.

Outside, the evening was slipping into darkness. Bulloch walked steadily towards his car, careful that no one should pay him any attention. 30 minutes later he was driving back towards the M6 heading back towards London. He started whistling to himself. 'That little scene is going to cause some confusion tomorrow morning!' he said to no one in particular.

It was gone midnight by the time Bulloch arrived back at the apartment. Dumping the bag containing Norris's box and the briefcase in his bedroom, he took a shower and went straight to bed.

Next morning, Bulloch took a leisurely breakfast. Seated as usual in the café, he scanned the morning papers for news of the mysterious deaths only to be disappointed. Back at the apartment, he examined the devices Jarvis had made, reviewing as he did so the instructions he had been given. Satisfied there would be no problems, he turned his attention to the carrier bag containing Norris's metal box and went into the kitchen. Using the sink, Bulloch washed the caked soil from the dark brown box, exposing the words 'Ammunition 7.62 Ball', indicating its original purpose. Placing the box on a tea towel, he unclipped the lid, pleased to see that the rubber seal had preserved the contents. On top lay what looked like two large white candles, but which the grease-proof paper identified as 'PE-4, 8ozs', plastic explosive. He put them on one side and explored further. In addition to the explosive, Steve's cache contained one hundred rounds of 9mm, fifty rounds of 5.56mm, two grenades and a tin of electrical detonators. At the bottom, wrapped in protective cloth, was a Glock 9mm pistol. Bulloch picked up the weapon, and began toying with it. 'Nice one, Steve. This will come in very handy.' Opening a carton of ammunition, he loaded the pistol before repacking the tin and hiding it in his bedroom.

For the remainder of the day, he sifted through the information Sir Gilbert had supplied, putting to one side anything he could use in Paris. By four o'clock he had had enough and decided to go for a walk. He picked up an early evening paper. The story was on the third page. It was a short article, describing how a man in his mid-50s, had died due to suffocation. The body had been found wrapped in cling film. His wife had been found in the bathroom, where it appeared she had taken her own life by cutting her wrist. It was assumed that the couple where acting out some bizarre sexual fantasy that had gone wrong. When Bulloch read the article, he smirked to himself. 'Who said you can't get away with murder? It just takes balls.'

Back at the apartment, he painstakingly cut out the article, treating it like some trophy. Discarding the newspaper, he reached for the phone.

'This is Bulloch. I have the equipment.'

'Did you encounter any problems?'

'No.'

'Good. Wait at the apartment. I will be there this evening.'

It was almost eight o'clock before Sir Gilbert arrived. He was carrying a small bag which he dropped casually at Bulloch's feet. 'It would seem the princess will be returning to London in five days time on the 31st of August. All indications suggest that she will leave the *Jonikal* early morning Saturday and fly to Paris where she will spend the night in Al Fayed's apartment on the Rue Arsene Houssaye where we now know he plans to propose to her. Given the amount of filth we have leaked to the newspapers, we believed that she would turn him down. However, we intercepted this communiqué this morning.' He dropped the folded sheet of A4 into Bulloch's lap.

'Fuck me,' said Bulloch after a few seconds of scanning the paper.

'Aptly chosen words,' Sir Gilbert continued. 'We are now totally convinced that on Monday the 1st of September the Princess of Wales will announce the news of her engagement to Dodi Al Fayed. Much is now riding on your plan. I want you in Paris by Friday. Accommodation has been arranged at the Concorde Lafayette. It is well situated and full of tourists, so you will not be out of place. Everything you need will sent to France using the diplomatic bag. Upon your arrival a Kawasaki ZX600 and communications system will be delivered to your hotel. I leave you to fit the ambush light. My operatives will deal with the hotel's Mercedes. Keep your mobile phone handy for any last minute instruction. If you do not hear from me, we will meet here tomorrow afternoon. It will be for the last time. Do you have any questions?

'Why do you want her dead in France?'

'It will make it easier to control circumstances after the event. Things do not always go according to plan and the French situation allows us a little more freedom for any mop-up operation.' Sir Gilbert studied Bulloch's face, waiting for a change of expression. When none was forthcoming he continued. 'I read the episode about Jarvis and his wife, rather odd.'

'Not really. The house is full of nude painting and weird art. Don't worry, there's no connection. Now would you like a demonstration of how the devices work?'

CHAPTER

9

'Here's a little box of tricks you might find handy.' Susan Greenwood passed the strange-looking electronic device to Cal.

'What is it?' Cal turned it over looking at it.

'As you seem quite determined to break into Harmsham Park, I thought you might need a little help. We don't want you getting caught, do we?'

Despite Susan's efforts the evening before, she had failed to dissuade Cal from his plan. If the truth was known, she admired his tenacity. What his father was going to say when he found out was another matter. Reluctantly, and only for the moment, she had agreed not to say anything. Now here she was helping Caleb.

'That little baby is basically a combination finder for any keypad operated system, similar to the ones you might find controlling Sir Gilbert's house alarm, which I believe is housed on the wall in the security office. You'll find that near the rear entrance,' she smiled.

'Do you have any further tips about the security at Harmsham Park?' Cal inquired, surprised by her knowledge.

'Only that the place is very well protected,' she went on to explain. 'Certain American dignitaries are invited there from time to time. I once attended a function there and, as my duty is to research, I researched. The grounds are completely surrounded by a high wall, with a secondary inner perimeter fence. In addition to this, Sir Gilbert has his own security people who are Section Five licensed. That means the guards are armed with automatic weapons. They also use dogs. From what I have seen, the security measures at Harmsham Park are good, but poorly managed. They rely too heavily on electronic devices. It's not just the alarm you must deal with, there are cameras all around the place. So, if you don't come under surveillance, set off the alarm, get eaten by the dogs or shot by the guards . . . you might stand a chance,' Susan shrugged. 'Still, it's your neck.'

Cal smiled. 'Would you mind showing me how this works?' he asked, studying the device. It was made of a dark green plastic material, measuring some 15 centimetres by 10, and reminded him of the old-fashioned photographic plates, used years ago. Fitted to one side was what looked like a small calculator.

Susan took the device from Cal. 'Come with me,' she commanded, opening the office door and stepping into the corridor, 'and close the door behind you.' As he watched, she pressed the plate against the entry control pad fixed to her office door. Almost immediately, four digits appeared on the screen of the calculator. Removing the device, she looked at

Cal. 'Key in those four numbers.' Cal did as instructed. There was a clicking sound. Turning the handle, she opened the door allowing them both back into the room.

'My God,' exclaimed Cal. 'Do you realise what you could do with this thing?'

Susan smiled, pleased with her showmanship. 'It's still fairly new and restricted to government use only, so be careful not to lose it. To operate it, you simply press the sensor plate lightly over any keypad. It reads the pattern of the buttons; those pressed the most times are detectable, weaker than the rest. And did you know most of us hit the buttons harder each time we key in a digit? This thing is so sensitive it is able to measure the resistance of each button. This not only gives you the four numbers, but also the combination in which they are used. Then, as if by magic, they are digitally displayed on the screen.'

'That is impressive,' Cal admitted.

'I must warn you, it's only about 90% accurate. That's why you get three selections. If the first one doesn't work, hit the key marked "retry" and it immediately gives you a second and third chance. After that, if the alarm is still going, get the hell out of there. Your father tells me you've been well trained in entry techniques, so you should have no problems with the rest of the systems.'

'Yeah, no problem,' Cal said absentmindedly, still twisting the gadget over in his hands, mesmerised by the ingenious device.

'One final thing. I believe Sir Gilbert keeps a safe in the library, so I have taken the liberty of putting together a few other items that might come in handy.' Susan reached into the small black rucksack and withdrew a camera. 'It's infra red, complete with infra red flash and film. You've got 36 shots.

There is also a night scope in there, but I guess you're up to speed on those. The rest is fairly straightforward.'

'Thanks a lot, Suzie, I really appreciate it,' Cal knew the risks Susan was taking by actively helping. Any incident connecting the American Embassy with a man of Sir Gilbert's status could have serious repercussions and could cost Susan her job.

'No problem. Just don't get caught,' she repeated. 'If, as we suspect, the Princess of Wales is in some sort of danger, we should try to protect her. I personally like the woman. Diana does almost as much to preserve the British Monarchy as the Queen. The American people like her.'

'It's Bulloch that I'm interested in.'

'Yes, I know. I just wish I was coming with you. Take care of yourself out there.' She reached up and kissed him lightly on the cheek. 'Oh, what the hell,' stretching on tip-toe, she pulled Cal's head forward and kissed him full on the lips. 'See you when you get back.'

'After that, you can guarantee it!' he beamed. Picking up the rucksack, he left Susan's office.

The light was rapidly deteriorating as the greyness yielded still further to the darkness that threatened thunderstorms. The tall grass lining the roadside verges swept back and forth in great waves as Cal drove carefully along the river valley. At last he noted the signpost for Manning's Heath and slowed the car almost to a halt. A small farm track ran over an old stone bridge 100 metres further on. Guiding the car into the rutted track, Cal crossed the bridge. He continued for a short distance, hearing the grass brush against the car's underbelly. Stopping by the edge of a wood, he parked under the shadow of a large oak tree. Taking off his shoes, Cal slipped his feet into a pair of soft-soled climbing shoes. They were perfect for breaking and entering. Taking the small rucksack supplied by Susan Greenwood, Cal locked the car and made his way back over the bridge. He checked the signpost before walking the remaining two miles towards his destination. The rain had subsided to little more than a thin drizzle but the wind had increased.

He made good progress, the full moon providing plenty of light. He surveyed the road ahead, feeling cold air chill his face, grinning at the sound that was made by the freshening wind. 'Best time to break in or out is on a windy night,' he recited the words from his escape and evasion training manual.

There was little or no traffic on the road, and when a vehicle did approach, Cal simply jumped into the roadside ditch and lay flat. At last he came to a small side road leading off to the left, a typical forest highway, albeit well maintained. He followed the ribbon of tarmac for some two hundred metres until the shape and lights of the gatehouse came into view. Walking on the grass verge, he got closer before ducking into the trees, watching the building for activity. Two large, ornate gates hung from the ball-topped pillars, with a small side gate on the left that allowed pedestrian entry into the grounds. Here the tarmac road ended and the surface reverted to the original, moss-grown gravel drive. It meandered between thickets of rhododendron, yew and laurel until at last, in the distance, some 200 metres away, Cal could just make out the lights of a large house. Moving silently, he progressed deeper into the forest. Above him the wind rattled hard, causing the trees to bend and creak, covering the sound of his movement. Stepping out of the wood, a small track separated the trees from the shadowy darkness of the wall that protected the grounds. Cal stopped, estimating his distance to be some 100 metres plus from the main gatehouse.

'As good a spot as any to gain access,' he thought to himself. The perimeter wall was constructed of stone and, although old, it looked formidable. Standing some three metres high, it would be easy enough to scale but he heeded Susan's warning of more sophisticated alarm systems on the inside. With his back to the wall Cal looked up, studying the forest that ran parallel to the obstacle. He searched left and right, trying to locate a substantial tree; one that would provide him with a view over the wall. His first priority was to check out a way in and avoid setting off the alarms. To his left, 20 metres along the wall, he found what he was looking for. Climbing the tree was exhausting work and Cal stopped when half way up. Perching himself carefully among the thick summer foliage, he rested a moment. He sat with his back against the trunk, feeling his heart race from the climb. As his breathing became regular, and the wind chilled the small beads of sweat that blistered his brow, he looked out towards the house. He had found his vantage point.

Removing his rucksack, he clipped the strap to a branch and took out the night scope. He felt the movement of the tree, and high above him the driving wind forced the moonlit clouds to race across the night sky, sending fleeting shadows into his hiding place. From his raised position, he was able to observe beyond the wall, noting the obstacles that barred his way. As described, a military-style wire fence had been erected, with coils of razor wire strewn across the top. As he looked closer, he identified the telltale flickering of sophisticated surveillance devices. Beyond this lay the vast lawns, festooned with abundant groves of seasoned foliage. In the centre sat the great house. It was a large complex, consisting of a grey stone-built, three-storey manor house, with smaller outbuildings at the rear. Using the night scope, Cal observed the main house, focusing on those rooms where light appeared. He detected movement, his attention drawn by the sight of two men talking in a ground floor room in what Susan had described as the library. Methodically, Cal turned his concentration to the rest of the windows and doors, though for the most part, the curtains were drawn. It was a strange contrast. The security system that protected the property literally buzzed with animate activity, while the house sat in the middle of the ornate gardens, with an air of eternity, as if, along with the trees and shrubbery, it belonged there.

Cal relaxed, and was considering his next move when, without warning, two powerful floodlights lit up the entrance steps and the front door opened. Cal had not noticed the waiting car, nor the elderly man dressed in a black tie and tails, holding open the rear door. Two men emerged from the house, walked down the steps, and disappeared into the car. He watched the butler close the door. Above the sound of the wind, he could hear the gentle hum of the engine as the vehicle crackled down the gravel driveway towards the gatehouse, disappearing from view. He swung the night scope back towards the house in time to see the butler disappear back inside, closing the large doors behind him. Cal continued his surveillance, noting the patio to the southern side – a large area paved with Italian flagstones, half of it enclosed with glass and housing a large indoor swimming pool. Satisfied with what confronted him, Cal decided it was time to make his entry.

He started to climb down when the barking of a solitary dog

made him freeze. He stood perfectly still, his feet firmly placed on a large branch, his body wrapped tight to the tree trunk. Below him, some 50 metres to his right, a man stood in the shadows by the fence. Straining, Cal could hear the guard's voice, commanding the dog. For almost five minutes, both man and beast stood motionless. Finally, they moved off, passing below Cal and heading towards the gatehouse.

Cal relaxed. He was about to continue his descent when he realised that the branch on which he was standing reached out over the wall. Although it did not pass over the inner fence, Cal estimated that if he held onto the branch above his head, the one on which he was standing would eventually rest on the top of the wall. Providing the branch would take his weight as far as the wall, he could jump the gap, clearing the inner security fence in one swift movement. Quietly, maintaining his balance on the branch above, Cal inched his way forward. As he neared the top of the wall, he stepped out and secured a foothold. He stood facing the wire fence. He looked down, checking the ground where he would drop. He braced himself. If he cleared the wire, he would land close to where a large rhododendron bush crept out from the lawn towards the fence.

Satisfied with his landing site, he steadied himself on the wall.

Bending his knees, and taking a deep breath he leapt forward.

It seemed like he was suspended in mid-air forever – a moment of panic as his right foot made contact with the razor wire, then he was over. He landed skilfully on the tips of his toes, relaxing his body, collapsing forward in a perfect parachute roll. Instantly he was up and running, diving flat into the undergrowth of the rhododendron bush. His body crushed dead twigs, and to one side he heard a solitary crack, as one of the small branches broke under his weight. Peering through the bush, Cal watched as a man emerged from the gatehouse. His head turned in Cal's direction, looking up at the shaking tree. Cal held his breath as the man took several paces forward, twisting his head as if curious. Then he looked at the bushes where Cal lay, crouched. The buffeting wind suddenly surged, beating the trees and causing the man to lose interest. He returned to his post. Cal let out a small sigh of relief, breathing slowly and deeply. Keeping low, he silently made his way through the bushes until confronted by the exposed lawn that separated him from the corner of the large mansion house. He stood for a minute surveying the surroundings, the fast moving clouds continuing to throw fleeting shadows in the moonlight. At the rear of the house, beyond the paved area and covered pool, he noted a number of outbuildings; offices, stables and the like but no sign of life. With one last scan, he ran silently across the grass until he reached the side of the building where he threw himself into the shadows. Treading carefully, Cal worked his way to the library window where he had seen the two men talking. The curtains were now closed. The shadow of a large yew tree growing close to the house offered Cal protection but no sooner had he moved than he heard a footfall crunch on the gravel path. He moved deeper into the inky shade as the shape of a man came round the corner. Cal stood very still, bracing himself for combat. The man walked on, then stopped some 20 metres away to look around. Even from this distance, the faltering moonlight was enough to show Cal that the man carried a weapon. The guard continued his patrol, passing the front of the house, making his way across the grounds. Moving quickly, Cal decided he would be safer inside the house. He cautiously turned the corner only to discover a narrow alley formed by the glass framework of the swimming pool structure which butted up close to the rear wall of the house. At the end of the alley, a dull bluish light flickered from a window. A similar shaft of light emitted from the half-open door, from where Cal assumed the guard had just emerged. Moving calmly, Cal made his way quietly to the window and looked in. He was not surprised to see several banks of television screens blinking blindly at the guard's empty seat. An inner door lay partly open, and although no light showed, Cal guessed it led into the main house.

Going through the doorway, Cal entered the security room. Immediately he recognised the illuminated alarm panel attached to the wall. Quickly checking the panel, he found the system in day mode, which meant that, although the sensors were blinking, they were nonetheless inactive. 'Sloppy bastards,' thought Cal. If the house were occupied, there was a chance that only certain rooms would be restricted. Still, he was not about to take risks. Moving fast, taking advantage of the guard's absence, he slipped through the inner door entering a small corridor. Several closed doors led off either side. Ignoring these, Cal ran lightly down to the end of the corridor where his way was blocked by a larger, more decorative door. He ran his hands around the outer edge, checking for contact breakers. Finding none, he took a deep breath and opened it. Stepping carefully into the dim light, he found himself standing in a massive hallway. The patterned, tiled floor was covered with large, luxurious rugs. To his left, a highly polished stairway stretched majestically to the second floor. Several opulent pieces of furniture stood guard in the hallway, while oversized paintings hung from the walls. He searched for the telltale glow of a security sensor. He could see none. From Susan's description, the library, or Sir Gilbert's office as she put it, was to the right about halfway up the hall. Cal found the door. It looked large and heavy, and appeared to be part of the original house. Praying that it did not creak, he paused for a moment before turning the brass knob. 'Shit.' It was locked. Checking quickly, Cal found that the old locks had been replaced with modern Yale-type fixings. He slipped his hand into his pocket, removing a small wallet; embossed with the initials H.P.C. 'Holden Pick Company', USA. The floorboards creaked menacingly as he knelt down and started to pick the lock. Cal selected two small tools. The first was a tension tool, the other known as a rake – both showed signs of excessive wear. Gently inserting the tension tool into the lock, he then used the rake to access the pins, which would normally be arranged by the serrated edge of a key. When the pins were seated correctly, the tension bar would turn the cylinder, opening the lock.

As he worked, Cal calculated the amount of time since he had seen the guard make his way to the gatehouse. He estimated that he had been no more than two minutes. If he could get this door open, maybe his luck would hold. 'Come on, you baby, sit down,' whispered Cal to the lock, trying patiently to seat the last of the pins in the tumbler. With minute pressure, he eased the pick gently upward, searching blindly for contact. Suddenly, the pressure on the tension bar gave way. Quickly, he turned the brass knob, this time the door opened. Cal entered the room, closing the door behind him.

The library was in total darkness, and Cal waited while his eyes adjusted to the gloom. To his left, at a height of some two and a half metres, the soft, red intermittent glow of a security sensor flashed out its warning. Dropping the rucksack from his shoulder, Cal took out what looked like an aerosol paint can. Walking towards the corner, he reached up and aimed the clear spray directly at the sensor face. He waited for a few seconds, his nostrils detecting the faint smell of almonds, then gave it another blast just to make sure. In the event that the guard returned and activated the alarm, the sensor would no longer detect his presence, although the system would appear to be working normally. Taking a small flashlight from his pocket, Cal worked his way forward, manoeuvring carefully past the furniture in an effort to avoid knocking anything over. At last he came to a broad oak desk situated in front of the bay window. It was here that he had seen the two men talking. Cal switched off the torch and risked peeking through the curtains. Outside the night had become overcast, rain droplets beating a steady rhythm against the glass. Cal reached up and unfastened the clasp that held the large sash window closed. Should there be any interruption, he needed an escape route.

Ensuring the curtains would emit no light to the outside, Cal switched the shaded torch back on. Systematically he cast the beam over the top of the desk. It was neat and tidy, with several envelopes, and two official-looking files centred on the blotter. Cal checked them, but they revealed nothing. He bent down and tried the first top left-hand drawer. It was locked. Once more Cal produced the small, black wallet from his pocket. A few seconds later and the drawer came open. Again he found nothing of interest. Progressing to the next drawer down – nothing. The bottom two drawers had been converted and made into one. It contained several files. Cal read through them and, although interesting, they contained nothing in connection with, or relating to, the Princess of Wales or Bulloch.

Disappointed, Cal replaced the files, and checked the drawers on the opposite side, again coming up with zero. He re-locked the drawers, leaving no evidence of his handiwork. Then, thoughtfully, he surveyed the room. Susan had mentioned a safe. If Sir Gilbert had anything incriminating to hide, it would very probably be in a safe. With no obvious sign of one, Cal reasoned it must also be hidden – a wall safe. He found it on his first attempt, traditionally placed behind a large oil painting. The picture was hinged at the one side, opening out like the cover of a book to reveal a modern safe. Rather than a lock or combination lock, the safe had an intricate-looking keypad. It passed through Cal's mind that Susan's observations during her visit to Harmsham Park had been more meticulous than she had let on. Searching in the rucksack once more, Cal withdrew the device Susan had given him. Holding it between the fingers of his left hand he switched it on then, using both hands, he placed it over the slightly proud keypad. Almost immediately, four digits flashed bright red on the small calculator display. Taking his time, Cal punched in the numbers. For a brief moment, nothing happened, then, with a soft metallic sound, the safe popped opened.

'Magic,' said Cal softly, putting the device back into the rucksack and glancing at his watch. It was 3.15 am. Outside the wind was driving the rain hard.

Cal set to work. It was not a large safe; its internal measurements were approximately 45 centimetres square, but it was almost full. On top lay an antique wooden box which Cal discarded, sensing it would contain only jewellery or other precious items. Below this sat several folders and a single box file. He removed them all in one lift, seating himself on the floor in front of the safe. Flicking the torch over the top cover of each individual file, he noted the clearly marked words OPERATION ROYAL BLOOD.

Most were stamped MOST SECRET while three were marked with the words, 'Sovereign Committee Eyes Only'. These he placed to one side while he examined the box file. It held several large, brown envelopes. Cal slowly emptied the contents of one onto the floor. A mixture of photographs and micro tapes fell from the envelope, evidence that someone had been doing an extensive bugging job. From the photographs it was plain to see who the target was. Cal had found similar pictures on Norris. He concentrated on the files. Those marked MOST SECRET appeared to be work carried out by the British Government. Still sitting on the floor, he threw the flashlight over the first file, and started reading.

He read for almost 20 minutes, his mind racing in disbelief, confused by what he had found. When he had finished, he sat in silence for a few moments, trying desperately to organise his thoughts. Then, delving once more into the small rucksack he grabbed the camera. The filtered flash allowed the infra red film faithfully to record the information in total darkness. Working his way through the documents, and limited to 36 shots, Cal selected papers that prompted the most interest. In particular, he recorded the most recent documents. These contained a detailed summary depicting every movement the Princess of Wales had made while in the company of Dodi Al Fayed. He finished the film by photographing the open wall safe – proof that he had indeed been in the house. When he had finished, he removed the film and secured it in the zip pocket of his trousers. Putting away the camera, he replaced the papers back in the file, making sure that everything was just as he had found it.

Finally he closed the safe, reset the combination, and snapped the painting back into place.

'All I have to do now is get the hell out of here,' he muttered to himself, doing a final check of the room.

He assumed that the guard would have returned to the monitor room by now and besides, the easiest way out was through the window. They may detect the open catch, but with no sign of forced entry from the outside, they would most probably put it down to sloppy security. Cal moved to the window, peeking through the curtains, checking the immediate area. The weather outside had not slackened; if anything, the wind had increased. Moreover, the moon had become obscured, plunging the grounds into total darkness. Lifting the lower half of the window, Cal managed to move it only a few centimetres before it jammed. Committed now, Cal shook the window, trying desperately not to make a noise. At last, with a sudden jerk, it came free, gliding up easily. It went too far. The rain rushed in, soaking the floor and curtains. Cal cursed. Luckily, the window was low enough for him to step directly out onto the ground outside. In one continuous movement he was out, closing the window behind him and stepping quickly into the shelter of the nearby yew tree. His senses detected no movement but, taking no chances, Cal moved cautiously to the front of the building. Looking around the corner, checking that the coast was clear, he crossed the open lawn with one quick dash before disappearing back into the cluster of rhododendron bushes. Crawling his way forward, he stopped when he could make out the perimeter fence and wall beyond. Cal was soaking wet from head to toe, and he decided to take a breather before making his exit. Resting for a while in the concealment of a bush, he listened for signs of danger, while pondering his next move. Over to his left, he could see light coming from the gatehouse window. With the weather so bad, he was tempted to try to sneak past, but the presence of dogs changed his mind. Sticking to his original plan would be the safest method of exit.

At their nearest point, the bushes in which Cal now sat were not more than six metres from the fence – and the fence was alarmed. Reaching inside the rucksack, Cal took out the metal bar that he had prepared earlier and unravelled the cord from it. Next he unclipped a small roll of canvas from the rucksack, securing it around his neck, letting it hang down his back like a cape. Cal stepped out from the bush and lobbed the metal bar at the fence. It hit with a clang and fell to the ground. Bright lights suddenly activated all along the metal fence. Inside the gatehouse an alarm was sounding. Quickly, Cal tucked back into the bush, tugging the cord and pulling the metal bar back in towards him. Silently, sitting deep within the bush, he waited.

Above the alarm he could hear the guards shouting and the sound of dogs barking. Behind him the house lights flooded out over the grounds. Secure in his hiding place and confident that the dogs would not detect him, Cal watched as three men appeared. They were walking steadily, using powerful torches to scrutinise the perimeter fence. As they came nearer, he could see they were all armed. Cal wondered what they would do if they managed to catch an intruder. Passing him by, they disappeared from view. After several minutes they returned, methodically checking the fence for any sign of entry. Finding nothing, they continued on their way back to the gatehouse and disappeared inside. Thirty seconds later, both lights and alarms ceased.

Silently, Cal crept from his hiding place, the metal bar in his right hand. Standing, he threw it vigorously at the fence. Metal hit metal with a resounding clang and the alarm triggered. Having repeated the procedure, Cal, swiftly pulled in the cord, before wriggling deeper in the rhododendron bush.

This time, the three men were moving quickly, running from the gatehouse following the line of the fence. Cal could hear them cursing as they checked for signs of entry. He watched as, once again, they walked back to the gatehouse.

Cal waited several minutes before repeating his action for a third time. Their reaction was slower, only two men appeared, neither seemed keen on getting any wetter. They ambled down the fence without really checking. When they were almost opposite Cal's position, the fence rattled slightly with the movement of the wind.

'Fucking weather, that's what's triggering the alarm,' Cal could clearly hear the man shouting above the rain. 'Go and tell him to turn the bloody thing off. We'll sort it out in the morning.' With that, one man walked back in the direction of the house, while the other returned to the gatehouse.

After fifteen minutes, confident that the system had been de-activated, he stepped out from his hiding place, and walked towards the fence. He threw the metal bar at the fence, and although he heard a distinct clanging noise, nothing happened. His deception had worked.

Cal approached the fence and started to climb. The rock climbing boots bit neatly into the chain-link fence and within seconds, he was standing near the top, just below the razor wire. Ducking his head down to his chest and using his right arm, he flicked the canvas cloak skilfully over the roll of razor wire. Unclipping it from his neck, the canvas provided a protective covering over which he could crawl. It was a noisy process, but Cal took his time, not wishing to become entangled in the razor-sharp wire. Safely on the opposite side, he grabbed the canvas sheet and shook it free before dropping to the ground. It took another thirty seconds for him quickly to scale the wall and enter the forest. He continued to move with care, until he reached the road. Although somewhat exhausted, he ran the rest of the distance back to where he had parked the car. He was soaking wet and his shoulder hurt like hell but, as he stripped off the wet clothes, a smile licked across his face. Two things gave him comfort. Firstly, he had not lost any of his skills. He had managed to get in and out of Harmsham Park without being caught. Secondly, he now had definite proof of a connection between Sir Gilbert and Princess Diana. The problem was what to do with the information.

Cal drove steadily, his mind preoccupied by what he had found. There was no mention of Bulloch working for Sir Gilbert, but he obviously was. And what of the Sovereign Committee? The files looked official, but how could you tell? From wherever their authority came, it would seem their sole purpose was to monitor the activities of the Princess of Wales. What continued to nag in the back of Cal's mind, was the part that Bulloch played in all this. He was not a private detective – Bulloch was an assassin.

He was still pondering his next move as he turned on to the M23 and headed for London and the warmth of his bed.

Alan Connors paced the grounds. He looked agitated. By 9.30 am he had been on the high ground from where he spotted Sir Gilbert's car returning from London. He had debated whether or not he should mention the incident. After all, it was not his fault but as Head of Security it would be wrong not to report the matter. Sir Gilbert had always treated him well and he earned good money with Phantom Securities. Honesty is always the best policy. He made his way towards the huge house.

'Come in, Connors,' Sir Gilbert's voice travelled the length of the room to the man standing in the open doorway.

'Yes, sir,' the man entered, walking briskly, stopping in front of the desk, standing almost to attention. Sir Gilbert favoured Connors' military style, which was matched only by the man's reliability and dedication. However, his usual briskness was tempered by a somewhat jaded look this morning. Connors resembled a faithful dog that had somehow let his master down.

'Well, what is it, man? Is something wrong?'

Connors hesitated, forming his words. 'When I arrived at the gatehouse this morning, sir, the night staff were just leaving. As a matter of routine, I checked all systems and found all the external alarms switched off. I immediately turned the whole system back on. When I questioned Jenkins, the senior guard on last night's shift, he said the high winds kept tripping the alarm, so he decided to shut down the perimeter detection devices.'

'From what time was this?'

'From between 3.55 am and 6.30 am this morning, sir.'

'Go on.'

'Well, sir, I did a quick routine check and everything looked normal. When I came to the house, the cameras covering the inside of the house, in particular the one in this library, had been activated. It had run for almost an hour.'

'You mean someone was in here last night?' Sir Gilbert's

face was turning bright red, his voice climbing in pitch.

'I'm not sure, sir,' Connors became nervous, 'but the tape has run. As yet I haven't viewed it. You were in London, sir, and no member of staff has a key for the library. But it could be a fault. The clock shows the camera active from between 2.36 and 3.42.'

'There is only one way to find out. I think it best we view the tape, don't you Connors?'

'Yes, sir, I'll set it up now,' Connors backed away towards the door. 'If you would just come this way, sir.'

Sir Gilbert followed Connors along the corridor into the small security office. Connors dropped into the only chair and reached across, flicking a couple of switches. One of the screens came to life. Almost immediately the figure of a man could be seen entering the library. 'Oh, no . . .' At sight of the intruder, Sir Gilbert let out a low moan. The man scanned around the room as if searching for something then, he walked quietly over to the desk. There was the odd 'click' as the man moved around the room. Connors looked at Sir Gilbert.

'Definitely a break-in, sir. A burglar by the look of it.'

'I can see that, you bloody fool!' said Sir Gilbert.

The man moved to the large desk and started checking through the drawers. He seemed organised, as if he knew exactly what he was doing. After checking several drawers and finding nothing, he moved away from the desk, probing deeper into the room. The beam from a small flashlight flickered in his hand as it swept across one of the walls, stopping suddenly as it spotlighted a picture.

'It's as if the man knows the safe's there, sir.'

'Be quiet!' Sir Gilbert snapped.

'Sorry, sir.'

The man stepped forward and felt round the edges of the painting then, gripping the left-hand side, he pulled the picture. It came away from the wall, swinging open on its hinges.

'Damnation,' said Sir Gilbert. 'What on earth is he doing?' The man looked to be placing something on the safe. Then the intruder tapped in the combination. In less than a minute the safe was open.

'He knows the combination, sir. How is that possible?'

'Stop the tape! Stop the tape now!'

Connors reached across, fumbling with the switch before finally stopping the tape.

'Do you want me to call the police, sir? Get them to come out and fingerprint?'

'It may have escaped your notice, but the man was wearing gloves. Just show me how to switch this thing back on and leave me alone.'

'Just press that switch there, sir. Press it again to stop it.'

'Right. Now I suggest that you get outside and check the grounds thoroughly. Report any signs of the intruder directly to me.' Connors was dismissed.

When he had gone, Sir Gilbert restarted the tape. He knew exactly the contents of the safe; a modest amount of money, a small box containing some of his mother's jewellery and a thick file marked 'The Sovereign Committee'. He watched in horror as the man ignored everything save for the file. This the intruder took and, sitting on the floor, proceeded to read the contents with the aid of his torch. When at last the man produced a camera, Sir Gilbert felt physically sick. There was no doubt in his mind that this man had taken exactly what he'd come for. He was no burglar. This man was a professional spy.

Sir Gilbert forced himself to watch every movement, until at last the intruder folded the file and replaced it in the safe. He had even used the combination to reset the alarm. At last the man had made his way to the window and disappeared. Sir Gilbert opened the door and walked into the corridor just as Connors returned. 'Rewind the film and bring it to me. I don't want anyone to see it, do you understand?'

'Yes, sir.'

Sir Gilbert stormed off in the direction of his office. The curtains had been opened, he could see the wetness on the floor below the window. On checking, he found the catch open. He turned and walked over to the wall safe. By the time Connors had retrieved the tape, Sir Gilbert had already confirmed the contents of the safe were still intact and was now seated behind his desk. Connors laid the tape on the desk in front of him. He was about to speak, but thought better of it.

'It would seem to me that this intruder not only made his way into the library via the hall door, somehow avoiding the house alarm, but he then opened my safe and left by the window, effecting his escape by making us switch off the perimeter alarm.' Sir Gilbert declined to say that the intruder had photographed a top secret file. 'As Head of Security, can you tell me how he did this?'

'I'm not sure, sir,' stuttered Connors. 'Jenkins told me he had shut down the fence, mainly because the high winds kept activating the alarm system. The alarm triggered at least three times.' Connors paused for a minute, desperately trying to think. 'The house alarm was still active, so were the cameras. I simply don't understand why the sensors didn't detect him. In my opinion, this was a very professional job, someone with a very good knowledge of alarm systems. I personally shut down the system this morning to allow the cleaning staff access. Might I ask sir, did he get away with much?'

'That's none of your concern. Sack Jenkins. That will be all.'

Connors turned and walked out of the room, grateful that he still had a job. Sir Gilbert took the small notebook from his pocket and leafed through the pages. He then picked up the telephone and dialled a number.

'Sir Robert Trescott's office. How can I help you?'

'Let me speak to Sir Robert now, please. It's Sir Gilbert.'

'One moment, sir,' there was a click, followed by a short pause.

'Gilbert, nice to hear from you. To what do I owe this pleasure?'

'We have a problem. An intruder broke into Harmsham Park last night.'

'Can't the local police handle it?'

'You don't understand – he didn't take anything. He just photographed the file. The Sovereign Committee file.'

'What? How did he get in? I thought your place was like Fort Knox!'

'It is. This was no ordinary burglar. He was a professional. We need to know who he is and for whom he is working – quickly. Lucky for us, he seems to have missed the security camera. It activates once the library door is opened. I'm having Connors bring the video directly to you. Be a good chap and see what you can make of it. Anything to identify this man, or a clue to his employers. Perhaps you could check out some of the other agencies. The Israelis, maybe. It seems someone has a vested interest in what we are doing. Give me an hour to sort out this mess, then I shall return to London. Let's arrange to meet in Mayfair, say around 12.30.'

He replaced the handset and scribbled out an address before calling for Connors once more.

'Get the film to this address without any further delay. Make sure that you personally give it to Sir Robert. He is expecting you.' Connors took the padded envelope and turned to leave. 'Oh, and Connors, tell my chauffeur I'll need the Rolls at around 10.30. I'll be returning to Mayfair.'

Sir Gilbert sat, pondering. He would have to remove the files, best give it all to Trescott, at least he could keep it safe. For a moment he considered calling the whole operation off, but he was somehow intrigued. Who had sent the intruder? How did they know about the file? At least, thought Sir Gilbert, there's no mention of Bulloch or his intentions in the file. At the very worst, if the whole thing became public, they could always say they were acting in the best interests of the country. Yes, he consoled himself, the damage wasn't too great, providing they could find the intruder and silence him.

The journey back to London had made him tired. his normally bright eyes were red-rimmed and expressionless, almost disinterested. Back at his Mayfair apartment, he sat at his desk, twisting the seat so that he could look out of the window and down at the rear gardens. Last summer had ruined the lawn; surprising that it had recovered at all, he thought absentmindedly. His gaze surveyed the finely kept grounds. Even now, despite the wretched weather, they looked neat and tidy. The flowerbeds were bursting with brightly coloured plants that had swollen to full summer bloom – the scene so typically English. He was half way through his first gin and tonic, and still daydreaming, when Robert arrived and flopped comfortably into a chair. Trescott refused the proffered drink. Lifting his briefcase onto his lap, he pulled out a large buff envelope and handed it across. 'There you are, Gilbert old boy, the best we can do with the quality.'

Sir Gilbert opened the envelope and took out two photographs. They were identical and, although grainy, they clearly showed the intruder's face. 'Can you trace him?'

'I've got everybody working on it now,' Trescott confirmed, 'but you realise I have to keep it fairly low key? At this stage I don't want to involve any foreign agencies. There is a chance that this man is not a freelance operative. In addition, I have arranged for an assessment team to evaluate the film. They should have something by tonight.'

'I certainly hope so.'

They discussed the problem for a further ten minutes before Sir Gilbert excused himself. 'I have a meeting at one o'clock, so you'll forgive me for being rude and asking you to leave, Robert.'

'I understand. I'll be in contact with you the moment I hear anything.'

When Trescott had gone, Sir Gilbert remained seated, leaning back in the leather-bound chair, he took another sip of his gin and tonic. The ornate clock, above the fireplace showed ten minutes to one. Taking a gold-plated pen from his pocket, he started to write down the details Trescott had given him. He hoped they could find the intruder. Unexpected distractions were very exhausting. Clipping the top back on his fountain pen with fastidious care, he returned it to his inside pocket. At last he roused himself. It was time to see Bulloch. He summoned the butler to call a taxi. One thing of which he was sure – he did not intend to cancel the operation.

Sir Gilbert stood in the Battersea safe-house looking out of the window. Somehow the Thames relaxed him; it was such a tranquil river. For a moment he admired the view, letting himself become engrossed, relieving the stress that threatened to consume him.

At last he turned, unaware that Bulloch had re-entered the room and was standing close behind him. The surprise made him jump and a muscle twitched under his left eye. He studied the man for a moment, realising, not for the first time, that Bulloch was a dangerous piece of work.

'I should remember that men of your ilk are somewhat inclined to indulge in crude forms of violence at the slightest provocation,' said Sir Gilbert, to cover his anxiety. 'You must forgive me, I am slightly on edge this afternoon. I have a tedious problem. There was an intruder at my country home. It would seem he was looking for something in particular.'

'Can you be more specific?' Bulloch inquired. 'You're a rich man, maybe it was just a burglar.'

'I don't think so. Would you look at this picture? When we find him – and we will – I want you to take care of him.' Sir Gilbert slid one of the photographs from the envelope and passed it across. For a moment Bulloch just stared then, very slowly, his face hardened. Bringing the picture up closer, he studied it in detail, as if he were short sighted.

'It can't be,' he growled.

Sir Gilbert did not miss the expression on Bulloch's face. 'You recognise this man?' he snapped.

Bulloch said nothing but continued to stare, his eyes drawn to the white splash of scar on the man's forehead. It was a wound he had created. The American had found him.

'Do you know this man?' demanded Sir Gilbert. Bulloch

snapped his head away from the photograph and stared blankly at Sir Gilbert.

'This is the intruder?'

'Yes.'

'I know him. He's an American. His name is Caleb Wesley. You remember my file you were so keen on reading to us in Paris? It mentioned that I shot an American during the Gulf War – that's the same man.'

'That's impossible.'

'It's him, I'm telling you. Look at that white scar on his forehead. It looks like a star. That's where I shot him. I knew he was alive, that's why Norris and I did a runner. I heard later, through the grapevine, that the bullet had travelled around his skull and exited at the rear. I thought I had killed him but I hadn't. What the fuck was he doing at your place?'

'Maybe he's looking for you,' said Sir Gilbert.

'Maybe,' replied Bulloch, calming himself, 'but I've never been to your "country home", so why would he be looking for me there? What exactly did he take?'

Sir Gilbert was thinking fast. He decided to tell Bulloch. 'He managed to get into my library, bypass all the alarms and open the safe by using the combination. He took no money, or anything of value' He paused for a second. 'There was a file – he photographed it.' Then he quickly added, 'Don't worry, there was no mention of your name in it.'

Bulloch was silent. If Wesley was hunting him, it meant he had revenge on his mind. But how had he found him? And who if anybody, was he working for? Bulloch felt the sudden desire to get up and run but years of training had taught him not to panic. Sir Gilbert seemed to have unlimited resources, best let him find the American. And when he did, this time he would make sure Caleb Wesley stayed dead.

'Find him for me and I will take care of the problem.'

They did not have long to wait. Trescott rang around four that afternoon. His voice sounded excited.

'Gilbert, we have him, but this may not be a simple as we first expected.'

'What do you mean?' Sir Gilbert asked with some apprehension.

'You were correct. The intruder was indeed Caleb Wesley. He is a major in the American Delta Force and the son of Dan Wesley, an American Military Officer stationed at their embassy in London.' Trescott went silent, anticipating the response.

'What? Are you absolutely sure?' Sir Gilbert was dumbfounded. 'We have been so careful about security? How on earth could the Americans possibly know of our intentions?'

'I'm not convinced that they do. A few days ago Wesley arrived from Colombia where he was training with the local army. He was operating near to the air crash site. It's possible he somehow became involved and recognised Norris. My intelligence appraisal team indicates it's the only logical link. This being the case, Norris may have been carrying information regarding to the Sovereign Committee, or the Princess of Wales. They also think that Wesley will have wanted to locate Bulloch by simply following the coffin back to England. Inquiries show that Norris was cremated near his home town of Stockport. Nothing special, just his mother, brother and sister . . .'

'Norris did not have a brother – that was Bulloch!' stormed Sir Gilbert.

'I see,' said Trescott, 'that would make more sense. However, we also know that Wesley arrived at Heathrow the day before the funeral. He's staying at the Marriott Hotel, where he rented a car from Avis, wait . . .' there was a short pause, '. . . a Red Vauxhall Vectra GLS, registration P437 HHW. We have just checked, and the car is parked in the NCP car park, at the rear of the Marriott.'

'Do you have any idea why this American should have searched Harmsham Park? I have been very discreet in my meetings with Bulloch. We only ever meet at the Battersea safe-house. He has certainly never been down to Sussex,' Sir Gilbert said, defensively.

'We have no idea how he made the connection. The appraisal team carried out a detailed examination of the film, and suggested that he was using state-of-the-art equipment. We know the CIA has been developing a device for reading push-button key-pads. We are almost sure this is how he opened your safe. The camera he was using was infra red, which would indicate that he came prepared to take covert photographs.'

'Are you saying that the CIA have somehow found out about the Sovereign Committee?' Sir Gilbert asked, feeling a sudden sickness in his stomach.

'We are not sure. It is highly unlikely that the Americans would risk such a politically dangerous act without concrete proof. Again, the appraisal team feels that this man could be working on his own initiative, but with access to specialist equipment. However, in light of the incident, I do recommend we suspend all further activities until we have established precisely who is involved.'

'I understand, Robert,' Sir Gilbert deliberated for a

moment. 'The princess is due back here Monday morning. Keep the team in place until then, after which you may stand them down. I'm going to send Bulloch away for a while. I'll have my men sterilise the Battersea safe-house tomorrow morning and bring the files to you for safekeeping. Oh, and leave the American to me, Robert.'

Sir Gilbert did not replace the phone, he simply pressed the button, broke the connection with Trescott and called Bulloch's mobile. Their conversation was brief, but enough to give a concise version of what he had learned, finishing with the details of the American's car.

'Leave it to me,' said Bulloch, 'and I'll do this one for free.'

Sir Gilbert continued. 'I have contacted Paris, all your requirements will be met. All equipment is in place and will be waiting for you. There is no need for any further contact between us. No doubt I will be able to track your actions through the media. Anything that happens to the princess will make world headlines.'

There was a short silence. Bulloch thought Sir Gilbert had hung up, then he heard him say, 'Good luck.'

Luck had nothing to do with this; slotting the American would be a personal pleasure. It was unfortunate that he couldn't do it face to face, but there was no time for anything elaborate. He would have to make a bomb. From now on, Diana took priority. All the same, reflected Bulloch, he was going to enjoy wasting Cal Wesley. Walking to the kitchen, he opened the fridge and took out a cold beer before setting to work. Like a child playing with a lump of Playdoh, he whistled happily to himself. Using the PE-4 he had recovered from Steve's cache, the bomb itself was easy enough to construct. The initiation device was beautifully simple; a wooden clothes peg, with two brass drawing pins pushed into the inner jaws of the peg would complete the electrical circuit and trigger the bomb. A small slip of plastic placed between the jaws, keeping the drawing pins apart, served as a safety breaker, to which he attached a length of fishing line. He finished off the device by pushing two large magnets into the soft explosive, before encasing the whole bomb in black masking tape, leaving only the battery connection exposed.

'You little beauty,' Bulloch said, admiring his work and walking through to the lounge. On the back of one settee lay the second-hand overcoat he had obtained in a nearby charity shop. The coat was a little old-fashioned, but it had several large pockets, and its length would serve to protect and keep clean the clothes in which he intended to travel. He placed the bomb into one of the pockets, before peeling off several strips of masking tape and sticking them to the inside lining of the garment. Everything was almost ready.

He would need sleep before his night's work, but decided it was still too early. Instead he sat down and reviewed his travel plans for the following day. His flight ticket lay in a white envelope, together with a timetable the issuing company had thought to provide. Bulloch discarded the envelope, placing the ticket in his briefcase, next to his passport. On top of this lay the file detailing the princess's latest movements. He had skipped through it briefly, but decided to study it in detail later. Finally, he removed the map of Paris from the wall and folded it neatly. The rest of the files he left heaped none too neatly in the corner of the settee. They were of no further use to him.

Then, for the first time since learning of Steve's death, Bulloch entered his friend's bedroom. He and Steve had been together for so long it felt strange without him. Bulloch inhaled deeply through his nose, hoping to sniff a familiar scent; there was nothing. He went to work. Through habit, neither collected personal possessions. In their profession, such things could identify a man. Working steadily, he checked every surface skilfully; dropping to the push-up position to check under the bed and scan the floor. Norris had taken most of his clothes with him to Columbia. What remained hung in the wardrobe. Bulloch examined each item of clothing with painstaking care. Finding nothing of consequence, he left the clothes for Sir Gilbert's men to remove. Back in his own room, Bulloch packed away his clothes, discarding the suitcase for a more manageable rucksack. Satisfied that all was in order, he placed everything in the hall ready for an early departure.

Assisted by a large Scotch, Bulloch lay on the bed and tried to sleep. He set the alarm for just after three which, if he could sleep, would give him a little over eight hours. But sleep was slow in coming, his mind constantly racing through his forthcoming actions. First he would plant the bomb and kill the American. When he had done that, and providing Sir Gilbert's arrangements held up in Paris, he would kill a princess.

'You are some man, John Bulloch. You really think you can pull this off?' He smiled at the challenge, gripped by the vanity and the confidence in his own ability. He experienced a strange sense of pride. The smile was still on his face as he fell asleep.

CHAPTER
10

London,
August 28, 1997

It was dawn when Cal arrived back at the hotel, and the city was already brimming with life. Parking the car, he went directly to his room and phoned Susan, arranging for them to meet at the hotel prior to her going to the embassy. Next he called room service and ordered a full breakfast. Stripping off his damp clothes, he dropped them in a heap on the bathroom floor before taking a quick shower. He was still getting dressed when a thump on the door informed him that breakfast had arrived. Placing the tray on the bed, Cal munched down the food with relish. He had just finished eating when Susan knocked on the door.

'So you made it back,' said Susan glancing through the bathroom door at the pile of damp, dirty clothes. 'Looks like you got a little wet. Did everything go okay?'

Cal gave her a brief outline of how he had entered the grounds, the details of what he had found in the safe, and finished with his bluff to get the fence alarms switched off. He could see she was excited, listening to his story in amazement.

'Wow. I'm impressed,' she glanced at her watch, 'but I'm late already and have to go. Give me the film and I'll get it processed by the time we go to see your father. Now, I suggest you get some sleep. You're going to need it.'

'And why is that?' asked Cal, the mention of sleep making him yawn.

'Because you're taking me out tonight,' she said, picking up the rucksack that contained the equipment she had provided and walking to the door.

It took most of the morning to get the film developed and then have the wording transcribed into a legible form. Susan Greenwood had undertaken this latter task herself. When she had finished she went upstairs, passing through the corridors until she stopped outside a large, well-polished redwood door. The small brass nameplate simply read Lloyd J Ramsey.

She now sat staring in silence at the ageing man opposite. He was slumped forward with his elbows resting on the desk, while the large mop of salt and pepper hair hung down almost touching his hunched shoulders. It made him look like an old Buffalo, thought Susan. Regardless of his appearance, Susan Greenwood knew this man had direct access to Washington and was widely tipped to be the next Director of National Security.

'Do you realise the position this puts us in, Susan?' he dropped the documents onto his desk. 'These documents could be official, and the people named here are very prominent, very important people.'

'Yes, sir.'

'While, I agree, they do show that the Princess of Wales is being watched, there is nothing to indicate that she is in any danger. In fact, these people could argue that they are protecting her!' The old man paused, studying her face.

'What about Bulloch?'

'We have no idea what Bulloch's role is in all this. There's no mention of him in here.' The old man tapped his index finger on the sheets of paper in order to emphasise the point. 'Phantom Securities is a respectable company. It has Section Five approval, and many of their contracts come from the government. Sir Gilbert is a prominent figure, not just in Britain, but worldwide. It is highly possible that the evidence you've found so far is part of some official operation. If authorised by the British Government, we could find ourselves in serious trouble very quickly. Britain is one of America's closest allies. To be seen spying on one of their covert operations could do immeasurable damage.'

Susan stood, leaning forward over the old man's desk. 'But what if Cal Wesley is right? What if they are planning to kill the Princess of Wales and we do nothing?'

Ramsey slumped back in his chair. When Susan had entered his office three days ago and presented him with the photographic evidence found on Norris's body he had deemed it worthy of further investigation. To this end he had instructed Susan to encourage Caleb Wesley to continue his search for Bulloch. Not that the CIA had any vested interest in finding the man, but more to uncover what the British security services were up to. His curiosity had stemmed from a report he had received two weeks earlier that indicated increased activity at GCHQ in Cheltenham. This was always a sure sign that the British were up to something. His own people had informed him that most of the traffic was being beamed over the Mediterranean. He was not America's head of European Intelligence for nothing. Piece by piece he could see a clear picture emerging. The problem now was what to do? If he confronted his counterpart in British Intelligence and the operation was genuine, where would that put him? He could imagine the hell the British would raise, especially when they found out how the information had been procured. The political repercussions were unthinkable. Yet, caution warned him that Susan had a point. If he sat on his butt and did nothing, he would never forgive himself if anything happened to that young woman. America had taken the young princess to its heart.

He turned his attention to the beautiful young woman standing before him. 'They never produced agents like her in my day,' he thought, with more than a little regret.

'I'll make some calls, Susan,' said Ramsey. 'You keep Caleb Wesley on a tight lead while I try to sort this mess out – and not a word of this to Dan Wesley. Make sure his son understands that.' The old man handed her back the papers, indicating that the meeting was over.

Susan returned to her own office and sat pondering. For some inexplicable reason she felt downhearted and somewhat penalised, 'That didn't go quite as planned,' she reflected. 'He should have been more positive.' She picked up the phone and dialled. It took several rings before Cal's voice answered. He sounded sleepy.

'Sorry to wake you but I just thought I'd let you know the photographs are ready and I have transcribed them for you.'

There was renewed alertness in Cal's voice. 'What do you think?'

'I think we need to have a long talk. I still have some work to do here,' Susan looked at her watch. 'It's almost four o'clock. Let's say I'll meet you in the hotel bar around eight.'

Despite her earlier disappointment at Lloyd Ramsey's response, both Susan and Cal were enjoying themselves. After drinks in the bar, they opted for supper in the hotel as opposed to going out, Susan delighting in the flourish with which Cal consumed his food. They talked continuously, their hands accidentally touching from time to time in a gentle, tactile manner. Cal told her of life in Delta Force, his time in the Gulf and his work in Colombia. In the telling, he added humour to the stories, and a thrill that brought them alive.

Susan told Cal about her early life in America and how she had eventually finished up working at the American Embassy in Paris. It was obvious from her sultry accent that the French blood Susan had inherited from her mother was a strong influence. For his part, Cal was content just to sit and listen to the lushness of her voice.

'When I first arrived in Paris I lived in a small two-roomed apartment but then the Embassy offered me this wonderful house to the north east of the city. The town Conflans Ste Honorine – that's about 30 kilometres from the centre of Paris, but my little Fiat is turbocharged and on a good day I can make it to work in under 40 minutes. It's a lovely place. It sits on the River Seine. You arrive in the town right by the river, and as you drive alongside it you will see hundreds of barges which have been converted into homes. In France they are known as *peniches*, and one of them has actually been transformed into a church. The quays alongside this part of the river are all planted with trees and flowerbeds and every Saturday they hold an open-air market.

'On the other side of town, where the tall houses give way to larger properties, the river forces you to turn left. You will see a sign for a mushroom farm. At the end of that road you will find my house. It's on the right, with its back towards an old quarry cliff and elevated enough to overlook the river at the front. On a clear summer's night I sit on the terrace and look at the Paris lights.'

'It sounds wonderful,' said Cal, prompting Susan to continue.

'You really must come over with me one weekend before you go back – I would love to show you the sights.'

'How can I possibly refuse such an offer? Now, what would you like for dessert?'

After they finished dessert and Cal had ordered coffee, the subject of Bulloch raised its head once more.

'So what do you intend to do now? Bulloch could be anywhere.'

Cal nodded his agreement. 'If he's working for Sir Gilbert Scott and is some way connected with this Sovereign Committee's operation, he has to be in London. He's most probably tucked away in some safe-house. Maybe if I shadow the Princess of Wales when she returns there might be a chance of spotting him, he's . . .'

Susan grabbed his arm, a look of inspiration warming her face. 'That's it, why didn't I think of it before?' She slapped her free hand against her forehead in mock stupidity. 'You said, among the items you found on Norris, there was a receipt from Oddbins, the off-licence in Battersea – that's a liquor store to you. Sir Gilbert has a safe-house near there!' She stood quickly, almost knocking over her coffee. 'Wait here, I'll be about ten minutes.' Cal watched in amusement as

Susan ran from the restaurant, causing several other diners to look in his direction. To assure everyone that this was not a lovers tiff, he ordered two brandies.

It was 20 minutes before Susan returned, charging back into the restaurant with the same speed she had left. Cal stood, as she approached the table.

'I've got it, look,' she handed Cal a sheet of paper. 'It overlooks the river, on the south side of Battersea Bridge road – top apartment.' She was breathless.

'How on earth did you get this? I thought safe-houses were supposed to be secret?'

'Maybe I've not been entirely honest about my job here at the embassy. Let's leave it at that.'

Cal folded the paper and put it in his pocket. 'You're a star. First thing tomorrow morning I'll check out the apartment. If Bulloch is there, then I'll go straight to the police. I don't care who he's working for – this time I'll nail him.'

'What about the pictures of Diana, and the stuff you found at Sir Gilbert's home?'

'From what you tell me, I think you can handle all that. All I want is Bulloch.'

'Don't count on me helping out tomorrow; I have an appointment to meet several Hungarian Generals. They're flying in to the military base at Brize Norton, which reminds me, can I borrow your hire car? It's a hell of a place to get to by train.'

'Sure, the keys are in my room,' Cal had spoken the words, without thinking, smiling when he realised the seductive interpretation. The thought made him blush a little. Susan saw his excitement. In her heart she had long since realised that Caleb was fast becoming very important in her life.

Slowly, the warmth she felt for this man was turning to passion. She could contain herself no longer. As Caleb finished his coffee, Susan seized her moment.

'Would you treat me to a night cap?' her hand reached across the table to hold Cal's.

'Sure,' Cal twisted in his seat, searching for a waiter.

Susan pulled at the hand. 'No, silly – I meant a night cap in your room.'

One prompt was all he needed. Cal signed the check and, still holding hands, they left the restaurant. Neither spoke as they entered the unoccupied elevator. The doors closed and without further hesitation, Cal kissed her tenderly. It was a soft, warm, embrace of dream-like passion. They parted only as the elevator stopped with a jolt and the doors slid open. They headed for Caleb's room.

The door clicked quietly shut behind them. For a moment they both stood, unsure. Cal moved towards her and they kissed, but only for the briefest moment. Then eager to be united, they undressed. Cal unbuttoned his shirt, discarding it on the floor. Susan caught her breath, romantic emotions giving way to physical reaction that started an intense ache within her. She opened her mouth as if to release some suffering and a deep sigh escaped. His body was strong and powerful, his muscular chest swelling as his breathing shortened. She watched as he stooped to step out of his trousers, before standing upright to face her. He was a rare man – a man she could love.

Cal studied her features and began to marvel. He had forgotten the pure oval of her face, crowned by the long black hair. Her perfect mouth crinkled at the corners when she smiled, revealing a set of tiny and regular, almost crystalline, teeth. She looked at him through dark, smouldering eyes. It was as if he had caught some fairy or angel amusing herself by playing at being a mortal. Her hands trembled as she undressed, her head remained bowed, as if concentrating on the labour. When only the transparent white scraps, that passed for her bra and panties remained, she raised her head and looked at him. He studied the swell of her breasts, and his eyes moved down to the flat of her belly. The vision he saw thickened the blood to his penis, which strained desperately against the fabric of his shorts. As if by some automatic reaction the sight of this made Susan's nipples harden, and her cheeks flushed bright pink. She rushed to hold him; gripping him desperately and feeling for the first time the warmth of her skin against his. In that moment she fell in love with Caleb Wesley.

They half walked, half fell to the bed. Then, in one swift movement, Cal lifted her, placing Susan's body beneath his, relaxing in the softness of the covers. He kissed her, his lips gently feasting on her mouth. Susan felt the warmth of Cal's body press upon her, and experienced the same trembles as when she had lost her virginity. It felt so deliciously sinful. She found herself desperately wanting to appear more experienced, more raunchy, more sensual, to please him. Instead she found the purity of love.

Her hand reached up and touched his chest, playing with the tussle of blond hair. She was aware that by some magic he had removed her bra, and that Cal was fondling her breast, his hand gently stroking the white flesh.

'You are so beautiful,' his voice was thick with emotion, his whole being engulfed by her exquisite body.

'So are you, Cal,' the ache in her belly echoed the yearning in her heart, as his hand continued to explore her body.

She lay trance-like, nuzzling her head into his shoulder as his hand reached lower. It tickled lightly over her tummy until at last his fingers worked their way under the top of her panties. She stiffened involuntary and for a fleeting moment a voice from another time summoned her back. Even now it was not too late. But Cal continued, unaware of Susan's insecurities, until at last his fingers buried into her most intimate folds. Her body shuddered as his full weight eased upon her. His hand moved deftly and her panties where gone, leaving her legs to spread without restraint. Taking the weight on his elbows, yet staying close enough for his chest to flatten her breasts, she felt his fullness press against her belly. Susan raised her hips for Caleb to penetrate her.

'Yes.' The single word sounded as if it had been sucked from her mouth.

Touching, groping, kissing in a delirium of passion, Cal moved in and out of Susan. She no longer felt alone, for the first time in years the union with Cal made her whole. The sensation rippled through every fibre of her body. Suddenly she was strong – he was making her more potent with every thrust. Her breathing became short, as somewhere in her abdomen the inexplicable eruption started in earnest. She crushed her face into his neck, gripping at his head, pulling at him. The continued with a increased passion. Susan panted ever faster, fairly screaming his name. In the final moment, Cal viciously flung her legs up over his shoulders, his hips rising from the bed. With four final thrusts, they reached their zenith and the warm surge filled them both. There was a moment of almost nothing, as if the world had gone away. Slowly, they relaxed into silence, collapsing, exhausted.

Cal rolled from her and Susan lay quiet, resting even though her heart was pounding. Slowly, as reality returned, she came back to earth. The emotional landing was bumpy and the tears began to flow, becoming uncontrollable, just as her passion had been moments earlier. Cal was confused. His arms reached out and he enfolded her within his embrace, hugging her tight, his voice whispered. 'What is it? What's wrong?'

'I'm happy. I love you, you idiot. I love you!' Susan's tears fell on his chest.

CHAPTER
11

London,
August 29 1997

Bulloch responded the moment the alarm went off. It was three in the morning. He awoke feeling fresh and ready for the task ahead. The same sense of purpose and urgency that used to grip him during SAS operations now filled him with vigour. The fact that he was about to murder several people added to his excitement and as he showered quickly, the imagined visions of Caleb Wesley's death made him laugh. Thoughts of the American entering his booby-trapped car filled Bulloch's head. He could envisage the sudden blast as the bomb exploded.

He finished shaving, collected his personal toiletries, and returned to the bedroom. Dressing neatly in slacks and sports jacket, he strode into the lounge and slipped into the old overcoat. Finally, taking one last look around the apartment, he shouldered the rucksack, picked up his briefcase and, without looking back, left the building. He would never return to the apartment. He knew that later in the morning Sir Gilbert would send men to collect the remaining paperwork, dispose of Steve's clothes and remove any trace of their presence. He could leave, confident in the knowledge that there was no trail behind him for anyone to follow and that his Swiss bank account had been increased by three million pounds sterling.

Bulloch walked to the car, breathing deeply on the freshness of the night air. He opened the rear door, dropping the rucksack and briefcase into the back seat. Two minutes later he turned the racy little Peugeot over Battersea Bridge and headed north through the streets to Hyde Park. Traffic was light and ten minutes after leaving the safe-house he was on the Hyde Park circuit. He chose a route that took him past the Marriott, driving towards the rear, where he entered the car park.

It took Bulloch several minutes to locate the American Embassy section, and identify the car Caleb Wesley had hired. It was the last car in the bay, tucked in nose first neatly against the rear wall. The light was poor and half shadows hid the car from sight. Slowly, Bulloch reversed his own car into the adjacent empty bay, leaving just enough room to open the door. For a moment he sat quite still, checking for noise, making sure he was not observed. Confident that he was alone and that the shadows would conceal him, Bulloch opened the briefcase, and took out a small torch. With the engine still running, he stepped from the car, instantly dropping to his knees. With the old overcoat for protection, he rolled onto his back and slithered under the car opposite. The work did not take long. Switching on the torch, he selected a spot directly beneath the driver's seat. Placing the torch between his teeth, he reached inside the overcoat and withdrew the bomb. The powerful magnets clamped the device in place with a dull clunk. Unravelling the fishing line, Bulloch stretched forward, attaching the line to the front drive shaft. Taking a small strip of tape from inside the coat lining, he secured the line to prevent it from slipping. Finally, checking that the plastic strip was firmly in place, he searched his pocket for the small nine volt battery. Bulloch had made many such bombs in his time. Connecting the battery was always a dangerous moment – if there was one simple mistake in the wiring . . .

'What the hell . . .'

He clipped the battery to the connection, taping it securely in place.

'One down, one to go.'

He slipped from under the car and stood up.

As he pulled out of the car park, the dashboard clock told him it was 4.30 am, two hours before his early-morning flight to Paris. He headed for Heathrow. Apart from several pieces of litter fluttering in the morning breeze, the car-lined streets of inner London were deserted.

'So far, so good,' mused Bulloch to the surrounding darkness.

Twenty minutes into the British Airways flight, Bulloch lay back, resting his head on the Club Class seat. He had declined breakfast, requesting only a mineral water. Inwardly, he felt a sort of freedom. His time in London had not been a happy experience. So much had happened. It was good to be leaving. He would do this job, then disappear somewhere exotic. He drank from the glass. He would touch no more alcohol until this operation was over.

Susan was still asleep when Cal slipped quietly from the bed. Tip-toeing his way to the wardrobe he selected a pair of slacks and a shirt, before taking the strange-looking vest from its hanger. Gripping the bundle, he stepped into the bathroom and pulled on the light before closing the door behind him. He showered; drying himself thoroughly. Then, slipping his arms into the bullet-proof vest, he adjusted the Velcro straps, pulling it tight close to his skin; it felt cold. Looking in the mirror, he could make out the tiny rips in the Kevlar material. He smiled, it had saved his life twice before. He couldn't be sure what or who he would find at the apartment. If he encountered Bulloch, the vest would come in handy. Pulling on a roll-neck sweater, he concealed the vest and finished dressing. Checking that Susan was still asleep, Cal slipped down to the restaurant and devoured a hearty breakfast.

It was just after nine o'clock when he re-entered the room and approached the bed. Susan stirred, rolling over to face him, the movement causing her fine black hair to spray fanlike over the pillow. There was a faint smell of her perfume mixed in with her body warmth, which stirred memories and excited him. Cal savoured the moment, watching as her eyelids fluttered open and shut, clearing the sleep.

'Good morning, I tried not to wake you.' He saw the tiny mouth drop open, emitting a small yawn. 'I've just had breakfast. Thought I'd give it an early start. Can I get you anything?'

'Oh, my head. I think I drank a little too much last night,' she smiled, reliving the memories, lifting her head a little. 'God, I feel awful. What time is it?'

'You look wonderful. It's just gone nine. What time do you have to leave?'

'I don't have to be in Brize Norton until one o'clock, so I figure on leaving around 10.30. If you're going now, don't forget to leave me your car keys – and I want a goodbye kiss!' Susan pouted her lips.

Resting on the edge of the bed, Cal took a handful of sheet, pulling it clear to reveal her breast. When she offered no resistance, he leaned over, but stopped when his face was just inches from Susan's. They were both silent, only their eyes transmitted the memories of last nights passion and the bond it had started to build. Brushing a strand of hair from her face, Cal kissed her lightly on the lips. There was a moment of hesitation, as if he was unsure of his feelings. Susan's comic insinuations were reassuring, 'Is that it? I give you my body and all I get in the morning is a little kiss? Typical, you're just like all the rest.'

She watched as his doubt changed to humour and he kissed her again, this time long and deep, rolling his body down onto hers. He felt the soft cushion of her breasts, and immediately became aroused. Sensing his excitement, she pushed him away.

'Down, boy. You've work to do, and I'm going to grab a little more sleep.' Susan rolled over, her head disappearing beneath the covers.

Cal paused a moment longer, letting out a deep sigh, before patting the round curvature of her hips.

'Take it easy. I'll see you this evening.'

Cal grabbed his jacket and left Susan to sleep.

Although partially awake, she found it difficult to move, as if held prisoner by the comforting warmth of the bed. Trapped beneath the covers, her mind drifted through animated thoughts of both past and present. In total contrast, her body ached from the physical activity she had embraced the night before, and it wanted to rest. She wished now that she had made love again this morning. 'You are undoubtedly the one, Caleb Wesley,' she thought to herself, allowing the fine pink tongue to run over her teeth. She tasted the residue of last night's interlude, and the smell of him still lingered in her nostrils. 'What the hell,' she said aloud, protesting against the lurking guilt that she had given herself too fully, too quickly. But she had not had made love like that for so long. Fogged by sleep, Susan let her mind revel in the memory of their loving – and it had been love, not just good sex. 'I'll get you, Caleb Wesley,' she vowed, throwing back the covers and stirring her sleepy body into action.

With an effort, she rose from the bed and, nursing her throbbing head, staggered to the bathroom. She was greeted by her reflection in the long wall mirror, and instantly cursed.

'You look like shit!' She laughed, realising how happy she felt. Her mirror counterpart stood laughing back. 'I know he likes me.'

She studied the long, unkempt hair which fell unrestricted down her back; it hung dark against the whiteness of her skin. Susan twisted her athletic body filling the mirror. 'Not bad for twenty-nine,' she muttered to herself, observing her features. The breasts were good, if a little small; she let her hands slide down over the firm, flat tummy. She turned to the side, looking down at her legs. 'Shapely,' she thought, 'even if a little too short.'

Suddenly she stopped daydreaming, looking at her watch she was reminded of the time and stepped into the shower.

By 10.30 am, Susan walked happily from the hotel. The

sun was shining, and the mid-morning traffic was moving normally. She walking briskly into the NCP car park and headed directly for the section reserved for the embassy. The bright red Vectra was parked at the end, sandwiched between a large Espace and the concrete wall. The Espace, she recognised, belonged to another member of the embassy staff and the driver had not been overly considerate when parking. 'Hope you've left me enough to get out, you son of a B,' Susan muttered, noting the lack of manoeuvring space. It was a squeeze just getting into the car, the door opening restricted by the badly parked Espace. On the first attempt, her coat caught and she fumbled to extract herself. Cursing, she made another attempt, this time wriggling her hips and twisting sideways until she made it, dropping into the seat with a winning sigh. 'Yes.'

The car was cold, and Susan shuddered, 'Someone's just walked over my grave!' Putting the key in the ignition, she started the engine and engaged reverse. Slowly, checking in both wing mirrors, she backed out.

'Oh, hell.'

She wasn't going to make it. Pulling forwards, Susan tried inching the car closer to the wall, hoping to create a wider gap between her and the neighbouring vehicle. She reversed again, smiling at her own dexterity. This time she was going to make it. A small snapping sound came from beneath the car, but any noise was hidden from Susan by the revving engine.

It took three turns of the drive shaft before the slack in the fishing line was wound up and the line became taught. The fourth turn gently eased the plastic strip from the jaws of the clothes peg allowing them to snap shut, completing the electrical circuit. Power from the nine volt battery ran its course, hitting the element in the tiny, five centimetre aluminium tube. It surged through the 1.6 ohms resistance, causing the element to glow white hot. This in turn burned the surrounding powder, known as PETN. The tube detonated. In a micro second it reached a velocity of over 24,000 feet per second. The white plastic PE-4 explosive that surrounded the detonator immediately reacted – the process of instantaneous decomposition had started.

The shock waves travelled outwards from the point of initiation, cutting through any steel, concrete and flesh that barred its way. The intense pressure pushed at the air, struggling to escape in such a confined space. Bulloch had placed the detonator at the bottom of the bomb, thus ensuring the shock wave energy was transmitted upwards . . . an SAS skill learned to achieve maximum devastation.

Susan Greenwood knew nothing of this. The blast alone had been enough to stop her heart and gel her brain. The blast split the car in two, throwing the roof back like an open can of beans. What remained of Susan's body passed through this ragged hole. In the process the tortured metal severed her left arm at the elbow. Her body finally stopped as it slapped into the concrete ceiling. Like some over-sized rag doll, it fell back to lie amid the wreckage.

'It's a bomb, sir. We will have to evacuate the building.'

The Marine paused for a moment in the open doorway of Dan Wesley's office, then urgently left to disperse the news.

'That's an understatement,' thought Wesley. The explosion had caused him to jump to his feet. It sounded so close. The shock wave had been strong enough to make the embassy building tremble. Standing by the window, he looked out at the billowing dark grey smoke which now spiralled high above the city. The sight of it troubled him. 'My God, let's hope there's no more.' The sound of running feet came from the corridor as others heeded the Marine's warning. Securing the papers on which he had been working, he followed the orderly exit, evacuating the embassy. There was no need to worry about security. The Marine contingent would not leave the building – bomb or no bomb.

He mustered with the others, standing in the sun-drenched gardens of Grosvenor Square. Some staff who had hurriedly left the embassy now stood around, huddled in small groups. Near the scene of the explosion people were running in all directions. Unseen sirens wailed, announcing the arrival of the emergency services, a chaotic scene in the making. Barricades started to spring up, forcing the embassy staff to move. People were checking roll calls, shouting out names.

Once a head count had been completed, most of the staff were dismissed and allowed home for the day. Those that remained found themselves in a nearby pub discussing how to treat the perpetrators of such work, waiting for the all clear. Dan Wesley sat among this group, talking with several other members of the Defence Attaché's staff who had joined in the debate. Due to the early morning trade, the pub was jam-packed and noisy, the clientele having been swollen to capacity by those who had been evacuated. Dan looked around as more people entered. Some, he knew were reporters, eager to get the story from the front line. It was through the latter that they learned the bomb had gone off in the NCP multi-storey car park and, as the Marriott Hotel was so close, it too had been evacuated. Dan was worried; there was no way of checking if Cal was okay and Susan Greenwood was the only one missing from the roll call, although her absence was accounted for by her journey to Brize Norton.

An hour after the explosion, the police asked for permission for their bomb disposal team to search the embassy. Because of security, there was some objection, until the police pointed out that the bomb had gone off in a car park space reserved for the embassy and that they had identified the victim. Despite the body being mutilated, they had found a handbag which contained Susan Greenwood's embassy pass. The bomb was clearly aimed at the American Embassy. Dan Wesley knew nothing of this until the Military Attaché arrived in person. He entered the pub, pushing his way through the crowded bar, then leaned over the table and addressed the small group in a whisper.

'Susan Greenwood is dead. The bomb was in a rented car. We have no idea what she was doing there.'

There was silence. Looks of disbelief froze the faces of those around the table. Dan Wesley was the one exception. He knew the truth. It was like finishing a puzzle, the last piece falling violently into place. There was only one question. He forced it from his lips.

'Was my son with her?'

The others looked at him with bewilderment.

'No. According to the police, Susan's was the only body found. It seems she was the only one in the blast area. What has your son got to do with this, Dan?' the Attaché asked, confused.

For a moment, Dan Wesley said nothing. He stood up, took the Attaché's arm and led him outside. Amid the blare of sirens, surrounded by the chaos of a disrupted central London, one thought echoed in Dan Wesley's mind – his son

had been right all along, Bulloch was here, and he was killing.
He stared at the Military Attaché, gripping the man's sleeve.

'Is Lloyd Ramsey still in the embassy?'

'As far as I know, Dan. Nothing would move that old goat.
What's all this about?'

'I think it's time I went to see him. There's something he
should know.'

'Tell me exactly what *you* know, Colonel Wesley,' Lloyd
Ramsey stood behind his desk, looking out of the window.
There were no vehicles and only the odd movement of a
running figure in the streets below indicated that anything
unusual had occurred. Behind him, he heard the voice of Dan
Wesley.

'During the Gulf War, sir, my son, Caleb . . .' Dan Wesley
talked for 15 minutes without interruption, ending with the
words, 'My son just wanted to catch this man Bulloch.'

Wesley turned away from the window and sat down.

'Did you know that your son broke into Sir Gilbert's
country estate the night before last?'

Dan Wesley raised his head as if he were about to rebut any
accusations.

'Don't worry. Although unaware of the fact, your son did
this with my full approval,' Ramsey assured Cal's father. 'You
may have guessed by now that Susan Greenwood worked for
me. She first came to me a few of days ago. Her story
answered several questions that had been bothering me for the
past two weeks. I ordered her to exploit your son's motivation
in searching for this man Bulloch. And now Susan Greenwood
is dead.' Lloyd Ramsey paused for a moment. 'Yesterday, I
ordered her not to continue until I had conducted some

discreet enquires . . . but now . . .' again the old man stopped. Susan's death had truly wounded him. 'Now, I think Susan took the bomb intended for your son, and the only person in the frame for this barbarous action is this man Bulloch.'

Finally, Ramsey looked up at the man sitting across the desk from him. In the six months he had known Colonel Dan Wesley, the man had proved to be a most resourceful and reliable negotiator for his country. He hoped the son would prove to be as good as the father. Nobody was going to get away with killing one of his agents – especially one he cherished as much as Susan Greenwood.

'I have contacted Washington. As there is no firm evidence of a plot to murder the Princess of Wales, there is little we can do. However, that does not stop us from finding Susan's killer. Your son will continue his search for this man Bulloch, but from now on he will do so under my direction.' Lloyd Ramsey saw the look of concern drawn on Dan Wesley's face. 'He's already on the case, Dan. We don't have time to brief anyone else. Besides, he seems to have done an exceptional job so far.'

On leaving Susan, Cal had taken a taxi, asking the driver to drop him off near the off-licence on the south side of Battersea Bridge. The morning traffic, hampered by what seemed like an endless tide of tourists, ebbed slowly along the embankment. It was after 10.00 am before he finally arrived. 'This is it,' he told the cab driver, pointing out Oddbins.

He stood with his back to the store, staring up at the modern apartment blocks opposite. The address Susan had given him was somewhere within the deluxe complex. For a moment Cal mentally prepared himself then, crossing the road, he went in search of Bulloch. The thought that he may be close to his old antagonist sent a feeling of excitement twisting through his stomach.

The blocks were built to house six individual apartments. Cal found the number, but discovered the ground floor door was locked and controlled by an entryphone system. Cal thought of picking the lock but, although the area was fairly deserted, he felt too exposed. He moved away to rethink. He had gone no more than 20 metres when a car pulled up violently, parking on the pavement in front of the block. A woman jumped hastily from the car and ran towards the door. Using her key, she opened it and disappeared inside. Cal turned around and walked to stand by the door. Through the glass panel he saw the woman coming back down the internal stairs. He pretended to speak into the entry system just as she opened the door from the inside. 'Thank you,' said Cal, grabbing hold of the door as the hassled woman pushed past.

Making his way up the two flights of stairs, he stopped outside number 12. There was no spy-hole in the door and Cal guessed that he would have a few seconds advantage over Bulloch when it came to recognition. Although unarmed, he took a small metal baton from his pocket and held it ready. If Bulloch became violent, he had the means to drop him.

Taking a deep breath, Cal braced himself. He knocked loudly on the door. There was no answer. He knocked again. Still nothing. Pressing his ear against the door, he listened, waiting a full minute. Returning the baton to his pocket, Cal searched for his lock-picks and set to work.

Using his index finger on the tension tool, he pushed the rake to the rear of the lock, before snapping it out over the pins. The cylinder moved a fraction – Cal repeated the process. Suddenly his index finger relaxed and the tension tool turned the cylinder, releasing the lock. He never quite understood why but the action always put a grin on his face.

Returning the picks to his pocket, he gripped the baton once more and made ready to strike. Gently pushing the door open, he stepped into the hallway, using the carpet to dampen his movement. He stood still, listening intently. There was no sound. He moved with caution directly through the archway, peering into the lounge. Moving swiftly, he examined each room in turn. The apartment appeared empty but from the mess he guessed that someone had recently been living there. Cal returned to the lounge.

A huge pile of documents was heaped onto one of the two matching settees. On the coffee table, a folded sheet of paper stuck out from an open envelope. Cal examined it. Although the ticket was missing, the letter was clearly from a travel company, confirming a flight for a Mr J. Rogers, travelling to Paris at 06.25 that morning. 'Shit.' Bulloch had already gone.

Disappointed, he dropped down on the settee, disturbing the paper pile, which lay half covered with a crumpled map. The movement caused several photographs to fall to the floor. At least, thought Cal, picking one up and looking at the woman in the pictures, he had the right apartment. He started to flip through each folder, briefly examining the contents. They were all very much the same, surveillance reports on the Princess of Wales and members of the Al Fayed family. A thin yellow folder stuck out from the rest. Cal laid it open on the table, to examine its contents. His forehead creased in puzzlement as he tried to understand how this information fitted into the picture. The folder held several sheets of paper that covered servicing aspects of various Mercedes cars.

Whatever Bulloch was planning was going to involve a car. Sabotage? Not his usual style . . .

The door to the apartment opened abruptly. Cal had been so absorbed in what he was doing he had not heard the key turn in the lock. Even as he stood, two men, both dressed in blue overalls and carrying large bags, entered the lounge. It was a moment of total surprise, not just for him but also for the new arrivals. Cal thought about running or diving out of the window and was still thinking of escape when one of the men spoke.

'Sorry, sir, they said you would be gone by now. We've come to collect the files and sterilise the flat.'

The two men looked uneasy, unsure what to do. On impulse, Cal picked up the envelope in which Bulloch's tickets had arrived.

'I forgot these,' he said, standing and walking towards the door. 'I would prefer you didn't say anything to anyone.'

'No, sir,' they waited until Cal had closed the door behind him. 'Call himself a bloody professional? Fancy forgetting his tickets?'

'Dopey bastard,' replied the second man, 'and look at the fucking mess he's left for us.'

Outside, Cal could not believe his luck. The two men had obviously no idea what Bulloch looked like. Elated at his narrow escape, he crossed the river, contemplating his next move. Suddenly he realised that this would be an ideal opportunity to have the police search the apartment. Considering the state of the place, the men would be there for at least an hour. What more evidence would he need? Looking at his watch, he thought of ringing Susan but she would be on her way to Brize Norton airbase by now. He started to run, searching for a phone box. Cal had no wish to involve his father any further but this was too good an opportunity to pass up. It took him five minutes to find a phone box that had not been vandalised.

Strange, thought Cal, there no answer from the embassy. He re-dialled making doubly sure he keyed the correct digits. There was still no answer. Searching his wallet, Cal found the card his father had given him and tried his mobile number. It rang several times before his father's voice finally answered.

'Dad, it's Cal – what the hell's going on? There's no answer at the embassy.'

'Caleb, where are you?' Dan Wesley's tone was harsh and unyielding.

Cal detected the stiffness in his father's voice and misinterpreted the manner for chastisement. His father had warned him about any further involvement in the case, but in light of his discoveries in the flat, he thought he could justify his actions. Cal was about to relay what he had found out, went his father interrupted. 'Cal, there's been a bomb, that's why the embassy is closed. A bomb went off in the car park at the rear of the Marriott hotel.' He let this information sink in before continuing. 'It was your car, Caleb. Your hire car . . . Susan Greenwood is dead.'

As his father's words registered, they deadened his brain. He felt detached from all around him – a paralysed consciousness. It was the same feeling he had encountered with the loss of his mother. The numbness filled his mind, leaving only a tapestry of fleeting imagery, snapshots of Susan, the love and warmth they had so recently shared. Outside the phone box, the traffic rumbled along the embankment, wheels squeaking harshly on the dry tarmac, yet to Cal there was only silence. A single echo resounded from his soul, 'Susan's dead. Susan's dead. Susan's dead.'

He stood, head bowed, the phone clutched tightly to his ear. Tears poured from his eyes and rolled down his cheeks to fall and pattern the concrete floor by his feet.

In the distance, he could hear his father's voice, yet the words made no sense. He required answers.

'What's happening, Dad? What the hell is happening?'

Dan Wesley could sense his son's anguish and pleaded, 'Take it easy, Caleb. Just hold on. Come back to the embassy. We need you here.' There was pain in his voice, a man wanting to share his son's suffering, as they had shared so much in the past. He waited for Cal to regain control.

'Bulloch's gone, Dad. He's killed Susan, now he's gone to Paris.' Outwardly, the anger flowed and within it fuelled a rage for revenge. Talking in short gulps, Cal informed his father about events at the Battersea safe-house. 'Susan said Sir Gilbert Scott owns it. From what I could see, it looks as if it's been used to plan this whole operation. Maps, tapes and files. This is a hit, Dad and we both know who the target is. We must do something!'

'We will, son. Compose yourself. Grab a taxi and come straight to my office. There's someone here you need to talk to.'

Cal replaced the receiver before taking out his handkerchief and mopping away his tears. Out on the pavement he stood and looked around, trying with some difficulty to concentrate. With a deep breath he focused on the two events that seemed to be engulfing him. Susan was dead and Bulloch was gone. He took several paces, regardless of direction. A gaudy sign hanging above an open doorway denoted the entrance to a small public house. Trapped between two large Victorian houses, 'The Stage Coach' gave the impression of being extremely old, echoing a past that stretched back long before the advent of the automobile. Cal needed a drink and a little time to bring order back into his life. He paused on entering, waiting while his eyes adjusted to the gloom. The pub was little more than a large, oblong room with a long wooden bar against the rear wall. Even though he could hear the road noise drifting in from outside, the mature wood-panelled walls gave the pub a feeling of tranquillity offering the sanctuary he required.

It was still early, the pub having only just opened. Apart from the barman and a couple of occupied tables, the place was deserted. Cal crossed to the bar and ordered a large brandy before taking a seat near the only window. He sat gripping the glass, making an effort to control his breathing. At the same time he gathered his thoughts. His mind was a jumble, struggling to accept Susan's death, and he found himself hearing her voice, smelling her perfume, feeling the touch of her lips. The tears threatened once more and with an effort he fought them back, gulping down half his drink in an act of suppression. At that moment, as if disturbed by Cal's presence, the man sitting at the next table stopped reading his newspaper, stood and left the pub. The discarded newspaper lay on the seat, its front page exposed clear enough for Cal to comprehend. At first he read without interest, then his eyes focused sharply on the words and flickers of recognition sparked in his mind.

The headlines proclaimed the love affair between Princess Diana and Dodi Al Fayed. Cal snatched at the newspaper, his eyes sweeping over the print, his mind registering snippets of information that told the story of the couple's latest holiday in the Mediterranean. The paper speculated on the possibility of marriage, a rumour based on the fact that the couple had visited a famous jeweller in Monaco and it was widely believed that the ring would be delivered to Paris ready for Al Fayed to propose this coming weekend. Filled with a new sense of purpose, Cal knocked back the remains of his drink and lurched towards the door. Inwardly Cal chastised himself, 'How could I have been so blind? All this time I have been looking for Bulloch when I should have been watching the news!' He ran into the street and hailed the first available taxi.

By the time Cal's taxi reached the American Embassy, the cordon that had been in place since the bombing was in the process of being partially removed. Taking the steps two at a time, Cal bounded through the front door and, after a brief word with the guard, made straight for his father's office. The relief at seeing his Cal alive was clearly illustrated on Dan Wesley's face as he bear-hugged his son. When at last Cal pulled away from his father, Dan Wesley, speaking in a whispered voice said, 'I'm sorry about Susan.'

Cal looked at his father. There was no way he could know of the commitment he and Susan had shared in the last 24 hours. He merely said, 'So am I, Dad, so am I.'

With that, Dan Wesley took his son up to the second floor and introduced him to Lloyd Ramsey. Cal had never been in a room where a man's presence was so dominant. He waited, absorbing the sense of distinction and authority pervading the office, while Ramsey and his father moved away to one side and talked in a murmur. Both men shook hands before Dan

Wesley turned to leave the office. As he passed his son, he placed his arm momentarily on Cal's shoulder.

'Good luck, son.'

Lloyd Ramsey sat down, indicating that Cal should do the same. He looked across at the young man opposite and, after several moments, nodded to himself as if confirming a decision. 'Tell me what you found at the Battersea safe-house.' The voice was coarse and challenging.

'Bulloch left for Paris early this morning.' Cal dropped the white envelope on to Lloyd Ramsey's desk together with the newspaper he had taken from the pub. 'I am convinced that he is going to kill the Princess of Wales.'

'Hold on, let's not get ahead of ourselves. Did you see anything other than this envelope to indicate that he had been at the apartment?'

'There was a whole heap of surveillance reports with photographs similar to the ones we found on Norris in Columbia and in the safe at Harmsham Park. I was in the process of checking out one particular file when two guys appeared. They mistook me for Bulloch. From what I could make out, the file contained diagrams for Mercedes electronic systems. Someone had hand written notes on the pages, but I never had time to read them. This all suggests some form of organised accident.'

Lloyd Ramsey was silent for a moment before expressing his theory for Cal's benefit. 'As I understand it, the princess is still in the Med were she spends most of her time on board Al Fayed's new yacht. So if, as you suggest, this man Bulloch intends to kill the princess in a car accident then it will most likely take place when she returns to Paris.'

'Precisely where Bulloch is at this moment,' declared Cal.

'In that case, we have to be careful. From what you and Susan have been able to ascertain and, bearing in mind the increased activity of British Intelligence, I believe we may have touched upon a deniable operation. The problem is, son, if I make waves at this juncture, the British will simply accuse America of involving itself in one of their operations. Likewise, they will terminate any shadow operation and that will be the last we see of your man Bulloch.'

'We can't just do nothing. Bulloch attempted to kill me, now he's murdered Susan. We can't let him assassinate the princess.'

'I have no intention of letting him get away with anything, Major Wesley, especially murdering Susan Greenwood. I have contacted Washington and, as of this moment, you are unofficially working for me. However, the rules are the same. You fuck up and it's your life on the line. The agency will deny ever knowing you.'

Ramsey's fingers tapped at the newspaper. 'If, as you assume, Bulloch is in France to kill the Princess of Wales, then you're our best hope of stopping him. Princess Diana and Dodi Al Fayed are due to arrive in Paris this coming weekend. Get close to the princess and you will find Bulloch.' Again Ramsey's fingers tapped at the newspaper. 'She will not be hard to find. The moment she touches down in Paris, she will be surrounded by the press. Use that to your advantage. Now, let's get down to business.'

Lloyd Ramsey spent the best part of an hour briefing Cal on his mission, providing him with a list of places the princess normally frequented whenever in Paris. 'You will leave for Paris immediately. It is obvious that the car bomb was meant for you – that means they know of your existence here in

London. I intend to pacify them a little, make them think you've been shipped back to the States. It should give you a little more freedom to operate if they think you're out of the picture.

'When you arrive at Charles de Gaulle airport, you will take a taxi to this address in the town of Conflans Ste Honorine.' The look of pained recognition on Cal's face was not missed by Ramsey. 'It's the house the department found for Susan. I know it may seem a little tactless but it serves our purpose. You'll find directions in here together with your flight tickets and 20,000 French Francs – that should see you through. I take it you have your own credit cards?'

Ramsey held out his hand, indicating that Cal should hand them over. He took out his wallet and did so, watching as Ramsey wrote down the number of his American Express card. 'I'll have your credit fixed just in case you need extra cash,' he said, tossing the card back across the desk. 'You will have to account for all your expenses, but you'll find me moderately generous. You might like to take a look around the Ritz Hotel, in which case you will need to find yourself a half-decent suit. As for transport, you will find a small car in the garage at the house in Conflans. A set of keys is secured in a box under the workbench at the rear of the garage. The same box also contains a weapon, together with sufficient ammunition.'

Ramsey handed over a mobile phone that had been sitting on his desk.

'Contact me the moment you find Bulloch or come across anything important. Likewise, I will notify you if anything crops up this end. I will try to organise some form of back-up in Paris, but for the moment you're on your own. When you find Bulloch, detain him if possible . . . kill him if you must. If you get into any trouble, make for the house in Conflans and we will get you out.'

Lloyd Ramsey thought that the British people had many virtues but there was one great anomaly throughout the nation. Theirs was not a classless society, the dichotomy never more blatantly evident than in that institution which the upper class and upper class aspirants referred to as 'The Club'. In Ramsey's eyes those who clung on to the outdated tradition of the gentleman's club did so because it was where deals could be struck and pacts made with fellows of the same rank or ilk. The club to which Sir Robert Trescott so proudly belonged was even worse than usual. It had a large reading room in which it appeared to Ramsey that at least half the occupied seats contained dead bodies. The bar was little better, frequented as it was by a regular patronage of 'old farts'. Ramsey had met with his British counterpart at 'The Club' twice before. On both occasions the atmosphere and clientele were swimming with self-importance.

Trescott met him in the 'saloon', a glorified title used to describe the club's large, pretentious bar. With a beckoning wave he gestured that Ramsey should seat himself in a large, high-backed leather chair.

'Would you like to eat? The food here is frightfully good,' invited Trescott politely, taking the seat opposite.

'No, thank you. A drink will suffice. A Scotch.'

Trescott looked towards the bar and raised his hand in a vague gesture. While they waited to order their drinks, Trescott decided to start the ball rolling.

'I trust this meeting is about the bomb this morning?

Terrible affair, absolutely terrible. I recall meeting Susan Greenwood at several embassy functions. She was such a pleasant woman. I'm so very sorry.'

'Thank you for that,' Ramsey dipped his head in acknowledgement.

'Of course, we have pulled out all the stops,' Trescott continued, 'but this is really a matter for the police and so far they have no idea who planted it, or why.'

'You're a lying son-of-a-bitch,' reflected Lloyd Ramsey to himself, but countered with a more acceptable response. 'Could have been the IRA, Iraqis or any Muslim extremist group. It seems that nowadays everyone and their dog wants to take shot at America.'

'It's a sad state of affairs,' agreed Trescott, who watched as the barman placed their drinks on the table. 'Anything from your end? Anything that might give us a lead?'

'No. Nothing at all.'

The reply had been short enough to convince Trescott that the bombing was not the main reason for Lloyd Ramsey's impromptu visit. He tried a fresh approach.

'So, Lloyd my dear chap, is there anything else I can do for you?' Trescott's voice was insultingly condescending, as if all was well with the world, in an effort to disguise his paranoia. Ever since the American had phoned requesting a brief get-together, Trescott had been worried. Although the bomb that had detonated earlier that morning had been close to the American Embassy, it was not like Ramsey to supervise such matters personally. It was obvious that the man had discovered something – possibly about the Sovereign Committee.

Ramsey did his utmost to render a look of embarrassment.

'It would seem that one of our military guys, a Major Caleb Wesley, was assigned to the anti-drugs programme in Columbia and became involved in the mopping up operation during the recent air disaster down there. While he was doing so, he discovered a body. The man was travelling on a British passport in the name of James Moore, but Wesley identified him as Steve Norris, an ex-member of your Special Air Service. I'm told that the man Norris and another soldier, a John Bulloch, tried to murder Wesley during the Gulf War.'

'This is most fascinating,' replied Trescott, sitting forward and feigning interest. Inside he felt physically sick. 'Do go on.'

'Well, that's about it, really. Major Wesley followed the body back here to the United Kingdom in the hope of tracking down this man's partner. To be honest, the whole thing is a bit embarrassing and the man has no official status here, but as his father is an old friend, I wondered if your department could help us find this man John Bulloch?'

'British, you say? In the light of recent events I can hardly refuse. However, it may take some time. The department is a little busy at the moment.'

Ramsey saw his opening and casually voiced his reply. 'Yes, we had noticed the increased activity over the Mediterranean. Something we should know about?'

'No, no, purely a British matter, don't you know,' Trescott's response was short.

'You don't get off the hook that easily, you bastard,' thought Ramsey. He pushed the subject a little further. 'Unless the Russians have launched a new submarine in the Mediterranean without our knowledge, the only interest British Intelligence could have in the area is this affair between your Princess of Wales and her new boyfriend. What's his name? Dodi Al Fayed?' Although Lloyd Ramsey had spoken the words in a light-hearted manner he knew from Trescott's expression that he had hit the jackpot.

Trescott swirled the ice gently in his drink as he rapidly regained his composure. He adopted a solemn face before answering.

'What I am about to tell you is in the strictest confidence. We believe there is a serious threat against the Princess of Wales. Unfortunately, she is besotted with this man and demands her privacy. She relies purely on the bodyguards supplied by Mohamed Al Fayed. For our part, the British Government would not be acting responsibly if we did not provide protection for the mother of our future King. It is as simple as that.'

'I understand, and thank you for confiding in me. Rest assured America has no wish to become involved in, as you say, a purely British operation. I am sorry to have bothered you with this man Bulloch.'

Trescott held up his hand. 'If, as you say, this man is in London, we will find him.'

'Thank you,' Ramsey stood offering his hand.

Trescott did likewise, shaking the proffered hand. 'Where is this Major Wesley now?'

'I'm having him sent back to the States.'

'It's not just the fresh air that tastes cleaner out here,' thought Ramsey, as he left the club. If Trescott had been running a double show, a black operation, and using Bulloch to do his dirty work, there was a possibility it would now be called off. However, for the time being, Bulloch gave him a legitimate reason for keeping Caleb Wesley in the field.

Bulloch had arrived in Paris mid-morning. As instructed, he had gone directly to the Concorde Lafayette, a modern hotel in the centre of the city. It was ideally located for his needs. His mood was relaxed and when he enquired at reception, he found that a room had already been reserved. There was also a message stating that a package was waiting to be delivered to him and giving a telephone number. From the security of his room Bulloch placed the call. The package would be delivered by courier shortly.

When the courier arrived, Bulloch recognised him as the same man who had made deliveries to the Battersea apartment. He gave Bulloch a large, black, canvas bag before handing over a set of keys. 'The bike is in the underground car park, bay C near the pay point. The exit ticket is tucked under the seat. I am to tell you that everything is bolted down safely.' With that the man turned and walked away.

'So Sir Gilbert's men have succeeded in fitting the explosive bolts,' thought Bulloch as he dropped the bag to the floor and slid open the zipper. He removed each item with care, placing them on the bed with silent approval. The black leather riding suit, together with a pair of high-fitting boots, looked sinister. Next, he removed the full-face helmet, noticing that the radio headset had already been fitted. Someone had even enclosed a short note on the method of operation and indicated the correct channel. Bulloch removed the coiled cable before placing the helmet over his head. It was a little loose but that was better than it being too tight. The lead to the radio hung down from the helmet, giving him about a metre of movement; it was capped with a multi-pin socket that connected to the radio. Turning the switch, Bulloch activated the radio. There was an immediate hissing sound in his right ear. He switched the radio off before disconnecting it from the helmet. He would not need the radio just yet.

Removing the helmet he continued his inventory. The ambush light was still in the original packing supplied by Jarvis while the Glock pistol and power glove remained wrapped in the Oddbins carrier bag. A smaller padded bag contained a professional camera, albeit battered and much used. On the bottom of the bag lay a buff-coloured envelope. It contained a new passport issued in the Republic of Ireland and bearing Bulloch's picture. There was also a neatly folded sheet of paper on which was written a series of numbers. Bulloch smiled. Upon Diana's death those numbers represented three million in Sterling.

Bulloch took a leisurely shower before dressing in light underclothes and donning the motorbike leathers. He was pleased with the comfortable fit. Taking the folded map of Paris from his briefcase, he tucked it inside his jacket. Finally, he grabbed the helmet and made his way to the elevator where he pressed the button for the underground car park.

The elevator door made a hissing sound as it closed behind him. The underground car park was vast and deprived of natural light, giving it a chilly air. The view from his hotel room, however, had confirmed that the weather above looked promising, and the roads would be dry. He spotted the car park pay point and headed towards it. The big blue motorbike sat close to the rear wall. The bike was, as requested, a Kawasaki XR 600. Bulloch paused to admire its beauty before taking a moment to check the bike over thoroughly. He knew it to be a powerful machine, capable of both cross country and on-road performance. His request that Enduro tyres should be fitted would also make the bike manageable if he hit wet roads.

Searching his pocket, he found the key and located the ignition. Bulloch, although a skilled rider, had not ridden a motorbike since the Gulf War. He savoured the moment before pressing the starter button. The machine burst into life, idling quietly. Kicking away the stand, Bulloch opened the throttle, letting the engine roar.

Engaging the gears he left the car park, throttling up the ramp before turning onto the main road and letting the motorbike race noisily down the Avenue de La Grande Armee. It was already midday and the traffic was heavy, although this would allow him time to examine the routes. When the time came he would need speed. As he circled the island with its famous Arc de Triomphe, the traffic slowed almost to a stop. Bulloch grinned; it was for this very reason that he had chosen a motorbike. Pushing the machine forwards, he rode easily through the blockage, emerging freely into the wide expanse of the Champs Elysees.

Ten minutes after leaving his hotel, Bulloch rode onto the forecourt of the Ritz Hotel. Easing back on the throttle, he let the bike roll into the main car park. The hotel looked impressive, its unspoilt beauty and traditional French features warranting its international reputation. Bulloch spent several minutes in silent study although his interest did not rest in any of Al Fayed's property but merely the routes that lay between them. He rode steadily, heading back down the Champs Elysees. As he approached the Arc de Triomphe for the second time he turned into the Rue Arsene Houssaye, where the Al Fayed apartments were situated.

By four in the afternoon, Bulloch had ridden at least once along every conceivable route the couple could possible drive between their main locations and favourite restaurants. When at last the summer heat had taken its toll he returned to his hotel. Back in the underground car park Bulloch positioned the bike with care, then took the lift directly to his room. Once there he stripped off his helmet and jacket, before removing the trousers and bulky riding boots – finally he headed for the coolness of the shower.

That evening, having eaten well in one of the hotel restaurants, he retired to the cocktail bar. Enjoying a relaxed disposition now that everything was in place, he was beginning to feel a little of his old self return. In an effort to recall his French he made a half-hearted attempt to strike up a conversation with the ageing barmaid. After several drinks the tête-à-tête became extremely cordial. The woman was mistaking Bulloch's intentions. She leaned over the bar and whispered, 'I get off in an hour – one thousand francs.' Giving him a seductive grin, she stepped back and went to serve another customer.

'You've got to be fucking kidding,' thought Bulloch, his character suddenly changing. The barmaid returned smiling, placing her hands on the bar and bending forward to expose her breasts. Her fingernails were painted bright red, a colour that clashed with the yellowish tinge of her tobacco-stained fingers. Bulloch's eyes rose to the level of her wrinkled cleavage. The skin looked artificially tanned and her sagging breasts stretched the material of her knitted sweater. It made him cold. Revulsion coursed through his body with an icy shiver. It was not a woman he wanted, it was another type of release and tomorrow, when he killed the princess, he would get it. Leaving behind the confused barmaid, Bulloch returned to his room and went to bed.

It was late afternoon when Cal arrived at Charles de Gaulle airport. He had never been to France before and the airport, with its system of tunnels and conveyers, reminded him of a 1960s sci-fi film. Going through passport control, he collected his baggage before making his way out of the terminal on the ground floor. Cal hailed a Mercedes cab from the taxi rank and gave the driver the list of directions supplied by Ramsey.

As they left the airport and took the A1 exit in the direction of Lille, Cal wondered what Bulloch was doing at that precise moment. He was still contemplating the problem when he noticed the sign for Le Bourget. Lloyd Ramsey had mentioned the small airport, specifying that Al Fayed's private aircraft often used it.

The cab continued down the motorway, passing through a heavily industrialised area before turning off in the direction of Pontoise. Eventually the cab pulled onto a smaller road and Cal saw the first sign for Conflans, shortly after he saw the river and Susan's words came rushing back to him.

'It's a lovely place that sits on the River Seine. You arrive in the town right by the river and as you drive alongside it you will see hundreds of barges which have been converted into homes. In France they are known as peniches, and one of them has actually been transformed into a church. The quays alongside this portion of the river are all planted with trees and flowerbeds . . .'

Cal's thoughts came to an abrupt halt as the taxi stopped in front of the house. He paid the fare and carried his bag up the drive. A small flight of steps led to a covered terrace that sheltered the front door. He fumbled a little with the keys as thoughts of Susan raced into his mind. Although it belonged to the agency, this had been her home.

Inside, the combined dining-cum-sitting room looked

spacious, neat furniture fitting well under a ceiling of exposed beams. Stylish curtains draped majestically over French windows that opened onto the terraces both front and rear. A study and kitchen were accessible through adjoining doors. To the left, a flight of wooden stairs swept up to the first floor. From here Call stepped timidly into the main bedroom. The large bed, covered with a pink silken quilt, filled the room. Beyond it were more French windows that led out onto the upper balcony with a view overlooking the river. One glance told him that this was Susan's room. He would sleep here tonight, but for the moment her memory was too overwhelming. Cal dropped his suitcase and went in search of the garage.

The basement beneath the house was divided in two, part being used as a laundry while the other half had been transformed into a garage. Parked in the middle was a white Fiat Uno. Moving around the car, Cal spotted the workbench against the rear wall. Dropping to his knees, he located the wooden box that had been secreted beneath the workbench. With the aid of a screwdriver he removed the box and placed it on the bench. As Ramsey had indicated it contained a spare set of keys for the car and the gun. It was a small, Czech-made Skorpion. Despite being no bigger than a handgun it was capable of full automatic fire. This made it ideal for concealment and Cal knew it to be formidable at close-quarters. The 20-round clips lay next to the pistol. He pocketed both keys and pistol.

At 4.30 pm Cal telephoned the Espadon restaurant at the Ritz, making a reservation for 8.30 that evening. Then, despite a reluctance to do so, he ventured upstairs once more and unpacked.

Cal drove the dynamic little Fiat towards Versailles. At the town of Le Chesnay he took the motorway towards Paris. Entering the Peripherique he emerged at Porte Maillot to be confronted by the Hotel Concorde Lafayette. Unaware of Bulloch's close presence, he continued down the Avenue de La Grande Armee, around the Arc de Triomphe and into the Champs Elysees. He approached the giant Needle in the Place de la Concorde and passed around the island, making his way up the Rue de Rivoli and into the nearby Ritz.

Cal made his way through he revolving door and into the grandiose lobby. Having asked for directions, he walked down the long, narrow wood-panelled lobby and past the garden courtyard that led to the opulent, mirror-walled dining room. He was shown to a table in the flowered garden where the temperature was a comfortable 72 degrees. A clear sky made the stars plainly visible. Susan should be here with him; she would have loved it. Shaking off the memory, Cal ordered.

For Cal the meal was incredible. He had never tasted such food – Paris's premier temple of gastronomy would linger with him forever. Nevertheless, despite the excellent food and the extravagance he had little trouble reminding himself as to his purpose here. He doubted that Bulloch was staying at the hotel. There were security cameras everywhere and he would not want his identity known. Finishing the last of his wine, Cal left.

The house in Conflans felt empty. He knew what was missing but there was little he could do about that. With Susan still in his mind he climbed the stairs and went to bed.

CHAPTER
12

Paris,
August 30, 1997

The small boat stayed within a half a mile of the *Jonikal*. There was no need to get any closer. For the past week the smaller craft had faithfully shadowed the larger vessel, moving first from Nice to Monaco and then eastwards across the Mediterranean to Portoferraio on the Italian island of Elba. Finally, the magnificent *Jonikal* had sailed into the calm, blue waters of Sardinia's verdant coastline. Although the *Jonikal's* security staff were constantly vigilant, the presence of one unmarked boat had gone unnoticed among the numerous pleasure craft the numbers of which had, over the past few days, been swollen by an influx of paparazzi.

The four-man surveillance team aboard the small boat was relaxed. There had been time to get a tan and, although the living conditions were cramped, they were at least comfortable. Working in shifts, the operation had allowed them time to swim or laze away their off-duty time. In the evening they had sat drinking beer as the moon's reflection sent ripples over the phosphorescent waters. Despite this holiday-like atmosphere, one pair was always watchful. The present observers knew that their part in this operation would soon come to an end. During the night they had intercepted several phone messages and learned that in a few hours Dodi Al Fayed would be taking Princess Diana back to Paris.

'This is the life – relaxing in the Mediterranean sunshine. I wish they would give us more jobs like this.' The man sat in the captain's chair perched on the small fly deck, his eyes closed while his face was turned towards the morning sun.

'It's okay if you've got plenty money,' the second man replied in a dour voice while peering into the vast lens which dwarfed his camera. 'They sleep in until ten o'clock then swim or jet-ski all day. Then they go ashore and stuff themselves. Just for once, I wouldn't mind walking onto that beach, sitting down at their table and sharing some of that champagne and caviar.'

'Whatever it is they're feeding them, it's doing their sex life the world of good. They were at it till half-three this morning. I don't know were that guy gets all his energy.'

'Ah, leave them alone,' retorted the photographer. 'If you ask me, those two really like each other. I'll have a bet with you that she marries him before the year's out.'

'Fuck off.' The man stood and climbed down from the fly deck. 'Don't try and con me. I read that bit of conversation from the intercept transcript as well – "We'll get married in November." Fancy some breakfast?'

'It's your turn to cook, so why not? How about a nice egg and bacon sandwich? I could just do with . . .' the observer paused. 'Something is happening. Time 10.03. Wake the others, we could be on the move soon.'

From the comfort of Harmsham Park, Sir Gilbert had watched the hunt progress. On the screen before him, several flashing numbers indicated the vehicles being followed, including Bulloch's bike and the Mercedes in which Diana now sat. Suddenly two of the numbers disappeared – Sir Gilbert held his breath. After several minutes the silence was broken. 'Zero, this is Echo-three. 10.03. Both targets on the upper deck, Tango-one is having breakfast, Tango-two is nearby making a call. You getting that?'

'Roger that, Echo-three. We copy. He's phoning Tango-five in London. Stay alert for any move. We want as much warning as possible this end.'

'Roger that, Zero. Echo-three out.'

'Zero, this is Echo-three. 12.20. We have movement. Looks like both targets are about to leave. Affirmative, they are getting into the launch. Do you wish us to follow?'

'Echo-three, negative. Stay in position just in case there's any last-minute change of plan. Once we have confirmed they are airborne you can return to Nice. Out to you. Echo-two, do you have?'

'Roger that, Zero. 12.28. The launch is approaching the jetty of the Gala di Volpe Hotel. A white Mercedes is waiting outside the hotel.'

'Zero, this is Echo-two. 12.31. Targets coming out of the hotel lobby. All units stand by. The Mercedes is moving off. I am in pursuit.'

'Roger that, Echo-two. Out to you. Echo-five, what is your location?'

'Zero, this Echo-five. I'm sitting at the road junction on the

S125. We will stay in front of them. It looks as if they are heading towards Olbia airport.'

'Affirmative, Echo-five. Good work.'

'Zero, this is Echo-two. 12.58. Target now approaching the main entrance of Olbia airport. They are going straight onto the airfield.'

'Zero, Roger that. Echo-five, can you go on foot?'

'Zero, this is Echo-five. 13.01. Confirm both targets have boarded a private Gulfstream Jet which was waiting on the runway.'

'Roger that, Echo-five. They have a flight plan filed direct to Le Bourget in Paris.'

'Zero, this is Echo-five. 13.29. The jet has taken off, heading north.'

'All stations, this is Zero. Stay in current positions until we have confirmation of touchdown at Le Bourget.'

Cal rose early. Feeling in a positive mood, he made himself some coffee, taking the hot mug out onto the front terrace. The morning air had mingled with the mist rising off the river adding a soothing chill to the atmosphere. Cal placed his mug on the table to allow the liquid to cool before he took a seat in one of the plastic garden chairs. The view before him was a backdrop of pale blue sky dominated by the yellow brightness of the rising sun. In the distance he could clearly see the towers and spires that made up the skyline of Paris. Raising the mug to his lips, he cautiously sipped his coffee while he formulated a plan.

His visit to the Ritz Hotel the previous evening had done little to further his efforts in locating Bulloch. He had, however, enjoyed the superb food and it was a good place to start. Ramsey seemed in no doubt that the princess would return to Paris sometime today. If this proved true, then there was the possibility that Bulloch would show himself. On all previous occasions in Paris the princess had stayed at, or at least visited, the prestigious Ritz Hotel. If Bulloch was planning some form of car accident, then Cal would need to be mobile at all times and ready for immediate action. He decided to return to Paris and walk the roads in the vicinity of the hotel. If possible, he would find some nearby parking. He could stake out the hotel while posing as a member of the press. Ramsey had mentioned that he would find a camera in the study. He knocked back the last of his coffee and went to look for it.

Paris, Cal discovered, was very much like London. In spite of the fact that most of the Parisians had by now deserted Paris, heading both north and south for their annual holidays, the city was still busy. It was tourists which filled the pavement cafés that festooned the tree-lined avenues; the tourists which packed the boats that sped up and down the Seine, passing alongside such magnificent bastions as the Notre Dame Cathedral; the tourists which sweltered in the mid-morning sun or sought shelter in the tightly-packed and dirty side streets. Summer in Paris had charmed the tourists and everywhere Cal looked it seemed jammed with vibrant crowds. If nothing else, Paris had a glorious heart.

'All stations, this is Zero. 15.20. Confirm we have touchdown at Le Bourget. Blue team, stand down. Repeat, Blue team stand down. Red team, the ball's in your court.'

'Sierra-one, Roger that. 15.22. There's a lot of paparazzi hanging around here. No sign so far of either target. Wait . . . we have a black Mercedes followed by a green Range Rover approaching the aircraft. Baggage now being unloaded and put into the Range rover. Both targets plus one pax now exiting the aircraft and getting into a black Mercedes. Three pax are getting into the Range Rover. Two police motorbikes have arrived. They are moving. I repeat, target is moving.'

'Roger that, Sierra-one. All mobiles, this is Zero. Keep the update coming.'

'Zero, this is Sierra-four. 15.28. Target now on the motorway. The police escort has now left them. Both vehicles are being harassed by the paparazzi. We're looking at a potential accident here.'

'Roger that, Sierra-four. Stay back. Do not become involved.'

'Affirmative, Zero. A black Peugeot has just cut right in front of the Mercedes forcing it to slow. Over.'

'Sierra-four and all units, this is Zero. Do not become involved. Stay back and shadow. Repeat, stay back and shadow.'

'Zero, this is Sierra-four. 15.39. The vehicles are splitting. The Mercedes has taken the Porte Maillot exit. The Range Rover seems to be heading for the city centre. Over.'

'Roger that, Sierra-four. Stay with the main target vehicle.'

'Stop! Stop! Stop! All stations, this is Sierra-four. 15.47. Target now entering main gates at Villa Windsor. Pull back and prepare for exit.'

'Zero, this is Sierra-four. 16.07. The Range Rover with two up has just passed our position and entered Villa Windsor.'

'Roger, Sierra-four. That vehicle went to the apartments and deposited the luggage plus two pax. Out.'

'Zero, this is Sierra-four. 16.18. Target is on the move. Repeat, target is on the move.'

'All stations, this is Zero. Stay back and provide loose cover. We understand that the target is now making for the Ritz Hotel.'

'Zero, this is Sierra-four. 16.28. Confirm targets have arrived at the Ritz. Entering through the service door at the rear.'

'Roger that, Sierra-four. Out to you. Sierra-seven, are you ready?'

'Affirmative, Zero. Standing by.'

By 3.30 in the afternoon, Cal's predicament was solved. After several hours of walking he located a parking lot on Saint Honore no more than 50 metres from Place Vendome. Large, five storey buildings lined the square on all sides and a tall column that occupied the centre served to form a traffic island. Cal crossed the road, making his way past the high class shops most of which were occupied by world-renowned, exclusive jewellers. Reaching the far side of the square, he came to the front entrance to the Ritz Hotel. He did not stop; his purpose now was to find a location from where he could observe the hotel without being too obvious. He found the ideal place on the corner.

Cal had been sitting at the pavement café for almost an hour. He had positioned himself in the shade of a colourful awning and, although some distance away, the table offered a clear view of the main entrance to the Ritz. If required, he could run to the car and be in a position to follow anyone leaving the hotel.

The best he could do now was to sit and wait for the princess's arrival. In this he was not alone – quite a few men whom Cal easily identified as paparazzi occupied a number of tables. The waiting was an occupational endurance for them, as this was an opportunity to earn money by photographing one of the world's most beautiful women. Sitting there in the mid-afternoon sun surveying people going about their business or pleasure, Cal found it difficult to imagine that somewhere out there lurked a cold-blooded killer. And Bulloch was here. Cal could almost feel the man's presence.

He had been contemplating having another coffee when a whole cavalcade of photographers in cars or riding motorbikes flushed into the Place Vendome. As if signalling the start of a race, several men leapt from their tables and ran towards the thickening cluster now gathering at the front of the hotel. Caught up in the drama, Cal dropped several francs on the table, grabbed his camera and ran after them.

The crowd was excited, pushing and greeting each other with words of encouragement and criticism. The doorman shouted to someone behind him and several staff members appeared behind the glass doors. Apart from the odd tourists who had joined the mob out of curiosity, the paparazzi were grouped in twos and threes who seemed to claim acquaintance with each other. Although Cal's understanding of French was poor, he was able to surmise that the press had followed the couple from Le Bourget Airport. *En route*, the princess and Al Fayed had given them the slip by suddenly turning off at Porte Maillot before going on to the Villa Windsor. Although not an organised group, when a shout went up, four men broke away and disappeared round the back of the hotel to cover the rear entrance on Rue Cambon. In each man's mind was the fact that two weeks ago a photographer using a long range lens had taken a picture of the couple kissing – it had earned the photographer over two million dollars. The princess would arrive soon and in those fleeting seconds as she and Al Fayed stepped from the car, another opportunity would present itself.

Cal was still making these observations when several mobile phones rang out in unison – the princess had arrived at the rear. Like a rushing tide, the pack swelled forwards only to fragment as individuals outpaced each other in the contest to reach the rear entrance first. Cal was carried along with the flood and ran with them. He turned the corner into Rue Cambon to find that the couple had already disappeared inside the hotel.

Dejected, the pack broke into several units, some staking out the front while others remained covering the rear. The older and more perceptive paparazzi knew that there would be no reappearance for at least an hour. They returned to rest and wait at the nearby cafés. Cal turned to follow this latter bunch, passing as he did so one of the paparazzi sitting astride a powerful motorbike. The man's right hand was pressed against his full-face helmet and Cal thought he detected the faint reverberation of a voice. If nothing else, thought Cal, the paparazzi were organised. Ramsey had been right – his best option was to stick with the media. He retraced his steps to the café across the road.

'What is the current position, Robert?' Sir Gilbert stood by the library window looking out over the splendid gardens of Harmsham Park. The fading sunlight highlighted the colours, turning the lawns into a vibrant map of green. By contrast, the room behind him housed several computers and bulky display screens covered half the far wall. Trescott and one of the operators was studying the electronic display, toying with a hand remote, enlarging the map of Paris until it showed the streets around the Place Vendome. From this room they could monitor and communicate with any of the surveillance units; listen to and record all the telephone calls; take pictures from security cameras and conversations from hidden microphones. Looking at it Sir Gilbert felt a real sense of power. Indeed, he was the power behind Operation Royal Blood.

Trescott had reacted badly to the bomb and his subsequent meeting with Lloyd Ramsey had caused him to panic. Now recent events proved his personal decision to keep Bulloch in the field were correct. In the past 24 hours there had been undeniable proof that the princess had consented to marry Dodi Al Fayed. Those in power had condoned his foresight at implementing Operation Royal Blood. He crossed the room, joining Trescott by the display.

'We have them housed in the Imperial Suite of the Ritz Hotel. They arrived there after paying a visit to Villa Windsor. So far she has made only one telephone call which was to a journalist, Richard Kay at the *Daily Mail*. The basis of that conversation confirms our earlier suspicions in that she will announce her engagement upon her return to England confirming that she intends to marry Al Fayed in the coming November.'

'I see,' said Sir Gilbert, inwardly gloating. He knew he had been right. 'I'm sorry, Robert, I didn't mean to interrupt. Do go on.'

'A table has been booked for 8.45 this evening at the restaurant Chez Benoit, close to the Pompidou Centre. Afterwards, they plan to drive to Al Fayed's apartment on the Champs Elysees. That is all we have so far. Oh, yes there was one other thing – at around 6.00 pm Dodi Al Fayed left the hotel by car. He only went across the square where he slipped into a nearby jewellers. La Place Vendome is full of jewellers. It would seem he was collecting the ring he had ordered at the Alberto Repossi boutique in Monaco. He did not take the ring with him but had it delivered to the Imperial Suite a short while later. We now have tracking and audio on all the vehicles they are likely to use.' His head turned to look at one of the projected computer screens. 'The disabling bolts have all been fitted.'

Sir Gilbert was pacing the room. 'Anything from your man inside?'

'No, we are still trying to contact him but he is not answering. Either it is too dangerous for him to do so, or he is getting cold feet. What about Bulloch?'

'The mobile phone we supplied him with is also being tracked. He has followed the target every inch of the way since they landed at La Bourget. His only request is that we should try and increase the media pressure. Apart from that, he sounded confident.' Sir Gilbert paused. 'Bulloch is a professional. He has proved that to me. When the moment is right, he will strike and not before.'

'I hope so. We can't allow her to make this announcement, even if it means bringing in a 'K' team to terminate her ourselves. The decision has been made,' Sir Robert Trescott sounded nervous. He wished he could share Gilbert's optimism.

'They're on the move!' the shout went up, like a hunt-master yelling 'Tally Ho' – the chase was on. The group of paparazzi reacted by dispersing, dashing off in different directions. Several ran for the same car park as Cal. On reaching his car, Cal switched on the ignition and engaged the turbo-charged engine. With a roar the small car lurched forwards. Seconds later he shot out onto the Rue de Rivoli. There was no difficulty in finding the princess. Both the Mercedes and its escort vehicle were surrounded by a mob of cars and motorbikes. As the cameras flashed constantly, Cal joined the swarm.

The procession swept up the Champs Elysees. At every set of traffic lights the Mercedes was forced to stop. This gave time for the bikes to move in. They snapped, darting back and forwards like jackals bringing down a running quarry. The endless popping of the camera flashes ceased immediately the lights turned green, allowing the cavalcade to surge forward once more. For the second time that evening, Cal wondered at the ingenuity of the press. Regardless of the escort vehicle the bikes were able to get in close. While the riders jockeyed for position alongside the Mercedes, the pillion passengers were free to snap shot after shot.

When at last the Mercedes pulled up outside the Al Fayed apartments the chase turned into an agitation of force. Cal could not believe the pushing and shoving that took place. Two bodyguards did their best to clear a way through to the front door but to little avail. Everywhere hands gripping cameras stretched over the mob, some almost touching the princess, blinding her. Cal stood on the fringe of the pack watching in disbelief until the couple was finally safely inside. Instantly, the pack relaxed, pulling back a little but waiting nevertheless, as if they had an animal trapped in its lair. At some stage, she would have to come out.

Cal walked back to his car and sat watching the group of paparazzi. Given France's strict laws on privacy, he wondered how they managed to get away with such behaviour and why there were no police present. Although she was in the nearby building, other than the photographs he had found on Norris, he had never seen the princess. Cal suddenly had the yearning to tell her, force her to stay put. But how could he?

His thoughts were interrupted by the sound of an engine starting. Movement in the shadows of an unlit side street caught his attention. Cal immediately recognised the man, despite the full-face helmet. It was the second time he had seen the right hand pressed against the helmet as though the wearer was listening to a guarded conversation. Without knowing why, Cal got out of the car and started walking towards the man. The closer he got the more he realised the difference between this man and the other paparazzi. The man was tall and well built. His outer clothing consisted of shiny black leathers. In the shadows, his face remained hidden by the closed visor. The right hand remained pushed against the helmet.

'He's paying someone to feed him information,' thought Cal. 'Whatever it is, he's keeping it for himself.' With 30 metres between them it suddenly dawned on Cal that the man was operating alone. All the other press bikes worked in pairs; driver and photographer. And why the secrecy? Despite working for different newspapers all the paparazzi operated on shared information. With the princess still inside the apartment why was this man suddenly departing? This mirrorball of information flashed round and round in Cal's mind. He came to an almost instant conclusion. At that moment of illumination, the man suddenly put the bike into gear and throttled away.

'Bulloch!' shouted Cal as the man sped past. How could he have been so blind, so stupid? The man had to be Bulloch and someone was passing him information.

Cal grabbed at the mobile phone clipped to his belt. It rang twice before Ramsey answered.

'I've found him. He's posing as a member of the press. '

'Are you sure it's him?' Cal went on to explain that although he had not seen the man's face, his actions all indicated that he was Bulloch.

'He's obviously monitoring the British surveillance operation. That's going to give him the opportunity to get in front at some stage and do whatever the son-of-a-bitch has planned. Your best bet is to stay with the princess until you pick up Bulloch. Once you have him, stick with him. I'll arrange some help. Let's see what the British do if we remove Bulloch from their operation. Call me the moment you have him sighted.' The phone went dead.

Cal suppressed the desire to chase after Bulloch. He had seen him twice while following the princess. He would have another opportunity. He returned to his car and waited until 9.30 pm, at which time the same two cars reappeared at the front of the apartments. Seconds later, two bodyguards emerged followed closely by the princess and Dodi Al Fayed. Dogged by the swarming paparazzi the cortège made its way back to the comparative privacy of the Ritz hotel.

Upon arrival, Cal was surprised to see that the ranks of the waiting crowd had doubled in size. Well-wishers and tourists now fought with the paparazzi in order to snatch a quick snap of Princess Diana and her new love. The situation was hindered by the presence of another car setting down its passengers at the front entrance, forcing the couple to remain in the Mercedes. It was an opportunity not to be missed by the paparazzi and several photographers rushed forward, bombarding the car with flashes. While hassled security personnel tried to keep them at bay, Diana leapt from the car and walked briskly into the hotel. Seconds later, Dodi Al Fayed followed. The show was over for the moment.

Cal scanned the immediate crowd at the front of the Ritz looking for Bulloch. He was nowhere to be seen. Walking to the rear, he checked the entrance where he had first seen the man sitting astride the motorbike – still no sign. At least while the princess was inside the hotel she was safe. If Bulloch was being fed information, he would know exactly when she left and in which direction she was heading. He would only surface when she was on the move. Once more, Cal was forced to wait. He parked his car for a second time and returned to the café.

'Yes, I appreciate how difficult it is for you to call me,' Trescott remained listening to the phone. He nodded his head. 'You must call me just before they leave.' Again there was a pause while he listened. 'Yes, yes but we paid you the equivalent of a £1,000 earlier today . . . very well, I'll see what I can do.' Trescott replaced the phone and turned to Sir Gilbert.

'It would seem that Dodi Al Fayed has lost his sense of humour. All this media attention is forcing him to rethink his plans.' Trescott read from the single sheet of paper on which he had been writing.

'What do you mean?'

'Our man tells me that they will be leaving the hotel and returning to the apartment around midnight. They intend to stage some elaborate plan to throw off the press. It involves taking a route along the bank of the River Seine – apparently the expressway has no traffic lights. This will allow the driver to speed up and lose the paparazzi. They mean to send the normal car and the escorting Range Rover from the front entrance as a decoy. Another Mercedes, also one which has received "special attention", will leave from the rear exit.'

'Most interesting,' muttered Sir Gilbert. 'I take it we are the only two who are privy to this information?'

'Yes. What do you have in mind?'

'If we say nothing of this and let this plan of Al Fayed's decoy both the press and our own surveillance units, that would present Bulloch with an ideal opportunity.'

'There's no assurance that either group will fall for the decoy ploy.'

'No but it should at least place the princess's Mercedes beyond the prying eyes of the press for several seconds. That's all the time they will need to cotton on to the decoy plan, but it's time enough for Bulloch to get to work, especially if he's pre-positioned.' Sir Gilbert picked up the phone and dialled. After some seconds, he asked, 'Where are you? I see. It would seem our friends are planning a little diversion, while in reality the target will be using the expressway along the northern bank of the Seine. We will try to give you five minutes warning so . . .' Sir Gilbert relayed the details Trescott had given him, ending with, 'Time is running out.'

Around 10.30 pm Cal noticed the paparazzi at the front of the Ritz were becoming excited. Paying for his drink, he walked across to rejoin the group only to find that four cars had been positioned close to the entrance. Several hotel security men were checking over the cars as if they were preparing to depart. One member was toying with the press, informing the photographers that the couple would appear within the next ten minutes. Despite the promise, nothing happened and after half an hour Cal wandered back towards the café.

A short distance away, Bulloch sat on his bike listening to the latest reports. It looked as if she was on the move. He strained his head to listen once more, cursing the loose headset.

'Zero, this is Sierra-seven. 00.15. Targets are preparing to leave. All units stand by.'

'Zero, this is Sierra-three. 00.18. We have a black Mercedes S-280 pulling up at the rear of the hotel on rue Cambon. Vehicle driven by hotel jockey who is now getting out of the car. Several paparazzi are close by.'

'Zero, this is Sierra-four. 00.20. We have two vehicles leaving from the front. No sign of targets. The crowd is so thick. Zero, we are in pursuit.'

This was it, thought Bulloch. That was the decoy leaving. The real vehicle would depart shortly. He let out the clutch and eased the bike forward, slowing by the pavement café before manoeuvring towards Place de la Concorde.

Cal had watched the paparazzi fire off a stream of photos as two cars roared away from the front entrance. Immediately, the bulk of the waiting group ran for their bikes and gave chase. He was about to do the same when a large and powerful motorbike slowed almost in front of him. It took Cal completely by surprise. Bulloch was so close he could have reached out and touched him. In that second the bike had roared off.

Cal ran for all he was worth. Jumping into the Fiat, he fired the engine and gave chase. Accelerating hard, he screeched into the Place De La Concorde only to be stopped by the traffic lights. Bulloch had to be close. Jumping from the car, he strained to look down the Champs Elysees. Bulloch was nowhere to be seen. The lights were about to change when he noticed the bike no more than 100 metres away. Bulloch had gone directly ahead at the island and was now stopped on the side of the road, sitting as if waiting for someone.

The lights changed and Cal pulled away. At the same instant, he saw Bulloch thrust the bike forward. He's playing cat and mouse with me, thought Cal. How the hell did he know it was me? Such was Cal's concentration he had not noticed the real focus of Bulloch's attention – a black Mercedes had jumped the lights behind Cal in an effort to shake off the pursuing paparazzi.

By the time Cal had turned into the long straight of the Cours la Reine he realised that Bulloch had slowed significantly, enough for him to catch up. A black Mercedes came speeding past in the fast lane. Almost at once Bulloch accelerated. In an effort to keep pace, Cal forced the pedal down to the floor, demanding every scrap of power the small Fiat had to offer. With Bulloch no more than 50 metres ahead, he entered a tunnel. Despite the diminished light Cal kept the speed up and, as he emerged at the other side, he realised that he was gaining.

A second tunnel was coming up fast. Both the Mercedes and the bike suddenly accelerated towards it. Cal drew alongside the Mercedes. The female passenger was giving him a sideways glance. The princess looked annoyed.

In that split second, instinct told Cal that Bulloch was about to strike. There was only one way to stop him – ram the bike. The road dipped suddenly and Cal fought to control the car. Next instant he was staring directly into the sun.

Bulloch had positioned himself perfectly. He had watched as the Mercedes jumped the traffic lights at the Place De La

Concorde and headed directly towards him. He immediately ripped at the throttle, leaning forward to counterbalance the front wheel lift. As the bike settled, he turned in Cours La Reine some 100 metres in front of the target car. The signals flashed through his brain as he recalled the data he had studied while checking the possible routes earlier that day. Two main opportunities came rushing back to him – both were perfect accident spots. As he raced through the first tunnel, he calculated the time and distance to the next one. A glance in the mirror clearly showed the headlights gaining on him. He adjusted his speed. He remained in the left-hand lane, making sure the Mercedes could not pass. The second tunnel was coming up fast. He checked the mirror again. He could now discern two sets of headlights. One of the paparazzi had somehow caught up. What the hell, he was committed.

Bulloch rolled the bike smoothly into the centre of the road, riding the white line between the two lanes. With 50 metres to go he let the bike run down the incline that led into the mouth of the tunnel. The speedometer read 82 mph. He reached down to pull the safety pin from the ambush light. His eyes flicked back and forth, tunnel to mirror, tunnel to mirror, watching as both cars behind him closed the gap. At 10 metres, Bulloch pressed the switch on the ambush light.

Two million candle power fanned out from the rear of his bike – an effect equivalent to looking at the sun for 10 seconds on a summer's day.

He saw the headlights in his mirror dance crazily as the Mercedes spun out of control. Jarvis's device had worked.

He accelerated away. A terrible noise of metal hitting metal echoed through the tunnel. He depressed the ambush light switch a second time killing the brightness. Checking in his mirror, the picture behind immediately told him the job was done. Lights swung through the air while bright red sparks ground away at the concrete and the car disappeared in a cloud of grey and white smoke.

Bulloch hit the brakes.

Although seeing the princess had warned Cal that Bulloch was about to strike, the ambush light caught him completely unawares. A gun or grenade he would have expected, but the light took him totally by surprise. In those final moments, he was pushing the small Fiat to its limit, finally drawing parallel with the Mercedes. Neck and neck, they entered the underpass.

He was just recovering from hitting the dip in the road when the ambush light triggered. The sustained brilliance of the white light, coupled with the darkness of the tunnel, rendered Cal completely blind.

With his senses reeling in confusion, he felt the impact and knew instantly that he had collided with the Mercedes. His head hit the Fiat's metal door framework and his body rocked violently. Suddenly the car broke free. Blind fear and his instinct for survival forced Cal to brake hard while holding the steering wheel in a vice-like grip. From all around him came the horrific sound of tortured metal. The Fiat continued its blind run for several more seconds until at last it hit the right-hand wall of the tunnel. The wheel jolted in Cal's hands but steadied as the contact with the smooth concrete wall slowed the car. With a final shudder, the Fiat ground to a halt, coming to rest just inside the underpass exit. Cal slumped forward against the wheel.

Bulloch had stopped close to the tunnel's central pillars and watched as the white car slid past, hugging the opposite wall. Turning the bike in a casual loop, he sped back towards the wrecked Mercedes. The large car hissed and groaned as boiling water bled from the radiator and twisted metal settled reluctantly into violently formed new configurations. Above all, the horn resounded like the dying howl of a wounded animal. The Mercedes had rebounded off one of the central reservation pillars before spinning round through 180 degrees and coming to rest against the north wall.

Bulloch stopped the bike and dismounted. Moving swiftly towards the rear passenger-side door, he immediately saw that it was virtually undamaged. It opened easily.

Diana lay before him. Trapped behind the front passenger seat, she was wedged in the floor well. The impact had twisted her body a full half turn so that she now faced towards the rear of the car. Her right arm was folded up behind her back. Compared to the other three occupants, Diana looked relatively uninjured. She was bleeding a little from the mouth and nose but there were few signs of severe damage. The head and shoulders of Dodi Al Fayed were slumped against the far door. Bulloch reached over, grabbing the body by the hair and pushing it back against the seat. Al Fayed was dead. Bulloch recoiled as an unfamiliar smell entered his nostrils; the interior was still thick with the escaped gas from the airbags.

He looked at the fallen shoulders of the driver. Bullock had seen enough corpses to know that this man was dead. The bodyguard appeared to have faired little better. From the massive facial injuries, Bulloch presumed that the man had gone through the front windscreen. If not already dead, he soon would be. It had taken no more than three seconds for the cold, calculating mind of the assassin to survey the macabre scene. Bulloch turned his attention back to Diana.

She had not been wearing a seat belt and the sudden impact had propelled her violently forwards into the back of the passenger seat. Her body was slumped, half on the edge of the rear seat and half in the footwell. Bulloch grabbed the blonde hair, using it to pull back her head. Without doubt, she was still alive. Releasing the head, he gripped her right hand, turning it to expose the palm. He squeezed the pad of her thumb and watched for a reaction; it remained white. She was bleeding internally.

Bulloch formed a fist and drove the weighted power glove into the exposed back with all the force he could muster. The impact was quick and brutal. The dull thud caused the woman involuntarily to arch her back and yielded a soft, whimpering sound. Her head fell forward. Bulloch was contemplating a second blow when headlights illuminated the car and the sound of motorbikes reached his ears.

He unzipped his jacket and removed the camera. Standing and taking a step backwards, he rapidly snapped off several shots. Behind him, he could hear the sound of running feet and abruptly he was jostled on all sides. Men pushed past him in their rush to get to the car. Amid erratic pushing and sporadic flashes, Bulloch edged further back. As more vehicles arrived he turned, heading directly for his motorbike. No one took any notice, their attention riveted on the wrecked car and its occupants.

With a final glance over his shoulder, he pulled quietly away. Reaching the exit he was about to push the machine hard when he caught sight of the white Fiat. He throttled back. His first thought was to silence the driver. It would be better if there were no witnesses. He swung the bike over, drawing to a halt by the driver's side door. The sides of the car had taken a battering but, miraculously, the car had somehow avoided serious impact with the tunnel wall. The man's head was slumped forward, his hands still gripping the steering wheel.

Bulloch contemplated putting a bullet into the exposed neck, but such an action would only serve to indicate that the tunnel incident had been something other than an accident. Suddenly the head swayed groggily and slowly lifted, stopping as it reached the headrest. The eyes opened. Through blurred vision, Cal Wesley looked up into the shocked face of John Bulloch.

The look of astonishment at seeing Wesley alive threw Bulloch for an instant. Then, shaking his head, he laughed, 'Got to hand it to you, Wesley. You're a hard man to kill.'

'Bulloch,' Cal's chest had impacted with the steering wheel and, while his injuries were not life-threatening, his breathing and ability to move had been seriously impaired. His voice rasped when he spoke. 'You bastard, I'll . . .'

Bulloch cut him short. 'Don't get all upset. Congratulations are in order – you've just killed the Princess of Wales.' It suddenly dawned on Bulloch that he had no reason to kill Wesley. By placing a single phone call to Sir Gilbert, they could accuse the American of causing the accident. 'See you in hell, Yank.' Bulloch drove his right fist into Cal's face. He sat for a moment, wishing he had time to finish the American off once and for all. Then, twisting the throttle, he roared the bike out of the tunnel.

From the comfort of Harmsham Park, Sir Gilbert had watched the hunt progress. On the screen before him, several flashing numbers indicated the vehicles being followed, including Bulloch's bike and the Mercedes in which Diana now sat. Suddenly two of the numbers disappeared – Sir Gilbert held his breath. After several minutes the silence was broken. 'Zero, this Sierra-four. 00.34. We have been following a decoy. We have now relocated the actual target which seems to have been involved in a serious road accident in the Alma tunnel on the expressway. Do you wish us to assist? Over.'

'Negative. Repeat, negative . Wait. Out.'

'Zero to all units. Abort the operation. I repeat abort the operation. No further transmissions. All units are to return to base. Sierra-seven remove all monitoring equipment as soon as possible.'

The blow from the power glove had landed on Cal's neck just below the ear. It had left him dazed for almost a full minute. As his head cleared, he became aware of the damage his body had suffered as a result of the crash. A vice-like grip seized at the muscles in his damaged shoulder; but the movement involved in attempting to sit upright relaxed his lungs. Cal inhaled deeply. With it came the pain. He exhaled with a forcible moan. Breathing evenly once more, he felt his strength returning. The thought of Bulloch helped to revive him and, although he felt his responses returning, his eyesight was still impaired. 'You've just killed the Princess of Wales.' The words echoed in Cal's mind.

He placed his hand on the door handle making to leave the vehicle, then hesitated. He was badly injured; if he left the car now he may not be able to return. Besides, Bulloch would not have left the princess alive. If she was dead, there was little he could do. He would be better off getting the hell out of there and reporting to Ramsey. Innocent or not, the presence of an American agent at the accident site would do little for public relations. He searched his pocket for the phone only to find that it had been smashed into several small pieces during the crash.

'If you get into any trouble, make for the house in Conflans and we will get you out.' Ramsey's words offered the only solution. He was certainly in trouble, and badly wounded. Struggling, he managed to sit up straight in the seat while his right hand searched for the ignition. A final glance in the rear view mirror revealed the presence of blue flashing lights. It was time to go. Cal started the engine and engaged first gear. Several weird noises erupted as the car pulled away from the wall, otherwise it drove well. Anxious to distance himself from the scene, Cal accelerated, exiting the tunnel and following the Avenue De New York. He had gone no more than 100 metres when he almost collided with a car which had entered from a side road. He cautioned himself to take it easy until his eyesight had completely returned to normal.

'Sir, I thought you should know. The British operation in the Mediterranean – all communications have stopped.'

'Run that by me again?' Lloyd Ramsey said, somewhat puzzled.

'The British, sir. Whatever it was they were doing, it's not happening any more. Complete silence.'

'What time was this?' Something had happened, he was sure of it.

'About ten minutes ago, sir.'

'Thank you. That will be all.'

'Yes, sir.' The man turned to leave, then stopped. 'There

was one other thing, sir. There's a breaking story on the television. Diana, the British princess, she's just been involved in a road accident in Paris.'

Lloyd Ramsey picked up the telephone in one hand while clicking the television remote with the other. The news flash was giving out the latest details even as he dialled the number of Cal's phone. There was no answer. Replacing the handset he phoned a second number.

'I think our boy is in trouble. Check out the Alma tunnel and the routes back to the house at Conflans. See if you can find him.' Ramsey slammed down the phone. The bastards had done it. He thought of phoning Trescott but decided against it for the moment, at least until he had found Caleb Wesley.

Cal came to slowly, his senses telling him he was lying down, and that the room was warm. His head swam with a sickening dizziness as he tried to sit up. He gave up when he found the effort too painful. He lay back, letting the numbness that hazed his vision clear a little. As he regained consciousness and as his eyes opened fully, his brain started to take in his surroundings.

He was lying in Susan's bed and the bedside clock told him it was 6.30 in the morning. Bulloch would be long gone by now but maybe they could still catch him. Cal was still speculating when he heard voices downstairs. It sounded like someone was on the phone. Cal tried to shout, clearing his throat in an effort to form the words. For some reason he could barely speak. He was about to try again when the bedroom door opened.

'So, you have come back to life, Major Wesley!' The voice was crisp and assured – a distinct American voice. 'My name is Paul Redford and this is Agent Johnson. We're from the Paris office. We received a message from Ramsey in London a little after midnight. He told us to come here. We found you unconscious, sitting in the car. Johnson and I carried you up here. It seems like you have been in the wars. I would say that you have three broken ribs and a dislocated shoulder – and that's just for openers.'

Cal's throat struggled to respond. With a painful heave of his chest, he forced out one guttural word, 'Bulloch.'

Redford nodded, his voice became solemn. 'We know about Bulloch. Ramsey has had people checking the airports all night. The French authorities are a little too pre-occupied to help at this moment, though. Princess Diana was involved in an accident a little after midnight. She died at 3.45 this morning. Ramsey wants to know what happened. You feel up to talking about this?'

Cal held up his hand for the man to stop. Gripping his throat, he whispered, 'Water.' Cal collected his thoughts while Johnson went to the bathroom and returned with a half-filled glass. Cal swallowed the tepid liquid in small mouthfuls and, while each gulp caused him pain, it eased the stickiness in the back of his throat. Relaxing, he told them what had happened.

They decided that Bulloch had been listening in to the British surveillance operation simply waiting for the ideal opportunity to cause an accident. 'I picked him up and followed. That's when the Mercedes came into the picture. The princess was sitting in the back. When I realised that he was about to make his move, I tried to ram him. Next thing I know there's this bright light and I was totally blind. I hit the Mercedes a glancing blow. Somehow I must have managed to stop my car. It's difficult to remember. I was blind throughout the whole thing. Next thing I know, Bulloch is standing there telling me I've just killed the princess. Then he hit me. I don't know what he used, but it was heavy and it hurt like hell. I only just managed to get back here.'

Redford disappeared back downstairs and once more Cal could hear him on the phone. Ten minutes later he reappeared, speaking to Johnson briefly before crossing the room to sit on the bed. 'There are a lot of ugly rumours going around at the moment and people are pointing fingers – mainly at the paparazzi. One thing Ramsey is adamant about is that we get rid of the Fiat and get you back to England ASAP. He also told me to remind you that you're still working for him. As such, you are bound by Federal Law. You're not to say anything. As far as the world is concerned, Major Caleb Wesley was never in France.'

'Thank you for letting me know. That information is most useful. No, she was not killed outright, but the damage was excessive and we managed to delay treatment long enough to ensure that recovery was impossible. Have a good holiday.' Sir Gilbert replaced the phone for a moment before making another call. 'A mobile phone just rang this number. Could you trace it for me? Thank you.'

Trescott looked in his direction, waiting for an explanation.

'That was Bulloch. He's safely away but rang to tell me that the American, Wesley, was following him in Paris,' Sir Gilbert smiled. 'Apparently, the American's car actually collided with the Mercedes.'

'Ramsey must have sent him,' said Trescott. 'He obviously has some evidence and was trying to expose our plot.'

'What evidence? Surveillance reports? Ramsey is hardly going to admit that he was spying on a legitimate British operation or that he sent this man Wesley to Paris. I mean, how would it look if an American agent was driving a car that collided with the princess's Mercedes, possibly even causing it to crash? With Bulloch gone, there is little evidence to implicate the Sovereign Committee.' The phone rang. Sir Gilbert listened for a moment before thanking the caller.

'It would seem that Bulloch phoned from Brussels airport. He's travelling on an Irish Passport under the name of John McAuliffe. I'm sure your department won't have a problem finding him.'

'No,' said Trescott. 'I'll get onto it right away.'

Leaving Trescott to tie up the loose ends, Sir Gilbert decided to go for a walk. Outside he strode across the landscaped gardens, feeling the springiness of the grass beneath his feet and the smooth air soft against his cheek. Near the wood, on slightly higher ground, he stopped to look back. The morning sun rose brightly in the clearness of an unclouded sky. In the distance he could hear the sound of sheep and the chirping call of birds. This was his England.

Below him, the old house stood as a timeless example of English architecture. Built centuries ago, it had stood the test of time, proud, a house with authority, a picturesque survivor of the past. History is made this way. He had no qualms about disposing of Diana. The news of her death made headlines around the world. Soon she, too, would become part of history. With her passing the monarchy was safe once more. Sir Gilbert Scott had done his duty.

Two hours and six minutes after leaving the tunnel, Bulloch was approaching Brussels airport. The only delay had been at the French border where they had checked his passport. As Bulloch drew level with the officer, he stopped the bike, leaving the engine to quietly idle. He lifted the helmet visor with his right hand. If the customs officer had noticed the glove covering his right hand was larger than its counterpart he made no comment, content to wait while Bulloch produced his passport. The Irish passport that Sir Gilbert had arranged passed as genuine. Two minutes later, Bulloch had crossed unhindered into Belgium, heading straight for the airport.

Sitting in the departure lounge, he drank from a bottle of beer while he phoned Sir Gilbert and relayed the fact that Wesley had been in Paris. He then dropped the phone on the floor, picked up the pieces and put them in the nearest waste bin. An hour later they called his flight to Thailand.

'You're a lying son-of-a-bitch, Trescott and don't think for one minute you're going to get away with it. I don't give a damn what you say, I know that you and Gilbert Scott arranged the death of the princess. That's your business, but Susan Greenwood is mine. She was an American, she was also a CIA agent. Now I want some answers from you.' When Lloyd Ramsey had telephoned his counterpart in British Intelligence, he had been angry – he still was. That the man had reached his office in less than 30 minutes spoke volumes about how heavily involved he was in this mess. With some small satisfaction, he watched Trescott flounder for words.

'I can only reiterate that the British government had nothing to do with the accident in Paris. Our operation was quite legitimate. While I am truly sorry about Miss Greenwood, that had absolutely nothing to do with us.'

'Don't give me that bullshit. I have enough evidence to implicate all those named here.' He threw down the list Wesley had photographed during his visit to Harmsham Park, and waited for Trescott to pick it up. 'How many of these names will

be knighted for their services in the next honours list, "old boy"?'
Ramsey's voice was full of sarcasm. 'Well, I've got news for you
and the rest of these gentlemen. The IRS is going to investigate
all their dealings in America, and I'll make sure that investigation
gets into the newspapers – their businesses will not be so
profitable from now on. Make no mistake, people will listen to
me.' He hammered home his winning point, discharging the
words directly into Trescott's face. Then, in a softer voice, he
added, 'If word of this every gets out, you can kiss goodbye to
your Royal Family. No one will want to know Britain.'

Ramsey slumped back into his chair. It had all been a
performance; there was no way he could ever tell anyone of
this, not even the President. It would be buried along with the
rest of his nation's secrets. He just hoped that his rhetoric was
enough to scare the shit out of Trescott.

Trescott was indeed shaken. Deep down he knew America
would never do anything to harm Britain and the princess's
death had been a private operation – nothing at all to do with
the British Government. Nevertheless, there were unfortunate
and embarrassing links to his department. His hands were
shaking as he picked up his briefcase and extracted a file.

'Perhaps this will help in some small way.' He placed the file
on Ramsey's desk, his hand visibly shaking. 'We have an SAS
unit working on Thailand's northern border – there has been
some discussion as to whether we should send in a team to
solve the problem. I thought it may give you some satisfaction
if you were to do it.'

Ramsey picked up the file and leafed through the pages,
stopping now and then to absorb more detail. After a couple of
minutes he dropped the file back onto his desk. His smile was
one of pure disgust.

'Not only does your shit stink, Trescott but now you want us to clean it up – you have some nerve.'

It was raining outside and Ramsey's office was cold. He had not offered Cal coffee, neither did he engage in small talk. When Cal had entered the room and taken the seat opposite the large ornate desk the old man had simply inquired about his health. 'How are you feeling?'

'Fine sir, the ribs are a bit painful but they're healing.' Cal had spent a month in the military hospital and another month getting fit again. It had been a lonely time; apart from his father he had received no visitors. The call from Lloyd Ramsey had been non-committal but secretly Cal hoped it would be some form of work.

'Good. What do you know about drugs?'

'Well, sir, I was part of the anti-narcotics team sent down to Colombia. We equipped and trained the special police units to combat the problem.'

'Yes. I've read your service record. It's impressive. What impressed me more, though, is how you handled yourself during the Bulloch affair. You're a good operator.' Lloyd Ramsey paused long enough for the words to sink in before proceeding. 'On an official note, the whole incident never happened and you will never talk about it again, not to me, your father – anyone. I want an operator I can trust.'

This was praise indeed coming from Ramsey. The mere mention of Bulloch, however, made Cal seethe with anger. He had been so close yet Bulloch had escaped. The British security services were now aware of Cal's presence in the tunnel, making it almost impossible for the Americans to make any sort of comment about Diana's accident (and what good would it do now? She was dead.) They had flown him out of

Paris later that same morning and secreted him away in a military hospital. That was two months ago and in all that time there had hardly been a moment when the thought of catching Bulloch had not entered his mind. He was brought sharply back to the present by Ramsey's voice.

'I want you to read this.' He handed Cal a thin blue file containing several sheets of paper. He waited patiently without interrupting.

Cal read in silence. The report told of the problems on Thailand's northern border with Burma, reflecting the growing concern with which the government now viewed the narcotics problem, in particular the avalanche of highly addictive methamphetamine pills produced in Burma for the Thai market. Over the past three years, the impact of methamphetamine abuse in Thai society had reached crisis proportions. Burmese-produced methamphetamine use had infiltrated homes, schools, offices and factories throughout the country. The pandemic of what in Thailand is popularly known as 'ya ba' or 'mad drug' had left in its wake a widening swathe of organised crime, official corruption, street violence and broken families.

Several insurgent groups inside Burma involved themselves in methamphetamine production and trafficking, but the overwhelming bulk of the 200 million or more methamphetamine tablets smuggled into Thailand each year were produced in areas controlled by the Wa group. Thai Army intelligence estimates indicated that some 50 methamphetamine and heroin 'labs' operated along the border opposite Chiang Mai and Chiang Rai provinces, most under Wa protection.

The report concluded with the fact that several Thai agents who had successfully infiltrated the Wa organisation in an effort to establish shipment dates and routes across the border, had suddenly disappeared. One agent who had managed to remain operable had passed a message indicating that the Wa had recently hired the services of a European assassin.

Having read the final page, Cal removed the photograph that had been attached to the back with a paper clip. The photograph was blurred and grainy and it had not been taken with a professional camera. Nevertheless, the picture clearly showed the face of John Bulloch.

'You want the job Major Wesley?'

Cal replaced the telephone and looked out of the hotel window. His room on the 14th floor gave him a wonderful view over the seething mass of humanity that was the city of Bangkok. Although his eyes took in the view, his thoughts were occupied by the phone call.

'There is a cowboy bar at the end of Soi 5. Be there at 7 o'clock this evening – do you understand?'

'Yes. Cowboy bar, Soi 5, 7 o'clock. Who is this?' The line went dead.

Although he had been waiting for instructions it had come as a surprise. It was not the call that worried him but the caller – the voice had been familiar.

Soi 5 was the small side street on which Cal's hotel was located. The cowboy bar was not far away. He left the hotel early, walking the short distance to the main road and, having crossed the busy street, made his way to the nearby group of bars. It was typical of so many areas in Bangkok; a collection of bars full of booze, drugs and naked young girls whose sole purpose was to satisfy the lusts and cravings of men and women from the west.

Cal pushed aside the curtain that separated the street-front bar from the more intimate atmosphere inside. The place was poorly lit apart from the raised platform in the centre which passed for a stage. Here, under bright spotlights, six girls gyrated their naked bodies to the musical beat. Cal eased himself onto a bar stool next to the stage and cast an eye over the establishment. It was fairly empty but the evening was still early. Apart from the 30 or so girls, there were no more than a dozen middle-aged guys in the place, most of them from Europe or America. Most looked well groomed and wealthy and each was being entertained by several girls.

'Hello honey you want a drink?'

Cal turned as a girl holding a tray ran her hand up his thigh, the smile on her face purposefully playful.

'Give me a beer,' replied Cal, removing her hand. She had no sooner gone when two more girls arrived, both competing for the best position on Cal's lap.

'Hello mister, what's your name?'

Cal smiled. It was hard to resist their impish faces and bold gestures, but he politely removed the girls from his lap.

'I'm waiting for someone.' They were both reluctant to go, but as the first girl returned with his beer they slunk away looking for another punter. Cal drank from the bottle and was quickly propositioned again.

'You looking for a good time, mister?'

The closeness and coarseness of the voice made Cal jump off the stool. He turned defensively only to find himself looking into the grinning face of Major Robin Carney. Cal's mouth gaped open in surprise. He was totally unprepared for Carney's sudden appearance. He had spoken briefly to the SAS commander at the end of the Gulf War and since that time they had maintained a loose contact. Cal had no idea what the SAS were doing here, and was unsure whether they could be trusted. Ramsey had merely said he would be contacted and Cal had assumed it would be by a CIA agent. His uncertainty caused a brief and awkward silence. As if he hadn't noticed Cal's hesitation, Robin Carney called the bar girl over and ordered two more beers.

Cal had always liked Carney but things had changed since the Gulf War – he needed to be sure. 'Are you involved in all this?'

Carney was still smiling. 'Involved in what? I don't know what's going on. I was told to get my backside down to Bangkok and meet up with you. We've been working up here for several months. You know the sort of thing – equipping and training mostly, similar to what we were doing in Columbia. Drugs are an even bigger problem here than they are in the West.

'Anyway, about a week ago I was instructed to send in a four-man team to a recce on a bar used by the Wa military. The request was to locate a spot from where the bar could be best observed. I thought it was a prelude to some form of cross-border strike. Then, yesterday, out of the blue, I was told to make contact with you in Bangkok. I flew down here from the northern border and arrived here about three hours ago. My orders are simply to help you. That's all I know – unless you want to tell me more?' Carney said, hopefully.

Cal looked at the man sitting opposite him. The racket in the bar faded as he tried to fathom out if this man was still his friend. So much had happened since they had last met. His faith in the British Government had been shattered, added to which Bulloch had once been a member of the SAS. Suddenly he smiled. Robin Carney was a good man and during the Gulf War he had done all within his power to find Cal. Yet, while instinct told him to trust Carney, there was a matter of national security at stake. He doubted if Carney knew anything about the incident in Paris and he intended to keep it that way.

'Sorry, Robin, it's just that you took me by surprise. You were the last person I expected.' He paused long enough for the smile to broaden on Carney's face, then added. 'It's Bulloch. He's working for the Wa – I'm here to kill him.'

'My God, so you finally managed to track the bastard down.' It was Carney's time to express surprise. 'Last I heard he and Norris were in the Middle East working for whoever paid the highest price.'

'Norris was killed in a plane crash in Columbia a few months ago. Bulloch, on the other hand, murdered a CIA agent.'

Robin Carney shook his head and raised his hand. 'I don't need to know any more, Cal. I was wondering why they instructed me to bring you a sniper rifle. I've got some other gear for you, too. Whatever you need, you just ask. I'll help any way I can. It's the very least I can do. I owe you – I'm the one who put you with Bulloch in the first place. Now how about we have a few more beers and sample the delights of Bangkok? I know this fabulous place called 'No Hands Restaurant'.'

Cal smiled, it was going to be okay.

'How the hell do we eat without using our hands?'

'Now that's the fun part. These girls . . .'

Next morning Carney and Cal drove to the military section of the airport and boarded a large helicopter. Both were dressed in jungle fatigues and carrying rucksacks; a large rifle case was slung over Cal's right shoulder. He had taken a quick glance at the weapon in the comfort of Carney's accommodation. Cal was impressed – a brand new Accuracy International PM. State of the art. Carney had also assured Cal that he would have time for a few zeroing shots once they had reach the jungle training camp. That would allow him to get to know the weapon as well as checking its calibration.

The helicopter was clearly marked with the logo of an American aid agency, as were the boxes that occupied most of the cargo area.

'Most of the methamphetamine and heroin "labs" are operating along the border opposite Chiang Mai and Chiang Rai provinces. Most are under the protection of the Wa army,' said Carney as he strapped himself into the canvas seat. He kicked one of the boxes. 'Don't be fooled by the labels, most of this is ammunition. We're training a special force unit to combat the drug trafficking, most of which comes directly over the border and down to the capital. We have a firm base set up not far from the border. I'll have the same team that did the recce take you in, from there on you're on your own. If you need to retreat in a hurry make directly for the border, we can cover you from there.'

Cal sat in his hide looking through the telescope, observing the small clutter of buildings which lined the jungle road. Intelligence had revealed that this location was the place for final preparation prior to the drugs crossing over the border into Thailand. The added attractions of a bar and brothel also made it a favourite with the soldiers of the Wa military.

Four days ago Carney and three other SAS men had led Cal over the border for a distance of about two kilometres. Here they had helped him set up a concealed position before leaving him to the loneliness of the jungle. From this vantage point, Cal could look down and observe the small Burmese roadside village. In the centre of the village, at a distance of little more than two hundred metres, stood the building which would be Cal's main focus of attention. It was a noisy bar that never seemed to close. Brightly coloured lights had been looped along the corrugated roof in order to attract customers, and several scantily clad girls appeared every time a vehicle pulled up out front.

Once settled, Cal began to concentrate on the routine which soon fell into a pattern. The soldiers would arrive in a wide variety of vehicles; sometimes even busloads at a time would descend on the village. They would all trudge into the bar and, after several hours of drinking, they would emerge and make their way across the street to another building which Cal assumed was the brothel. There was a constant movement throughout the small village, but the main activity seemed to be between four o'clock in the afternoon and dawn. Cal had adjusted his sleeping hours accordingly for fear of missing Bulloch who, to his disappointment, had not so far shown himself.

As the light began to fail and evening grew darker, Cal removed the telescopic sight from the sniper rifle, replacing it with the 'Nite Watch' sight. This unique night viewing device had been specially adapted to fit the Accuracy International PM, allowing Cal to shoot even in complete darkness. Waiting in the jungle had given Cal time to reflect, pondering all that had happened over the past few months. With Bulloch his thoughts went further back to the Gulf War. Somehow this man always had the upper hand. No matter what Cal had done, Bulloch managed to outmanoeuvre him. Perhaps he had been too soft or too naïve – either way this time Bullock was going to lose.

It was gone midnight and Cal was beginning to feel the strain of the constant observation. Laying the rifle across his lap he stretched and flexed his arms. At that precise moment a Toyota Land Cruiser drove into the village and stopped outside the bar. Cal eased the rifle up in time to see two men climb out of the Toyota on the side nearest to him. One of them spoke to the driver who, crunching the vehicle into gear, drove off. As it cleared his line of sight, Cal noticed that a third man had been in the Toyota. In the green glow in the night sight's eyepiece, the man's white shirt shone brightly, making him stand out. With a chill feeling the adrenalin rushed through Cal's blood – it was Bulloch. He spoke to the two other men, who laughed in reply before stepping into the bar. There had been no chance for Cal to get off an accurately aimed shot. But when Bulloch re-emerged he would be ready. Cal had fantasised about this moment for days and planned the shot with great care. In his mind he had already pulled the trigger a thousand times. While a head shot at this range would not be a real problem, he could not afford to take any chances. He would shoot Bulloch in the chest. Then when he was down he would place the killing shot, making absolutely sure.

The door to the bar clattered open several times over the next couple of hours, disgorging drunken soldiers and prostitutes, but Bulloch was never among them. Cal could barely contain himself and each time the door opened he raised the rifle and sighted on those entering his killing ground. Then Bulloch appeared. The noise of the door crashing open once more alerted Cal who immediately raised the rifle. Bulloch was staggering a little, borrowing support from a young girl trapped beneath his right arm. Cal dropped the sight from Bulloch's face down to his chest and waited for him to step down onto the street.

'Wait . . . wait,' Cal cautioned himself, while taking up the first pressure on the trigger. 'Now!'

But Cal did not fire. Instead he watched as for one fleeting second Bulloch stopped and looked up directly towards him.

'He knows I'm here.'

Cal squeezed on the trigger and felt the rifle kick back into his shoulder. At the instant of firing he lost sight of Bulloch. There was chaotic movement as the body spun and fell backwards. Cal steadied the rifle. Bulloch had landed face down, his head towards the bar. Beneath him the girl struggled to free herself.

All Cal's senses screamed at him, 'Go for the head shot now!' He quickly aligned the sight, but the girl was still trapped and struggling to get free. He had no desire to harm her. With cool determination, Cal let the crosshairs slip down Bulloch's back until they rested at the base of his spine.

'The first one was for me, this one is for the princess . . .' he squeezed the trigger.

All this had taken just seconds, but by now the girl had become hysterical. Armed soldiers spilled out of the bar and into the street. Seconds later they were pouring fire into the surrounding hillside. Girl or no girl there was only time for one more shot. Cal moved quickly, placing the sight in the middle of Bulloch's head.

' . . . and this one is for Susan.'

With a coldness he had never felt before, he eased off the shot. The rifle kicked, then settled and Cal watched the drama unfolding in his night sight. The girl had managed to free herself and most of the soldiers, despite being drunk, had run for cover – Bulloch lay alone and unmoving.

For what seemed like eternity Cal stared through the sight, mesmerised by the prone body of Bulloch.

It was over.

Only when several bursts of automatic fire sliced through the nearby foliage was Cal jolted back to reality. Within seconds he had packed up his rucksack, cradled his rifle and was making his way back towards the Thai border. As he picked his way along the track in the darkness of the jungle, Cal's feelings were a bewildering mixture of both elation and apprehension. Bulloch was dead, of that he was sure. The score had been settled. Why then did victory lack any feeling of comfort or well-being? It was a question that gave rise to another. Why, at the moment of firing, had Bulloch looked up at him? Suddenly Cal's senses detected movement on the track ahead. His troubled thoughts evaporated as he calmly took cover, melting into the jungle to observe the approach of a lone figure.

Despite the mask of camouflage cream which covered Robin Carney's face there was no disguising his concerned expression. Cal whispered a greeting as Carney drew closer.

'Thought I'd come to meet you,' Carney's voice was hushed to avoid the sound carrying in the still night. 'Mission accomplished?'

'Mission accomplished,' replied Cal.